MEXICAN WHITEBOY

MATT DE LA PEÑA

MEXICAN WHITEBOY

EMBER

Text copyright © 2008 by Matt de la Peña
Cover art copyright © 2009 by Nick Haas

All rights reserved. Published in the United States by Ember, an imprint of Random House Children's Books, a division of Random House, Inc., New York. Originally published in hardcover in the United States by Delacorte Press, an imprint of Random House Children's Books, New York, in 2008.

Ember and the E colophon are registered trademarks of Random House, Inc.

Visit us on the Web! randomhouse.com/teens

Educators and librarians, for a variety of teaching tools, visit us at randomhouse.com/teachers

The Library of Congress has cataloged the hardcover edition of this work as follows:
Peña, Matt de la.
Mexican whiteboy / Matt de la Peña. — 1st ed.
p. cm.
Summary: Sixteen-year-old Danny searches for his identity amidst the confusion of being half-Mexican and half-white while spending a summer with his cousin and new friends on the baseball fields and back alleys of San Diego County, California.
ISBN 978-0-385-73310-6 (hardcover) — ISBN 978-0-385-90329-5 (Gibraltar lib. bdg.) — ISBN 978-0-375-89118-2 (ebook)
[1. Identity—Fiction. 2. Self-acceptance—Fiction. 3. Racially mixed people—Fiction. 4. Baseball—Fiction. 5. Fathers and sons—Fiction. 6. Cousins—Fiction. 7. National City (Calif.)—Fiction.]
I. Title.
PZ7.P3725Mex 2008
[Fic]—dc22
2007032302

ISBN 978-0-440-23938-3 (tr. pbk.)

RL: 6.0

Printed in the United States of America

16

First Ember Edition 2011

For the de la Peñas,
my endless inspiration
(y especialmente mi abuelita
Natividad Burgos-de la Peña)

Danny Lands in
National City

1

Dressed in a well-worn Billabong tee, camo cargo shorts and a pair of old-school slip-on Vans, Danny Lopez follows his favorite cousin, Sofia, as she rolls up on the cul-de-sac crowd with OG swagger.

A bunch of heads call out to her, "Hey, Sofe!" "*Yo,* girl!" "There she is!" and wave.

Sofia waves back, pulls Danny by the arm toward a group of girls sitting on a blanket in an uneven semicircle. *"Oye putas,"* she says. "Yo, this my cousin Danny I was telling you about. He's gonna be staying with me for the summer." She smiles big—proud, Danny thinks. "Yo, cuz, these are my girls." She points them out and rattles off names: "Carmen, Raquel, Angela, Bee, Juanita, Flaca and Guita."

"Hey," the girls singsong in unison.

Danny nods with a shy smile, aims his eyes at the asphalt. He feels the heat of their stares and for a second he wishes he could morph into one of the ants zigzagging in and out of tiny crevices in the street. Their little lives, he thinks, totally off the radar.

Danny's sixteen, a shade over six foot and only a year younger than Sofia, but unless he's on a pitching mound he feels like a boy. He's long and thin with skinny arms hanging down skinny thighs—his arm length the reason he can fire a fastball so hard. His shoulders are wide, but his muscles have yet to catch up. Sometimes when he sees himself in a mirror it looks like his shirt is propped up by an upside-down coat hanger. Not a human body. Doesn't even look real.

And Danny's brown. Half-Mexican brown. A shade darker than all the white kids at his private high school, Leucadia Prep. Up there, Mexican people do under-the-table yard work and hide out in the hills because they're in San Diego illegally. Only other people on Leucadia's campus who share his shade are the lunch-line ladies, the gardeners, the custodians. But whenever Danny comes down here, to National City—where his dad grew up, where all his aunts and uncles and cousins still live—he feels pale. A full shade lighter. Albino almost.

Less than.

"And just so you know," Sofia adds, "Danny ain't no big talker, all right? He's mad smart, gets nothin' but A's at the best private school in San Diego, but don't get your *chones* in a bunch if you can't never pull him into a convo." Sofia looks prettier than Danny remembers. Less of a tomboy. Her hair long now, makeup around her eyes.

Carmen clears her throat, says: "He don't need to talk to give me no deep-tissue massage." She gives Danny an exaggerated wink.

"Ain't need no words for us to soak in a nice Jacuzzi bath

together," Flaca says. She reaches out, puts her hand on one of Danny's Vans. "We can just sit there, Papi. Backs against them jet thingies. Take turns sippin' a little white Zin and shit. How's that sound, beautiful?"

Danny gives her a polite smile, but inside he's shrinking. He's trying to suck back into his shell, like a poked and prodded snail.

Behind his back he grips his left wrist, digs his fingernails into the skin until a sharp pain floods his mind, makes him feel real.

Angela and Bee comb Danny over with their almond-shaped eyes, devour his out-of-place surfer style like a pack of rabid dogs. Danny cringes at how different he must seem to his cousin's friends. They're all dark chocolate-colored, hair sprayed up, dressed in pro jerseys and Dickies, Timberlands. Gold and silver chains. Calligraphy-style tats. Danny's skin is too clean, too light, his clothes too soft.

"*Que putas,*" Sofia says, slapping Flaca's hand away from Danny's shoe. "Leave my cuz alone already. He only just got here today." She turns to Danny, says: "I see my homegirls gonna try and corrupt you, cuz. Better watch it, though, these *heinas* got mad STDs."

"Say what!" Carmen shouts.

"For real, I seen 'em jumpin' off like fleas." Sofia plays like she's swatting germs out of the air, stomping them on the ground.

Danny sees all the girls are laughing so he laughs, too.

2

As Sofia switches topics, brings up their annual summer trip to the Del Mar Fair—"Speaking of alcohol, Flaca, which one of y'all's sneakin' in the thermos of jungle juice?"—Danny eyes a group of guys playing stickball at the mouth of the cul-de-sac. A wave of butterflies passes through his middle. *His game!* His pitching arm starts to tingle, his right elbow and fingertips, like he's already gripping the seams of a baseball—a Pavlovian response, he thinks, recalling his psych teacher's chicken-scratch scrawl on the chalkboard. The guys playing stickball are all Mexican except the one waving the bat around—he's black. Danny watches one of the Mexican kids lob a meatball down the middle and the black kid smack it over the roof of the house. Watches everybody react. Start dancing around, showing off.

He'd give anything to be out there playing instead of standing here watching. Trying to maintain this smile out of respect. He digs into his wrist some more with his nails. Breaks previously broken skin and pulls away. A smear of blood he wipes away with his other hand, rubs off across his dark jeans. Back home his mom is always on him to stop digging, but that only makes him want to dig more.

Danny looks around the cul-de-sac. Everyone is Mexican. The girls, the guys, the young kids, the mailman—even the mangy chocolate Lab tied to a lamppost, sleeping. He spots a pretty girl chasing a little boy across the cul-de-sac. She's tall and thin, Mexican like everybody else, but different. She's lighter, too, like him. Straight black hair past her shoulder blades. White tank top and long flowing green skirt. She calls after the little boy in Spanish, motions for him to stay off the lawn of a neighboring house, but when the boy suddenly plops down on his diaper in somebody's carefully manicured flower bed, all she does is laugh.

She picks the boy up, brushes off his bottom and leads him back to her beige towel.

Danny gets a strange feeling in his stomach. A knot. He wonders since she's light-skinned if she has a white mom, too. Like he does. He watches her carry the boy back to her blanket and sit down. Then he turns back to the guys playing stickball, wonders if his dad ever played here. If his dad ever stood on the exact section of cul-de-sac he's standing on right now. He pictures his dad's face (like he *always* does) the last time he saw him. They were on the steps outside their old apartment. Three years ago. He wouldn't look up or say anything. They just sat there together, cars driving by, the sun going down, a beer dangling from his dad's right hand.

The next morning he was gone.

But the reason Danny's chosen to spend this summer in National City, instead of in San Francisco with his mom and sis, is because he's got a plan. He's gonna save his money and fly to Mexico. To Ensenada. He's gonna track down his dad and spend some quality time with him. So they can get to know each other again.

"Yo, check my new tattoo," Flaca says, pulling her jeans halfway down her butt, revealing the letters *OTNC* written out graffiti style.

"Ooh, that's tight," Sofia says, gently touching the skin around the swollen letters. "Lo's bro did it? Bet it hurt right there, girl. It's all fleshy."

"Nah, Lo's older brother's good, Sofe. I could barely feel the needle—"

"Stop lyin'," Carmen interrupts. She turns to Sofia, shaking her head. "I was right there with her. She was bawlin' her eyes out before he got halfway through the *O*."

As everybody laughs at Flaca, Danny glances over at the guys playing baseball again. Nobody plays stickball in Leucadia. Why don't white kids play stickball? he wonders. Maybe because they have real baseball fields. Or because the houses are too nice. Or maybe they've just never thought of it.

He turns to check on the girl with the kid again, feels the knot rise, then cuts back to the game.

Home Run Derby:
Uno's Time Has Come

1

Uno steps up to the makeshift home plate again, an over-turned metal trash can lid, and waves a duct-taped bat through the strike zone. He stretches his shoulders, hikes his Raider jersey sleeves up his black arms and points, Babe Ruth style, to the centerfield fence—an old two-story house with security bars on all the windows, Mr. and Mrs. Rodriguez's place.

"Yo, put one in your boy's wheelhouse," he says as Chico moves toward the pretend pitching rubber, a section of curb to the left of the Rodriguezes' crumbling driveway.

Chico pulls a couple more tennis balls from the mailbox and shoves them into the web of his glove. He pimps his Dodgers cap to the side a bit, says: "I'm gonna put it right down the middle, *vato*. But I ain't so sure 'bout you havin' no wheelhouse."

"Already got four dongs to your one, Chee. Wha'chu want, baby?"

"But you ain't no finisher, Uno." Chico turns around to the eight or nine neighborhood kids spread across the front lawn behind him, says: "Least that's how I heard it from some of my homegirls at the mall last night."

Everybody laughs.

Uno straightens up. "You ain't gotta go to no mall to investigate that shit, Chee. Ask around the house, homey—both your sisters know how I got it."

Everybody breaks up again, including Chico, who shakes his head and taps a heel a couple times against the curb behind him. He grips the first tennis ball and lobs it toward home plate.

Uno watches it travel through the air, takes a wicked swing and connects. But he gets a little underneath the sweet spot, and instead of sending it over the roof like he did the last two, he lifts it high into the sky—like a firework, pre-explosion.

All the neighborhood Mexican dudes on the lawn spring into action. Some have mitts, others just their bare hands, but they all call for the ball as it begins dropping back down to earth a few feet in front of the nativity scene Mr. Rodriguez keeps up all year round.

"I got it, *ése*!"

"Yo, *aplacate*! That's me!"

"This one's mine, *vato*! Clear out!"

The tennis ball's headed straight for Big Raul's open mitt, a baby-fat seventeen-year-old rap wanna-be from down the block, when his best friend and biggest nemesis, Lolo, swoops in at the last second and snatches it with a bare hand. Lolo raises the ball up over his head as he turns to a disappointed Raul. "Ha, *bola de pan*! I catch so easy! You no fast enough!"

Lolo's five-ten and lanky. The youngest son of separated Mexican immigrants. He's got a shaved head and ridiculous homemade tattoos running up and down his forearms and shoulders—the price he's had to pay for having an aspiring tattoo-artist big brother who needs an occasional practice canvas.

"Why you always be fightin' fools for the ball?" Raul shouts back. "He ain't any more out if *you* catch it!"

"You mad 'cause you no fast enough, *croqueta*."

"Whatever, man."

"That's one down!" Chico shouts toward the lawn, extending an index finger toward the blurry summer sun. "Time to send this Uno fool packin'."

2

It's another home run derby Saturday on Potomac Street in old-town National City. The neighborhood kids all competing in baggy jeans and oversized white tees or throwback jerseys for the hat stuffed full of one-dollar bills and hanging off the faded bird feeder. At the outset of every derby each guy tosses two bucks into the pot, like an entry fee, and before the first pitch the kid with the best grades, usually Skinny Pedro, tallies up. Launch the most tennis balls over the Rodriguez house and you go home thirty, forty bucks heavier in the pocket.

Night before last, Uno put some thinking in before he closed his eyes in bed. This summer's derby was his to dominate. He easily had the most power. These days he hardly even recognized himself in a mirror. He'd be toweling off after a shower, and he'd stare at his upper half—seemingly overnight he'd gone from skinny-ass mess-up to a six-foot-two seventeen-year-old with crazy cuts. Like the fading pictures he keeps in his sock drawer of his old man, Senior, back when *he* was young. Not only is Uno the only black kid in the neighborhood—or *negrito,* as the old Mexicans call him (even though his moms is Mexican, too)—he's also stronger, quicker, taller, a better fighter. It's his time. This summer he's gonna clean fools out.

But Uno knows the derby's about more than just making some cash or building a rep. It's also about groups of neighborhood girls scattered around the cul-de-sac, gossiping, sipping ice-cold Kool-Aid out of old Gatorade bottles. It's about the two or three crews of young bucks, *los ratas,* hanging out on stolen bikes, pulling drags off stolen cigarettes. The few non-athletes walking from group to group like social free agents. It's about Uno's fifteen-year-old stepbro, Manuel, sitting on the open tailgate of Mr. Rodriguez's Ford F-150 with a half-peeled orange in his lap, cheering: "Hey, batter, batter! Swing!"

Doesn't matter *who's* at the plate, Manny's cheering.

Everybody shows up to check out the action on the lawn, sure, but they also come to chill, to shoot the shit, to draft game plans for nighttime activity.

Uno knows his derby facts better than he knows the stuff they teach in school. Is he solid on his Civil War dates? Nah. But he knows Mr. Rodriguez is a retired fireman. Mrs. Rodriguez, a retired special ed teacher. Knows they've hosted the derby for going on ten years now—their own son, Marco, having started the Potomac Street tradition back when *he* was coming up. Knows Marco is now a first-year resident at some hospital for kids in Albuquerque—the derby continuing on in his absence.

Some of the faces change each summer—new kids show up, old kids disappear—and many of the rules morph and evolve with each new generation, but three things have remained constant since that first summer:

1. There's always a hatful of one-dollar bills on the bird feeder.

2. There's always somebody interrupting the action on the grass to crack on somebody else.

3. And every kid who participates in even one Saturday derby during any given summer shows up to help repaint the outside of the Rodriguez house, top to bottom, the week before school starts back up.

3

Chico lobs in another meatball, and Uno takes another vicious whack. This time he kisses yellow felt with the sweet part of his bat, sends the tennis ball rocketing into the sky. All anybody on the lawn can do is watch as the two-week-old Wilson Titanium sails high over the roof for Uno's fifth dinger of the afternoon—more than double the next highest tally.

Uno megaphones a black hand around his mouth and makes fake crowd noise as all the little Mexican boys race around the side of the house to retrieve the battered ball.

The only person celebrating more than Uno is Manuel, who springs to his feet on the tailgate, gripping the last couple sections of his orange, and calls out in a warped Mexican accent: "Going, going, gone! Going, gone! Ahhh yeah, Uno!"

Manuel may be a little slow in the head—that's how the white social worker explained it to Uno the first time he visited his stepbro at Bright House—but Uno couldn't care less about that mess. Manny's his people for life. It doesn't mean nothing to him that they aren't even blood. That's why he breaks into a little chicken dance around home plate. Manny goes crazy for his chicken dance.

Some of the neighborhood girls point at Uno and laugh. One of *los ratas* does a wheelie as he cuts through the middle of the playing field on his BMX. All his boys crack up, wait for him to circle back, and then they ride away together.

Chico pulls another ball out of the mailbox and waits for Uno to end his made-for-Manny dance. "Yo, you need to act like you been there before, *cabrón*." He takes a short walk to his bag, pulls out a towel and wipes a glaze of sweat off his brown face.

"The derby ain't just about winnin', Chee," Uno says, stopping abruptly. "You know that. It's about winnin' with style. Puttin' on a little show for the peoples." He waves a hand toward all the groups of kids scattered throughout the cul-de-sac. "You just pissed 'cause your boy's always the main attraction."

Chico makes his way back into pitching position, impatiently watches as Uno leads his little bro through an elaborate home run handshake.

Only thing that gets Uno to stop dancing is when he spots Sofia watching, some light-skinned Mexican skater-looking kid standing by her side. What's up with *this* pretty boy? he says in his head. Sofe gots a man now?

For some reason, this thought stops Uno's dancing midstep. It irritates him, though he couldn't tell you why.

He picks up the bat and steps to the trash can lid again. Waves through the strike zone a couple times and waits on Chico's delivery.

The Shot Heard Round the Cul-de-Sac

1

When the black kid finally makes another out, Danny and Sofia watch everybody switch around. Then Sofia shoots Danny a quick smile, marches right in front of the makeshift home plate and calls out to all the guys: "Yo, who's winnin' this bullshit?"

Uno, back on the lawn now, punches the inside of his mitt and cocks his head to the side. "Who you *think*, Sofe? You saw that last one I put in the upper deck, right? I was sendin' you an SOS, girl."

"Hmmm, missed it," Sofia says, winking at Raul as he steps into the batter's box with the duct-taped bat. "Funny, isn't it, Raul? How I never actually *seen* all these home runs Uno supposedly hits?"

"Makes you wonder, right?" Big Raul says, nodding. "It's like, do a tree falling in the forest really make a sound if there ain't nobody there to see it?"

"*Exactly!*" Sofia says, turning back to Uno. "What Raul said."

"What's that shit supposed to mean?" Uno says.

"Raul's mad deep," Chico says. "He writes poetry."

"I write *rhymes*," Raul says, lowering his bat. "And y'all just too simple-minded to catch my flow."

"Anyway," Sofia says, "this is my cousin Danny. He's staying with me for the summer. Oh, and by the way, he's better than all you fools at baseball."

Danny watches all the guys on the field turn to check him out. He lowers his eyes, kicks at a small piece of glass lying in the street.

"You talkin' crazy," Chico says, approaching Sofia from the house.

"Sofe don't know nothin' 'bout no baseball," Skinny Pedro says.

"I know you *suck*!" Sofia shoots back.

Everybody cringes and puts a fist to their mouth. "Oh, damn!" they all say, pointing at Pedro, laughing.

A few of the guys hug Sofia and shake Danny's hand, introduce themselves. Raul and Lolo try to run him through a neighborhood handshake and laugh when he fumbles it three straight times.

"Your cuz, huh?" Uno says, flipping Danny a tennis ball.

Danny snatches it out of the air, feels his right arm come to life, the pace of the blood in his veins quicken.

Uno smiles. "You want in, homey? Gotta put down some paper."

"Four bones for virgins, right?" Chico says.

"Nah, it's a fiver this summer," Uno says.

"Here," Sofia says, pulling two crumpled ones out of her pocket. "Ain't nobody hustlin' *mi familia*. It's two!"

Chico takes the cash, walks it to the bird feeder.

Uno looks Danny up and down, says: "Matter of fact, GQ, you up next. Right after Heavy D here."

Danny shrugs.

"Watch, he's about to do you guys," Sofia says to Uno.

"Yeah, okay." Uno holds his glove out for the tennis ball.

Danny tosses it back, watches everybody move into position on the lawn as Raul steps up to the trash can lid and takes a practice swing. He watches Uno snap the tennis ball in and out of his glove a couple times as he follows Sofia with his eyes as she walks off the playing field.

"Ready, Biscuit?" Uno shouts, turning back to Raul.

Raul nods.

2

Uno tosses the first pitch.

Raul doesn't move his bat off his shoulder, lets the tennis ball cross the plate unharmed.

"Wha'chu want?" Uno shouts. "Why you always scared to swing the bat?"

"Nah, I just needed one to get my timing," Raul says.

"That's really gonna matter, Biscuit? You never hit more than two in a Saturday. I got six right now. Do a little math, baby."

"You ever think maybe today's my day?"

Uno scoffs, looks back at Chico, who shrugs.

Sofia shakes her head, says to Danny, "Uno talks so much shit. I can't even handle it sometimes." She pulls her cell out

14

of her bag, flips it open to check a text. Closes it back up. "He's got all these other *vatos* talkin' shit, too. They all think they're black now."

They watch Raul swing at the next pitch, hit a little dribbler a few feet in front of his Timberlands. Uno rushes the tennis ball, scoops it and fires it at Raul as he's rumbling toward the garage door. The ball smacks him right in the ass. Raul trips and falls to the ground, clutching the back of his jeans.

Everybody on the lawn falls over laughing.

Danny and Sofia laugh, too.

"You're outta there!" Manuel shouts from the tailgate.

Raul rolls over, cringing. "Damn, Uno. Why you gotta throw it so hard?"

"I thought you was gonna make it."

Raul struggles to his feet, shaking his head. He makes his way back to the plate. Picks up the bat and wipes his sweaty forehead on his shirtsleeve. He reaches around and rubs the back of his jeans a little, then flips Uno off.

Uno and Chico slap hands, laughing.

Sofia turns back to Danny, still grinning. "Rules are like this," she says. "Each guy gets only one time hitting. And only two outs. You make an out when somebody either catches it on the fly or pegs you—like Uno just did Raul. If you make it to the garage door before they hit you, though, it's not an out. Whoever hits the most over the roof wins."

Danny nods.

Sofia links arms with her cousin again as Raul steps back up to the trash can lid. He spits in the direction of Uno because Uno's still bent over laughing. But all that does is make Uno laugh even harder.

Danny peeks back over his shoulder at the Mexican girl with the little boy. She's reading a magazine now. Her legs crossed, hair pulled back in a rubber band.

He feels the knot again. And for the first time he wonders if maybe it's because she's so pretty. There was only a couple Mexican girls at Leucadia Prep, and none of them looked like this.

He turns back to the lawn as Raul pops one in the air. The ball doesn't get much lift, and Skinny Pedro brings it in easy.

Uno immediately aims a finger at Danny, barks: "You up, GQ."

3

Pulling a couple fresh tennis balls from the mailbox, Uno shouts over his shoulder at Danny, "Where you want these, first-timer?"

Danny grips the bat, shrugs.

"Come on, dawg. You want 'em low? A little inside so you could pull it? Right down the middle? Talk to me."

"Just throw it already," Sofia pipes up from the sideline. "It don't gotta be all technical like that."

"I'm tryin' to hook your boy up, Sofe. Tryin' to be nice for once, *damn*." Uno turns back to Danny, says, "What's it gonna be, homey?"

Danny loosens his grip on the bat and forces a smile. He shrugs again, stares at the duct tape and wonders how he's gonna pull this silent thing off down here. Back in Leucadia, he made a pact with himself. No more words. Or as few as he could possibly get away with. When his dad spoke at all, he mostly spoke Spanish, but Danny never learned. All he had was his mom's English. And he didn't want that anymore. Up in Leucadia it was easy. Nobody paid him any attention anyway because he was Mexican. He roamed the school halls with his head down like a ghost. Drifted in and out of class-rooms without a peep. Nobody even saw him as a real person. But down here, where everybody's skin is dark, everybody seems to be coming at him.

He glances at a little red Honda parked down a ways in the cul-de-sac, sees a Mexican guy in a Padres cap leaning against the passenger door with his arms crossed. Guy looks just like one of the scouts that used to show up to watch Kyle at Leucadia Prep. Danny used to wonder about him because he seemed out of place with the other scouts. Why would he be down here, though? Danny wonders. Maybe this is where he lives.

Danny steps to the trash can lid and swings through a couple times, stretches his shoulders. Feels the nerves in his stomach climbing up into his chest.

Uno turns to Sofia, laughing. "What up with your cuz, Sofe? Cat got dude's tongue?"

"Just pitch 'im the damn ball," Sofia says. "You talk too much. Maybe he could teach you somethin'."

Uno lobs the first pitch right down the middle.

Danny follows every inch of the yellow felt's flight but doesn't take the bat off his shoulder. Instead he visualizes contact. Pictures the barrel of the bat meeting the rubber ball and where. Pictures finishing with perfect follow-through.

Raul gathers the ball on the short hop a few feet behind the plate, tosses back to Uno.

Danny watches Uno snatch the ball with his glove and shoot Sofia a look.

He doesn't swing at Uno's next pitch, either. Instead he measures the slow arc. Shifts his weight from his back foot to his front foot just before the ball crosses the trash can lid. He plays the contact out in his head but doesn't take a swing.

When Uno gets the toss back from Raul this time, he

throws his hands in the air and spins to Sofia. "I know you ain't brought me another punk too scared to swing. Bad enough I gotta deal with Biscuit back there. I ain't got time for no nervous cats."

"Come on, cuz," Sofia calls out. "Swing at one."

The guys in the field grow noticeably restless. Lolo stands up straight, throws a dirt clod at Chico, who ducks at the last minute. Rene sits down on the grass, reties a loose shoelace. Skinny Pedro isn't even paying attention. He's poking around the nativity scene, talking to himself in Spanish.

Danny waves the bat through the strike zone again. Looks back at the Mexican scout look-alike.

Uno stares in at him, says: "You plannin' on swingin' at *all*, homey?"

Danny nods.

"Sure 'bout that?"

Danny nods again.

Uno rolls his eyes, wipes forehead sweat on the shoulder of his jersey.

Manuel hops up and down on the tailgate. He cups his hands around his mouth and yells: "Hey, batter, batter. Swing! Batter!"

Danny looks over his shoulder at Manuel. Turns his head and sees all the neighborhood kids watching from the cul-de-sac. The girl with the kid. He takes a deep breath, another practice swing. Wonders what these people think of him. The new kid. The light-skinned kid. Wonders if any of them will be his friends this summer—though it's pretty tough to make friends now that he doesn't talk so much.

Uno says something under his breath to the guys on the lawn behind him. Everybody laughs. Then he turns around and haphazardly tosses the next pitch.

4

Danny waits on this one. Makes out white seams in a sea of yellow felt. Spinning through the air like a softball. Like a beach ball. Like a big spinning globe, the planet Earth. He locks in. Shifts his weight quick and turns on the pitch, drives the barrel through the zone.

Crushes it.

A muted gunshot sound carries across the lawn as the ball explodes off Danny's bat. Everybody looks up as the tennis ball soars above their heads, a tiny dot in the bright blue sky. A distant commuter plane. A drifting bird. One of the hawks his dad used to stop and point out whenever they walked through the canyon.

The ball clears not only the Rodriguez roof but the roof of the house behind the Rodriguez house, too. It ends up on another street altogether, at a different address.

Danny watches his long ball clear both roofs. Watches the expressions change on all the guys' faces. He holds his breath for a sec. Holds on to the feeling of perfect contact swimming through his arms and shoulders. His chest. A tiny man-made earthquake inside of his body.

When Danny was a kid, his dad told him being a great pitcher is better than being a great hitter. The guy on the mound controls the entire game, he'd said. Controls the pace. Who sees what pitch. Who has to dive out of the way to avoid taking one in the back. And then he dropped it. Never brought it up again. But Danny always remembered. That night he put the bat down and decided to become a pitcher, what he is today.

Secretly, though, it still makes him feel alive to crush something with a bat. Almost as much as striking somebody out.

Danny realizes that everybody in the entire cul-de-sac is perfectly still, silent. Like statues. And they're all looking at him. Like people looked at Kyle Sorenson, the best player at Leucadia Prep.

The guys on the field turn and look at each other.

Uno stays staring at Danny.

The silence is finally broken when Sofia shouts: "Ha! See! I told you! I told you! Go 'head, Uno, throw him another one! He's about to swipe all y'all's *billetes*!"

Danny steps away from the trash can lid. He pretends to concentrate on the barrel of his bat, but secretly he's watching the guys on the lawn. There's nothing better than the shocked looks on their faces. Makes his breaths come quicker. Deeper. Makes his skin tingle and his heart pump harder.

Rene starts toward the fence but stops suddenly, turns to Uno. "Should I go look for it?"

Uno shakes his head. "Forget it." He reaches into the mailbox and pulls out a new tennis ball.

A buzz starts spreading through the different groups scattered around the cul-de-sac. A few people move closer to the action on the lawn.

Manuel climbs off the tailgate and stands behind Danny's back shoulder. He starts chanting, louder than usual: "Hey, batter, batter! Hey, batter, batter!"

Uno steps up to the makeshift mound, tosses another pitch.

Danny smashes this one, too, sends it flying well over both roofs again.

Sofia jumps up and down, laughing and pointing at Danny. "Show 'em, cuz! Who's nervous *now*, Uno?"

Carmen and Flaca jump with her.

The guys on the field back up against the house, far as they can go.

Uno pulls another tennis ball. He winds up and throws this one harder.

But Danny cranks it again. Sends the tennis ball even higher than the previous two. It doesn't clear the second house this time, doesn't go as far, but it takes forever for it to finally fall behind the Rodriguez house for another home run.

The Mexican boys all race around the house to retrieve it.

Uno's face goes blank as he walks toward the fence, waits for the kids to come back with the ball. He walks around the mailbox, avoids all eye contact.

"That's three," Chico says, a slight smirk on his face. "No outs, either, eh, Uno?"

"About to catch you, Uno," Raul says.

"He ain't catchin' a *damn* thing," Uno barks as one of the boys drops the ball into his open mitt. He walks back to his pitching spot, wiping his increasingly sweaty brow on his jersey sleeve. Looks at the ball.

Sofia jogs over to Danny. She holds up his right arm and squeezes his muscle. "Ooh, you in trouble now," she yells out to Uno. She kisses her cousin on the cheek and then hustles back to her girls, all of them giving each other girly high fives.

Uno kicks the toe of his Nikes against the crumbling curb, ignores Sofia.

Just as Danny steps to the trash can lid, Uno fires a tennis ball as hard as he can at Danny's chin.

Danny dives backward, onto the asphalt. Looks up at Uno, who's staring him down from the curb.

"Wha'chu doin', kid?" Uno shouts. "Why you fallin' like a little bitch? That wasn't even close."

"Uno!" Sofia yells.

Raul catches the ricochet off Mr. Rodriguez's truck. He walks out toward Uno shaking his head. "Come on, man! Just throw it regular, like Chee did for you."

"I *am* throwin' it regular."

"Gotta give him a chance to hit," Raul says, tossing the tennis ball back to Uno.

"I *am*."

Raul pats Danny on the shoulder as he marches back behind the plate.

Danny takes a practice swing, prepares himself for the next wild pitch. He can see in Uno's eyes, the guy's not gonna let it go down like this.

5

Uno winds up and fires another fastball inside.

Danny tries to turn on it, but he gets jammed. Hits the tennis ball with the inside part of the bat, near his hands, and the bat goes flying.

The ball soars high into the air. All the guys on the lawn crane their necks as they wait for it to finally start dropping back down to earth. When it does, they jockey for position. Lolo leaps into the air and snags it with a bare hand again, holds the ball high above his head. "See, I catch another one! Ha ha!"

"That's one!" Uno yells in the direction of Sofia.

But Uno's smile quickly vanishes when Chico shouts: "Yo, man! The bat got Manny!"

Everybody turns to Manuel, who's holding his bloody face in his hands, the bat lying still beside him. He pulls his hands away to look up for Uno, total shock in his eyes. Blood streaming down his face and neck, soaking his white T-shirt.

Uno, Chico and Raul rush toward him. Marco and Lolo hustle after.

Uno lays Manuel on his back in the grass, holds his face still to look over the damage. His nose is totally busted, blood streaming out of both nostrils. His lip is split. One of his two front teeth has snapped in half.

Uno rips off his Raider jersey and presses it against the bridge of Manuel's nose. "Call your brother!" he shouts at Chico. "Tell him we need his car. Go!"

Chico races off to his bag to get his cell.

Uno caresses the back of his brother's head. "You're gonna be all right, Manny. I got you."

Manuel looks up at Uno, eyes wild with fear. "I didn't mean to do it, Uno."

"I know you didn't," Uno says.

"I'm sorry," Manuel says, tears welling in his eyes now, running down his face and mixing with the blood. "I'm sorry."

"It's *okay*, Manny," Uno says. "Just don't talk no more. Here, keep the shirt against your nose. I got you." He tries to smile.

Danny moves closer, looks at all the blood on Manny's face and feels his stomach drop. What has he done?

"I didn't mean it," Manuel says to Uno again. "I was cheering like you said I could, and I didn't mean anything."

"It's *okay*," Uno says. "Come on, no more talkin'."

He tells Chico to keep the shirt pressed against his brother's nose and then rushes Danny, shoves him with both hands. "The fuck you doin', man? Why you throw the bat at my little bro?"

Danny backs up a couple steps, surprised.

Sofia pushes in between them and starts screaming for Uno to step off. "It was an accident, Uno! You think he did it on *purpose*?"

Uno shoves Sofia out of the way and gets in Danny's face

again, pokes a finger into his forehead. "Answer me, bitch! Why you throw the bat?"

Danny backpedals, puts his hands up and says: "I didn't mean to." But his voice comes out too weak to be understood. He looks over at Manuel, lying limp in Chico's lap, then back at Uno. *I'm sorry.*

"Nah, you gonna *tell* me about it. You messed up my little bro's face."

Sofia pleads with Uno, fights to get between them.

"Talk, bitch!" Uno shouts, and he shoves Danny again. "Say somethin'!"

I'm sorry. I'm sorry. I'm sorry.

"Talk, bitch! Why you throw the bat at my little bro?"

Danny glances at the guys watching from behind Uno. He's about to say he's sorry again, louder this time, so he'll be heard, but it's too late. Uno's already gritting his teeth. Uno's already stepping forward with all his weight, delivering an overhead right that smashes flush into Danny's face. Snaps his head back. Buckles his knees.

6

Danny hits the pavement in a flurry of blackness, the back of his head whiplashing against a patch of dirt next to the crumbling curb, making an awful cracking sound. Like a bat smacking a baseball. A lightning flash goes off in his head.

Raul and Chico rush Uno, hold him back.

Sofia screams him down in Spanish at the top of her lungs.

Kids around the cul-de-sac rush the scene to get a better look at what's happening.

Carmen holds Sofia away from Uno. But Sofia kicks and elbows her way out of Carmen's grasp. She runs at Uno, throws a wild open hand, which Uno catches. Raul pulls Sofia away as she screams: "Hit *my* cousin, *pinche puto*! I'll kill you!"

Uno shouts back, "Look at my brother, Sofe! He's bleedin' all over the place!"

Danny's vaguely aware of the commotion building around him. He knows he's been hit. Punched. Saw the fist just before it landed. Knows he fell, that a mound of dirt caught the back of his head like a stiff mitt. Knows there was a loud crashing sound in his brain. But he doesn't know if he's hurt yet. Doesn't know if he's awake. He hears people above him. Sees their images. Muddled voices and shadows moving around above. The packed dirt under the back of his head. The warm liquid running down his neck. Sweat? Blood? Running into his mouth. Salty. Smell of copper. Pooling under his matted hair. Staining the cul-de-sac.

Somebody is lifting his head off the sidewalk, setting it on a towel. A girl's hand. Nail polish. Red. He doesn't look up to see whose face it is. Just stares at her red fingernails. So red. Shiny.

He concentrates on his breathing, the air going in and out of his lungs. Then he closes his eyes so he can rest a second.

Dear Dad:

    I keep thinking about the last time you and me walked home from the Digueño baseball field. I was even skinnier back then, my ribs sticking out all over.

    Mom was gone that week, but nobody ever said where she went or why. She was just gone, and you were watching us.

    We were walking together and you told

me, "I did somethin' crazy, boy. And some shit's gonna change 'cause of it. Soon. I just wanted you to hear it from me first, all right?" I nodded, trying to think what was up. It was the most you'd ever said to me at one time. And then two weeks later you were gone.

Lately I've been playing your words back. Over and over, in my head. I've been analyzing not only what you said but how you said it. Trying to figure out what you meant that day. And I think I finally got it. You were talking about me!

At the time I was too dumb to get it. I was more concentrating on the strides you were taking. I was trying to make mine long enough so that the shadow of my steps matched up with the shadow of yours. But now I'm older.

I remember then you stopped cold and pointed to the sky. You'd spotted a hawk gliding overhead. Your favorite thing in the world. Instead of looking at the hawk, though, I stared at your face. The leathery brown skin. The stubble on your chin. Your strong cheekbones and dark eyes. Mom always said you had a face like an Indian. I was thinking in my head: Do I have a face like an Indian, too? When I grow up will my face look like my dad's? Will my skin get dark like his if I stay in the sun all day?

7

Danny pops open his eyes, looks into the sky, but instead of finding the hawk he finds the face of a girl. *His* girl. The one with the lighter skin. Her eyes locked on him. And she seems so concerned. Her shiny hair falling toward his face.

And her mouth is moving. He can't make out what she's saying because she's clearly speaking Spanish. But he realizes she's even prettier up close. She's the prettiest girl he's ever seen. At any of his schools. In any of his towns. Her eyes so big and brown, almost like a cartoon, but in a good way. Her face so perfect. It makes him feel something in his chest again.

She looks away for a second, at somebody else, and then comes back to him.

Suddenly he's aware of the pain in his jaw, the scary numbness at the back of his head. And the girl looks genuinely worried. About him. For some reason her worry makes the back of his head hurt less.

He tries to smile. So she'll know he's okay. He's gonna be fine. But instead he closes his eyes again. . . .

Finally I looked at the sky, too, that day. Like you. And we watched the giant black bird soar over a pack of thick trees and back again. Measuring the sky with its wings.

But I have something I wanna tell you, Dad. I know why you said that to me now. About how things were gonna change. You were telling me you were going to Mexico. You were sick of living in a city with so many white people, with a white wife, with two kids who were half white. You wanted to be around more Mexicans. Your real family. But what I wanted to tell you, Dad, is how much I've changed since that day. How much better I am. How much stronger and darker and more Mexican I am. Matter of fact, just today I knocked some kid out. A big black dude who was trying to mess with Sofia. I pushed him and yelled at him in Spanish and then I punched him right in the face, Dad. You should have seen how fast this kid fell to the asphalt. And then I just stood over him, waiting to see if he'd try to get up.

I wish you knew that about me back then. I wish I would have told you. But at the time I didn't know you were leaving. So I just stood there with you. Both of us watching that hawk. And when it finally dove behind the pack of trees and was lost, you lowered your head and continued walking.

And I followed you.

Spaghetti
with Meatballs

1

"A leopard can't never change his spots," Senior says, stopping Uno from crossing against the light by snatching an elbow. He fingers the crosswalk button with his free hand, shaking his head. "That shit's real, son. Trust me. A leopard's spots come from nature, and nature's unnegotiable." He lets go of Uno's elbow and subtly crosses himself with a forefinger, points to the clouds.

Uno nods at his old man, looks both ways—not a single car in sight.

He slips off his baseball mitt and tucks it under his arm, wipes an ashy hand across his face. As his old man goes on a little more about leopards he glances down at a broken forty bottle lying at the mouth of the gutter, right under his kicks.

Wonders how much alcohol must be flowing through National City's gutters after an average Friday night. Probably enough to give them guppies swimming around down there a nice little buzz.

Ever since Uno can remember, the first Saturday of every month his biological father has driven down from Oxnard to pay him a visit. Senior has a whole new family now—a pretty black wife and a brand-new baby boy—but the guy still makes an effort to see his firstborn.

Senior will pull up in his old-school Chevy Impala at around noon, crank the parking brake across the street and tap his horn. To avoid dealing with his moms, Uno will hop through his bedroom window, and the two of them'll walk the eight blocks to Tony's Barbecue on Honeysuckle Street. They'll grab a table in back, eat a plate of hot wings and a couple po' boys and "discuss" Uno's self-image.

But this week's discussion is going down a different road. Since they last saw each other, Uno's been in trouble twice. First he got questioned by the cops for the incident with Sofia's cousin at the derby. Whole thing turned into a big mess, and he regrets it. Luckily, the kid didn't press any charges, so nothing happened. But then a week later he gave some frat dude a beat-down outside the Horton Plaza Mall. Gave him a nasty gash under his left eye, dislocated his jaw. A couple security guards caught the tail end of the altercation, rushed the scene and contained them both until the cops showed. When Uno wouldn't fully cooperate with the cops' tired line of questioning they cuffed his ass, shoved him in the back of the squad car and took him to the station, where he had to stay overnight.

Uno's mom and stepdad didn't show up until the next morning. Before he saw them, he overheard his moms asking

one of the cops at the front desk, "Lemme ask you this, offi-
cer: what happens if I *refuse* to take my son back?"

2

The walk sign lights green and Uno and his old man cross together. After a few rare seconds of quiet, Senior gives Uno a
little whack to the back of his dome. "Why you lookin' at
your glove for, boy? You should be lookin' in my eyes. The
answers isn't in some game, they in the pupils of men who
seek the path to wisdom. Men who learned how to accept
they spots, learned how to make the best of 'em, learned to
love 'em."

"I *am* lookin' in your eyes, Pop," Uno says, rubbing the
back of his head.

"Man is his own best doctor," Senior says as they continue down the block, side by side. Uno's every bit as tall
these days, but his skin is still a couple shades lighter—the
Mexican brown of his mom's side diluting some of Senior's
shiny black. "They got mad drugs now, right? Ritalin, Vi-
codin, Zoloft. A kid gots some extra energy these days and
they wanna pump his little ass full of chemicals. But lemme
ask you this, Uno: Who benefits more from all these prescrip-
tions? The patient or the doctor? Is they tryin' to help this little youngster? Or control his ass? It's a simple conflict of
interest we talkin' 'bout."

Senior taps at his right temple twice with two fingers,
raises an eyebrow at his son. "A wise man don't just consider
the shit he sees, Uno, he considers what's *behind* the shit he
sees."

Senior's a distinguished-looking, reformed-gangster type.

Always shows up to see Uno looking polished: a perfectly pressed button-down tucked into a pair of Dickies, clean Timberlands. Keeps his salt-and-pepper crop cut close to the scalp, his silver sideburns and goatee meticulously sculpted. Only things disorderly about the man these days are the thick tattoo running across the front of his neck *(NANA RIP)* and the long, jagged scar running from his chin to his upper ear.

Uno's mom claims the cheek scar is the work of Senior's own father, Senior senior. According to the story she tells, pre-Jesus, Senior was the biggest black gangster in San Diego: "Get a hold of that man's rap sheet if you want the *truth*, Uno. Got more pages than any of them books he claims he reads: selling drugs, shooting up liquor stores, jacking cars, burglaries, even tried to rob his own father one time. Bastard was in prison the day you took your first breath, Uno. You remember that next time *tu papa* comes breezing down here talkin' like he on some kind of moral high horse. Nuh-uh, *mijo*, he don't fool me. I know what's in that son of a bitch's heart."

When Uno and Senior reach Senior's old Impala, they settle onto the curb next to one another. Senior lists a few more drugs abused by doctors, but Uno's attention drifts elsewhere. He steals a quick glance at his old man's profile. Follows the path of the scar, top to bottom, then looks away. As a kid he used to have this crazy recurring dream: Some blur of a hooded black man was chasing him through a dark cemetery. No matter what kind of moves Uno put on or how fast he ran, the guy would always be gaining on him. Finally he'd leap at Uno's feet like a football player, drag him down by his ankles. Pinned to the ground, Uno would look up at where the guy's face should have been, but there *was* no face. There was only this huge scar, shaped just like Senior's, floating around inside an otherwise empty hood. At that point Uno would let out a punk-ass scream and wake up.

3

Senior reaches into Uno's glove and pulls out the beat-up baseball. He spins the seams around in his fingers for a sec and then studies the scuffed-up label. "I'll tell you who makes out on them drugs, boy," he says. "The American aristocrat. You ever heard that word, Uno? *Aristocrat?*"

"Nah, Pop."

"Means rich people. White folks livin' in them big-ass houses you see in places like La Jolla. Folks who don't care nothin' for nobody with a little color to they skin. See, I been doin' a grip of reading, boy. I got all kinda bookshelves in my house. Filled to the capacity with books. A wise man always surrounds hisself with the right type of biographies."

Uno nods. A fly lands on his knee, but he manages to chase it off without his old man thinking he's not paying attention.

"Now, I used to go down the same lonely and loveless road you travelin'," Senior says, taking Uno's chin in his hand. Forcing eye contact. "When I was seventeen like you I used to throw down, take people's shit. Used to smoke anything I could roll up in a Zig-Zag. But I didn't love nobody. I didn't love *myself.*"

"I hear ya, Pop," Uno says, looking into his old man's cloudy eyes.

"Now I work a hard, honest day's work. People come to me and say, 'Senior, why you don't never use none of your sick days or vacation days?' I tell 'em, 'Because I found myself in my work. In being a provider. In being a responsible human being.'" Senior releases Uno's chin, flips back his baseball.

Uno slips the ball into his mitt, nodding. Sets his mitt in his lap.

"I know how hard it is, son. You see yourself in them thugs you roll with. You find acceptance. Reinforcement. I been there and back, two times. But answer me this question: you roll with suckers, play sucker games, come up with sucker schemes—what that makes you, boy?"

Uno shrugs.

"Makes you a *sucker*, motherfucker!"

Senior's deep, raspy laugh sounds just like his old Chevy engine turning over.

Uno laughs a little, too, but inside he's trying to figure out what his old man's talking about. Sometimes he wonders if he has a learning disability or something. He knows Senior's dropping mad knowledge, but he can't ever seem to scoop it up, make it stick to his brain.

Uno slips on his mitt again, pulls out his baseball and tosses it back in. He glances across the street. Still no sign of his moms. A group of Mexican kids walk past the house, one of them taps the mailbox. The kid glances at Uno, gives him a what's-up with his head. Uno recognizes the dude from the neighborhood, nods back.

4

"What up with Manny?" Senior says. "You lookin' out for your little bro like I told you?"

"Course I am, Pop," Uno says. "Moms and Ernesto got him stayin' in some halfway house for retarded kids, but I visit him. He took one on the nose at the derby couple weeks back. He all right, though."

Senior scoffs, shakes his head. "They put little man away, huh? Bad business." He leans forward, says: "I want you to look at me, boy. I want you to look right in these two eyes I got."

Uno sits up a little straighter. He hooks his arms around his knees and tries to look even deeper into his pop's eyes than he already was. How can he show Senior he's looking even deeper?

"I love you, son."

Uno cuts away from his old man's eyes. He pulls the ball from his mitt and tosses it back in, mumbles: "Me too, Pop."

Senior snatches his boy by the chin again, forces eye contact. "You heard what I just told you, boy? I *love* you!" He pauses a few seconds, adds: "Just like I love Jesus! He felt powerless, too, you know. Like you and me. When he took the most messed-up suckers and died for them, he died for *us!*"

Uno tries to nod, but his old man's got a pretty tight grip on his chin. The most he can manage is a little facial vibration in his dad's callused hand.

"It's on you, boy. You already know the answers—look at your pop, Uno! You can't give in to them feelings that say you ain't good enough. That you ain't mean just as much as the American aristocrat. It takes a murderer to be isolated from the rest of society to understand what wrong he done."

Uno swallows, tries to nod.

"You wanna evolve, son? Or you wanna stay the same? It's on you, man. I could serve you spaghetti every night, right? Seven days a week, plain old tired spaghetti. But say one night I throw some meatballs in the mix. That's a change, son. . . . That change is in *you!*"

Uno tries to nod.

"That change is God."

Uno clears his throat. He starts to say something, but Senior's not done.

"A man cannot run away from the first light of dawn for forever, son. You fake it till you make it, know what I'm sayin'?"

When Senior lets go of his chin Uno nods.

Senior picks up a rock and tosses it down the road. "I want you to come live with me, Uno. Already talked with my wife and my baby. We extending that invitation to you as a family. You pull together five, six hundred bones over the summer, like a deposit, a show of good faith, and you can come live with your old man. See, I believe in you, Uno. And I'll always be here for you."

Uno feels something tighten in his chest, his throat. He sticks the baseball in his mitt, pulls his hand out and scratches the side of his shaved head.

"You my gift to the world, boy."

Uno looks up at his old man, mumbles, "Thanks, Pop."

"Don't you never forget that."

Uno nods.

Just then, Uno's mom comes storming out of the house, torn screen door whacking shut behind her. "Uno, you come on in now! You been listening to this nonsense long enough!"

Senior stands up, brushes off the back of his Dickies. "Oh, that's how it is, Loretta? You eavesdroppin' on people?"

"Didn't have no choice! The whole damn neighborhood heared you blabbering on like some kinda minister. But you *ain't* a minister, Senior! You're a plain ol' garbage man." She starts across the street. "Uno, you better get inside and finish cleaning up that bathroom. You ain't done by the time Ernesto gets home you gonna be in some trouble."

"Hell with Ernesto!" Senior shouts. "This *my* son!"

"Ernesto's twice the man you ever were." Loretta takes Uno by the elbow, pulls him to his feet.

Senior jerks Uno out of his mom's grasp. "You treatin' the boy like a bitch. No wonder he's actin' out."

"He acts out 'cause he got a good-for-nothing black bastard for a father."

"Bitch, if I didn't have the Holy Ghost . . . I swear to God."

"Oh, now you wanna threaten people," Uno's mom says, backing up. She spins around and marches back across the street, barks over her shoulder: "We'll see about them threats when I call the cops."

Uno watches Senior key open his car door, slip into the driver's seat, slam the door shut and start the car. The roar of the engine reminds him of Senior's laugh, but the look on his old man's face couldn't be more serious.

Senior rolls down his window, says: "You gonna come live with your old man, Uno. In Oxnard."

Senior peels away from the curb and speeds up and over the hill, out of sight.

Uno starts walking up the same hill, on foot.

Loretta flings open the screen door again. She steps out onto the porch with the cordless pinned between her ear and shoulder, shouts: "Where you think *you're* going?"

"Out."

"Where?"

"Out!"

She pulls the phone from her ear, holds it by her side. "That man comes down here once a month, Uno! I'm here *every single day*! You think about that!"

Uno ignores her words, continues up the hill.

5

Uno's mind is a mixed bag as he veers right on Twenty-eighth St., heads toward Las Palmas Park. His old man has never said anything like that before. That he's a gift. That he should move up to Oxnard. And why does his moms always have to start bawlin' the guy out like that? Almost every Saturday his old man comes through it ends up with the two of them yelling. And Uno's stuck in the middle. One pulling his left arm, the other pulling his right. Like it's some kind of tug-of-war between black and Mexican, and he's the rope.

When Uno's a few blocks from the park he reaches down, picks up a couple stray rocks and shoves them in his mitt, next to his baseball. He pictures Senior's scar, remembers those dreams he used to have. But how's he supposed to raise that much paper over one summer? Five hundred bones isn't no joke. Imagine how many money pots he'd have to win during Saturday home run derbies. And then he decides what he's gonna do. He's gonna move up to Oxnard. With his old man. He's gonna figure out a way to get that money.

Uno pulls one of the rocks from his mitt and fingers it a bit, flips it over in his hand. Then he turns quick and fires it at an apartment building, hard as he can. The rock flies through the security bars of a second-story window and crashes through the glass, setting off a howling alarm.

Uno drops the rest of the rocks and tears down the road, laughing his ass off.

He cuts into the mouth of Las Palmas Park, slides down the ice-plant-covered hill, races across the weed-infested base-ball field and leaps the crumbling fence along the first-base line. He ducks under the rusted bleachers, chest heaving in and out, heart pounding in his throat. And he can't stop laughing. Why's he laughing? He's already on probation. How's this shit funny?

He watches the hill for a squad car or a couple cops on foot, trying to catch his breath. Scans the sky half expecting a helicopter to come through aiming a high-powered spotlight down onto the field. But there's nothing in the sky except a couple puffy white clouds. The foot cops'll probably show up any minute. They'll slip down the ice plants after him clutching their guns. Or their clubs. Or the guy who lives in the second-story apartment he just nailed will appear at the top of the hill gripping a bat.

Either way, there'll be someone looking for him. And soon. He knows that.

Uno stays tucked under the bleachers for hours. Picturing his moms pulling him up by the elbow. Senior's face when he rolled down his window. The Impala speeding over the hill, out of sight. The rock crashing through the window. Manny's bloody face and Sofia's cousin hitting the ground after he punched him. He pictures these things over and over while he waits for the foot cops. Or the helicopter spotlight. Or the guy who lives in the apartment.

But nobody ever comes.

Stuck in
Uncle Tommy's
Apartment

1

After Danny's trip to emergency, where he took five stitches under his left eye, ten in the back of his head—where he had to talk to cops and fill out paperwork and look his uncle Tommy and uncle Ray dead in the eye and lie—since then Danny's spent almost two full weeks hiding out in Tommy's National City apartment in a sort of depression. At least that's what he's decided to call it. Depression. He's never actually been depressed before, but his mom has. And when *she's* depressed she refuses to go to work or the grocery store or the bank or anywhere else. She gets stuck inside the apartment, day and night. Inside her room. Underneath the covers. Like she's sick. Only she's not really sick. Not physically, anyway.

"Don't worry," she always says when Danny stands at her bedroom door. "Seriously, Danny, go throw the baseball around at school or something. I'll be fine. Mom's just sort of stuck right now."

Ever since his dad took off, Danny's drifted apart from his mom. He hardly even acknowledges her presence these days. She's the reason he went quiet in the first place. The reason his dad's gone. The reason he's whitewashed and an outsider even with his own family. But whenever his mom got stuck it was another story. It was hard to stay mad.

And here he is stuck himself now. Meaning he's depressed. Because all he's felt like doing for the past five days is hiding out in Sofia's bedroom, on his cot, digging into the inside of his forearm with his nails to remind him he's a real person.

He has to keep away from people so he can think things over.

2

Wasn't three weeks ago that Danny was standing along the chain-link fence of Leucadia Prep's brand-new, state-of-the-art baseball facility, watching the team practice for playoffs.

He was always on the outside at Leucadia Prep, but it didn't *get* more outside than having to watch the varsity baseball squad take the field without him. Daily. While he stood on the wrong side of the chain-link in his generic private-school uniform: white short-sleeved collared shirt tucked into pleated khakis, navy blue tie knotted at the neck and falling toward the school-emblem buckle of his belt.

This had been Danny's spot since Coach Sullivan pulled

him aside after the last day of tryouts—in front of everybody—patted him on the back and tried to let him down easy.

"Listen, son," he'd said, walking Danny off the school's manicured infield. "You got great stuff. You really do. But you have to learn to keep it in the strike zone. A high-speed fastball doesn't do me a whole lot of good if it's three feet off the plate. You get what I'm saying?"

Danny nodded.

"Do me a favor," Sullivan added, unlatching the gate and pushing it open. "Spend the year working on your control, your location, and let's try this again next year. Okay?"

Danny nodded and stepped through the gate, secretly digging nails into forearm.

Sullivan pulled the gate shut behind him.

Over the course of the three-day tryout Danny had struck out three batters, walked four and *hit* seven. He lit up the radar with his fastball, sure, but he couldn't put it where he wanted. Not the greatest situation when you consider Leucadia Prep baseball was perennially top ten in the state. When you consider that every other hopeful pitcher had an important business-suit dad cheering him on from the stands, chatting up Sullivan the second there was a break in the action.

When you consider Danny was the new kid. Again. His third school in three years. The semi-mute Mexican kid. The kid whose dad, Javier Lopez, not only had failed to show up in a suit but had failed to show up at all. To anything. Three years and counting.

So there Danny was, standing at the fence watching Kyle Sorenson pick up a bat to take batting practice. It was the team's last practice before they went to the state finals in Fresno. Danny's last chance to watch Kyle in the batter's box. According to *Street and Smith's* big preseason baseball issue,

Kyle was the number one outfield prospect west of the Mississippi. *Baseball America* had Kyle penciled in as a surefire top five pick in the upcoming MLB draft.

The entire Leucadia Prep outfield retreated at the sight of their big cleanup hitter. They shifted left and positioned the heels of their cleats just inside the warning track. Scouts, scattered throughout the brand-new bleachers behind home plate, sat up a little straighter. They opened their eyes a little wider, folded up well-worn newspapers and set aside Styrofoam cups full of sunflower seed shrapnel. Coach Sullivan emerged from the dugout, pulled off his cap and ran his fingers through his rapidly thinning hair.

Kyle was eighteen but looked like a full-grown man. Blond crew cut and a square jaw. Biceps the size of most kids' thighs. Broad shoulders like a running back posing in full pads.

Danny studied Kyle the way his fellow honor students studied their biology textbooks.

When Kyle was finally set, chin to left shoulder, knees slightly bent, aluminum bat pointing up at the heavens, the batting practice pitcher threw one right down the pipe. Kyle took a vicious cut, smashed the ball a mile high.

The pitcher snapped his head around to watch the flight of the baseball. All four infielders looked straight up, watched the ball shoot up into the afternoon sky like a 747. The guys in the outfield watched the ball soar well over their heads. Coach Sullivan took a step forward and watched. Mr. Sorenson, Kyle's defense-attorney father, followed the flight of the ball while offering the only technical commentary he could these days, "Way to keep your head down, Ky." Several scouts stood up as the home run ball broke up a small flock of pigeons over the faculty parking lot behind centerfield. A pen-pocketed math teacher looked up, fumbled with his keys, opened his car door and ducked into the driver's seat for cover.

Even Kyle himself followed the ball's rainbow arc across the bright blue North County sky.

Only person who *didn't* watch the ball off the crack of the bat was Danny. He started out in the same place as everybody else. Followed the pitcher's leg kick, the pitcher's release point, the pitcher's follow-through, the spin of the baseball's seams, Kyle's stance, Kyle's swing, but at the point of contact, when everybody else looked west to see where this particular Sorenson bomb would land, Danny stayed with Kyle.

He studied post-swing mechanics: Where did his follow-through leave him? Where did his bat end up? His feet? His shoulders? His hands? His head? His eyes?

But Danny was looking for more than just technical answers. He needed to figure out how Kyle got there. How he became a great player. A star. Because that's exactly what *he* had to become. And it wasn't for his ego, so that everybody in school would stare at him and talk about him the way they did with Kyle. No, he needed only one person to look.

3

That night Danny's mom had arranged a big dinner party. He and his sis were finally going to meet the new boyfriend.

Danny walked to the door, put an eye to the peephole and got his first look at Randy. Guy was standing in the hall business-suit slick, just like he'd suspected. Gray three-piece, sophisticated glasses and clean-shaven face. A bottle of champagne in one hand, bouquet of roses in the other.

Watching Randy run a hand through his short sandy-blond hair, Danny shook his head. The way his dad might. Of course, he thought, a *white* guy. His mom had dated nothing but white guys since the day his dad disappeared. Yeah, *she* was white, and Danny himself was *half* white, but it was still disrespectful. She knew how pissed his dad used to get when he caught some white guy checking her out.

All she had to do was go back to that day in Del Mar when they were at the beach and his dad rose up on some muscle-bound white guy for whistling. His mom was sobbing as she pulled Danny and Julia around to the other side of the public bathroom. She went to her knees clutching Julia to her chest and shouting "I'm sorry!" over and over. The sound of punches landing and shouting and then sirens and cops shouting. Danny's mom said she was sorry, over and over, throughout the entire thing. While the cops handcuffed his dad and pushed him into the back of their squad car by his face. "I'm sorry, Javi!" she said. "I'm sorry! I'm sorry! I'm sorry!"

But was she *really* sorry? Danny wondered as he stood at the door, peering through the peephole. Because here she was again, inviting another white guy into the apartment.

4

Danny puts his fingertips up to his stitches, feels the jagged threads weaving in and out of his skin.

Sofia walks in to check on him again, but he pretends he's asleep. He feels her standing over him, staring down. Feels her touch the top of his head. "We saved you some tacos, cuz," she says. "I'll bring 'em to you when you wake up, okay?" He feels her stand there a few more seconds and then walk back out of the room.

Danny opens his eyes. He's so lucky he still has his dad's family. The Lopezes. Throughout all the moving around they did after his dad left, the different towns and high schools and apartment complexes, Danny's relatives made sure his mom still dropped him and his sis off in National City for Thanksgiving and Mother's Day and every other Christmas. Where all his *tíos* and *tías* and cousins are cracking on each other and playing horseshoes in the dirt alley behind the house and eating baby empanadas and toothpick-stuck chorizo bites off plastic trays. Where they are drinking home-made horchata and Pacifico and Bud Light and tequila with lime—always tequila. And since their snaps are a random mix of both Spanish and English, Danny gets only half of every joke. Not enough to laugh. But he laughs anyway. He points at whoever's currently taking the heat, puts a fist to his mouth and says in his head, Oh, shit, that's *cold*! He slaps Uncle Ray's hand and laughs some more, but they know he doesn't quite have the whole picture.

And he knows they know.

This is why sometimes he feels as out of place at his grandma's as he does at Leucadia Prep.

And when his grandma passes out homemade tortillas, hot off the griddle, she does it based on family rank. It's a subtle and unspoken ranking system, but one each and every person in the house understands. And 'cause he's so *guapo* and gets such good grades and lives in such a better neighborhood these days—and 'cause in a weird way Grandma's almost *ashamed* of being Mexican—he's always the first to eat. Even before his uncles. His dad when he was still around.

And sure, that's when it *seems* like he belongs, but it's more complicated than that.

His uncles and cousins may smile and nod and even crack on him some—"D-man, Li'l D, D-money, roll it up right, man, fold it at the end, here do like this, homey, with your fingers, don't hold it like no white boy now or else the butter's gonna drip right out the bottom, get all over your hand"—but all he wants to do is give that tortilla right back to his grams. Hold off till the next round. Have her offer that first one up to his dad instead. Or Uncle Ray. Or Sofia and Veronica. Uncle Tommy and his new wife, Cecilia. Even Veronica's gangster boyfriend, Jesus. He'd just as soon wait till *everybody in the house* had one in their hand before he did.

And if people only knew how that felt. Having the whole family stare at him and his tortilla, these people he adores.

That's when he wishes he didn't get such good grades. When he wishes he lived even closer to the border than *they* did, in a one-room shack in the worst barrio this side of Tijuana. Dirt floors and no running water. When he wishes he got in more trouble at school, maybe a suspension on his record for fighting or bringing a switchblade to class. Maybe he could cuss out one of his private-school teachers in the hall during lunch: "I ain't gotta listen to you, white bitch!"

'Cause the very things Grandma gushes over are what shame him most. Such a good little boy. Such a pretty boy. Look at him doing all his homework before bed, studying for that big English midterm, taking out the trash without even being asked. Look at him writing letter after letter to his dad, even though his dad never even said goodbye to his bitch ass.

If it came down to a choice, it wouldn't *be* a choice. That top-tier tortilla? The butter running all down his fingers now, down his arm? Nah. To be a real Lopez, though—*that's* what he'd pick. A chip off the old block. One of the cousins from *el barrio*.

Things aren't always as they appear. Try inside out. Try hung up in plastic like a pair of Randy's dress slacks and put away for a special occasion—when all Danny's ever wanted to be was a pair of Grandma's worn-out house slippers.

47

And what's interesting is the way they all genuinely want him to succeed, to rise above the family history. Be the first Lopez to go to college. Come back one Mother's Day as a doctor or a lawyer or a dentist. A wealthy businessman. Hey look everybody, it's Professor Lopez! Look at him, Grams! The son of a bitch is pulling up in a *brand-new Lexus*!

But at the same time, he bets they subconsciously resent him, too. He's almost sure of it.

Take two Mother's Days ago when Uncle Tommy pointed to a line in the sports page and said, "What's this mean, Danny? 'H-o-l-i-s-t-i-c-a-l-l-y'?"

"Holistically," Danny fired back (he was still talking at that point). "Since the Padres are so young this year, the writer's urging fans not to get caught up in wins and losses but to consider the bigger picture."

Uncle Tommy nodded.

Danny's heart dropped.

Tommy slapped Danny on the back and said: "How you turn out to be such a smart motherfucker, D? I *know* it wasn't nothin' to do with your pops."

Danny shrugged and told him: "I ain't that smart, Uncle Tommy."

And he *ain't*!

Talkin' like that to grown folks. What he should've done was act like he'd never even *seen* that word before. Stared at it just as perplexed as his uncle. Offered to pull the dictionary off the bookshelf he'd helped his dad build next to Grandma's bed.

But it was too late. The damage had already been done. And when his uncle went back to the rest of his article, the rest of his beer, Danny went back to the rest of his life—seemingly on the inside of *la familia de Lopez,* but really on the outside.

5

In the bathroom, Danny applies the special ointment the doctor gave him for his stitches. But also still thinking things through. He dabs the cream on with a Q-tip, checks the mirror, screws on the lid and drops the tube into the drawer. He leaves the bathroom and heads back to his cot.

But just as he's leaving, his uncle Tommy is heading in. Tommy looks like he means business, has his cap turned backward, a day-old *Union-Tribune* tucked under his arm. He gives Danny a little fake jab on the walk-by and then pulls the door closed behind him. Before Danny can get to his cot, though, Tommy swings the door right back open, gasping for air. "Goddamn, D!" he shouts. "What the hell died in *your* ass?"

Danny stops cold in Sofia's doorway, turns to his uncle confused. All he'd done was put ointment on his stitches.

"Cecilia, baby," Tommy shouts, "the poor kid musta been backed up from here to Tijuana. You tellin' me we can't pour his irregular ass a bowl of bran flakes in the morning? Get him a mug of green tea? Jesus Christ, baby!"

Sofia and Cecilia start laughing so hard they're doubled over in the living room. But Danny's just standing there barefoot and shell-shocked.

"Sofe, where's the yellow police tape I swiped off that fire truck last Halloween? I'm serious, baby, go get it for your old man. Danny messed up my john so bad I gotta caution it off for the night."

It isn't until Uncle Tommy joins in on the laughter, goes back into the bathroom and closes the door behind him that Danny gets the joke.

For a few seconds he watches Sofia and Cecilia laugh, and then he laughs, too. Even though it sort of pulls where his stitches are. After a few seconds he ducks back into Sofia's room, lies on his cot and goes back to his thinking.

6

After Julia and Danny cleared the table of dirty plates, stacked them in the kitchen sink, Wendy tapped a fork against her half-empty wineglass and said: "Kids, come take a seat. Randy has a very important announcement to make. I want you to give him your undivided attention."

Danny and Julia took their seats.

Wendy turned to Randy. "Floor's all yours, babe."

Randy set down his wineglass and wiped his mouth with a napkin. He cleared his throat. "Danny. Julia. First off, let me just say thank you for a truly wonderful evening. Hearing about your baseball talent and academic success, Danny. And Julia, your interest in modern dance. I mean, no wonder Wendy just beams whenever she mentions you two."

Randy smiled, pulled the bottle of champagne out of the bucket of ice and wiped down the base with a hand towel. "Now, your mom and I have known each other for something like six or seven months."

"Seven and a half," Wendy said. "But who's counting?"

"Right. Seven and a half. Exactly. Not a ton of time in the grand scheme of things, I suppose. But I'm a firm believer in going with your gut. I got to where I am today by doing just that. And, not to pat myself on the back or anything, but I'm doing pretty darn well, I'd say. I own a beautiful three-bedroom condo on Russian Hill in San Francisco. My bedroom window takes up an entire wall. Get this, guys. Every morning I wake up, roll over in bed, and *bam!* There's Alcatraz. I have a decent amount of capital invested in coastal real estate—anyway, you get the idea. I don't bring all this up to float my own boat. No, I bring it up to illustrate the power of going with one's gut. And my gut in this case, Danny, Julia . . ." Randy looked at them both, one at a time, and then turned to a grinning Wendy. "Well, my gut tells me the feelings I have for your mom are the real thing."

The little grin on his mom's face bloomed into an all-out smile. She reached across the table and covered Randy's hand with her own.

Randy flipped his hand over to squeeze Wendy's hand. With his other hand he pulled the champagne bottle closer. "In light of this, last week I asked your mom to come live with me for the summer. In San Francisco. If things go well, which I fully expect they will, the move will become permanent. In the meantime, we're looking at the summer as a kind of a trial run. I've already paid the rent on your apartment here through September. If for any reason we feel the situation isn't working out, *any* of us, we simply go back to the way it was. You guys follow?"

Danny and Julia looked at each other. They looked at their mom.

"I'm not sure I've made myself clear," Randy said. "I'm inviting *you two* to live with me as well. One of my closest friends in the world, Mark Jenkins, has two children around your age. He has a real beat on the teen scene, I guess you could say. Anyway, we sat down a couple days ago and made a list of things you kids may be interested in—camps you could attend, sports teams you could join, dance classes, Julia, that you could sign up for. San Francisco is an amazing city full of wonderful opportunities. And I want you two to feel as welcome as your mom. This is a *package deal.*"

"But at the same time," Wendy added, "I've spoken to

your uncle Tommy and Cecilia, and they're more than happy to take you guys in for the summer. I want you guys to have a choice."

Danny looked at Julia, whose face had gone totally pale. He looked at his mom—she was smiling ear to ear and looking at Randy. At that moment he wanted nothing else to do with her ever again.

"The choice is yours," Randy said. "I'm a firm believer in presenting people with options. Even children. Choice gives a human being a sense of empowerment."

"But San Francisco. . . ," Wendy said, shaking her head. She giggled and squeezed Randy's forearm, didn't finish her sentence.

"Now, your mom and I figure it's only right to give you some time to mull things over. We've just thrown you guys a pretty good curveball, right, Danny?" Randy laughed a little, winked at Danny. "It's only fair we give you time. Why don't we say Friday. Sound good? Friday we'll all touch base again and talk more specifically about our proposed arrangement."

"But do understand," Wendy said, "if things work out between Randy and me, we'll be—honey, I'm not being too presumptuous, am I?"

"Baby, you're not being presumptuous *enough*. We'll be a family. Plain and simple. I want to spend the rest of my life with you."

Danny looked to Julia, who was staring at her empty plate, fighting back tears.

Wendy reached out, took Randy's hand. "God, sometimes I wonder if you're for real. It's like any second I'm going to wake up and *poof*, it'll all have been a dream."

"I'm not going anywhere, sweetheart. And neither are your two beautiful children." Randy reached for the champagne bottle, started working at the cork.

Wendy jumped to her feet. "This is all so exciting! Listen, you two think it over, okay? We'll talk again on Friday. Like Randy said. But right now I wanna hear some music. Something happy. Something with a little bit of soul."

She danced over to her CD stand and ran a forefinger down the titles. She turned to Randy. "How about a little Al Green, baby? Doesn't that sound nice?"

"Sounds *perfect*," Randy said, popping the cork.

Wendy pulled out Al Green's *I'm Still in Love with You* and cued the title track. When the first notes came over the speakers she covered her heart with both hands and sighed. Then she turned up the volume and danced by herself, in front of the window overlooking the parking lot.

Danny watched Randy watch his mom. He felt so mad he wanted to throw something at the wall. Break something over Randy's head. But he just sat there. He turned to Julia. She was still staring at her plate. He reached under the table and touched her hand, and instead of looking up she squeezed his hand back and began to cry without making any sound.

Randy stared at Wendy and chuckled a little under his breath. He shook his head, said: "Just look at her, guys. *That's* the reason I fell in love with your mom."

He shook his head again, said: "That. Right there."

A few days later Uncle Tommy and Sofia came to pick up Danny. Julia decided to go with their mom and Randy to San Francisco.

Uno and His Peeps Talk Summer Jobs

1

From a sitting position on the curb, Uno pitches a rock after a passing minivan. The van continues on, untouched, as the rock skips to a stop halfway down the block. He turns to Chico, says: "How's that gonna fly, man? You know I ain't got no rig."

"They *give* you a car," Chico says, pulling his hands from his pockets. "Isn't that right, Raul?"

Raul nods. "Some of 'em do. Not pizza places, but the higher-class ones."

"And you'd make mad tips," Chico says.

Uno stretches out his right shoulder. He picks up another rock, fingers the edges for a sec and then flings it across the street.

The fellas are sitting on the corner of Twenty-eighth and Potomac, discussing Uno's financial situation. All three of them dressed in jeans and white T-shirts. Their Timberlands at the edge of the street. Raul has a generic fitted cap turned backward.

It's late afternoon and behind their backs the sun is slowly falling from the sky. The air is warm and heavy. An occasional burst of wind scoots an empty McDonald's bag along the sidewalk across the street.

"But you can't be countin' on no more derby wins," Chico says. "Not with Sofe's cousin around."

Uno rolls his eyes. "Dude hit a couple out—"

"He hit *three* out," Raul interrupts. "And he wasn't done yet."

"Hit deep ones, too," Chico says. "Cleared the *second* roof, man. Nobody's ever done that."

"I was trippin'," Raul says.

"Yo, when he hit that second one?" Chico goes on. "I was like, 'Oh, damn!'"

"Whatever," Uno says. He throws another rock into the street. "Anyway, I ain't sure I could be no delivery boy. Imagine I gotta take food to some little cutie, man. Showin' up in some stupid-ass uniform. Nah, that ain't my skeeze."

"That's they fantasy," Raul says. "Some fine-ass mom asks you to bring in her food. Says, 'Sure is hot out there, young man. Can I offer you a beer or something? Be nice to cool off for a minute.'"

Everybody breaks up a little at the breathy female voice Raul puts on.

Chico flicks on his lighter, lets it die out. "'Why don't we throw those sweaty clothes in the wash, young man? I'm sure my husband has a robe somewhere you can borrow.'"

"'Go on, honey. Step out of them pants. I won't look.'"

Raul slaps hands with Chico, says, "'Wow, you have such big muscles for a high school boy. Do you lift weights? Come here for a minute, I wanna feel them for myself.'"

The guys crack up for a sec, then Uno says, "Y'all *sellin'* me."

"Right," Raul says. "Yo, what's better than gettin' paid to do up some old broad's fantasy?"

"Them moms got skills, too," Chico says. "And they get mad lonely playin' Legos all day."

Uno scoops up another rock, hucks it into somebody's yard. He stares at the pavement, his smile slowly fading, tries again to picture what Oxnard might look like. For some reason the first thing he always thinks of is a big, clean church. Stained-glass windows. Senior standing in the middle of a bunch of black folks, singing along to some old-school hymn. Then he imagines the big grocery store Senior told him they moved next to. No bars on any of the windows. A real new one with bright fluorescent lights inside. Neat rows of food. Maybe there's a Mexican sweet-bread shop next door. A place to rent movies.

Uno's pulled out of his head when Raul nudges him with an elbow and nods to the street.

Uno looks up, spots Sofia and Carmen Rollerblading down the hill together.

At first the girls are just laughing and blading and don't notice Uno and his crew. But just before they pass, Sofia glances left and comes to a screeching halt.

She says something to Carmen and then skates up to the boys. She puts on a fake smile. "Hey Raul. Hey Chico."

Both guys say hi back.

Then she turns to Uno, lets her smile fade. "My cousin's hiding out in the apartment right now. Took mad stitches in the back of his head. His left eye's all black and blue and he won't come out 'cause he's ashamed of what happened."

Uno looks at the pavement.

"I'm gonna tell you now, Uno. If you ever pull some shit like that with my cousin again, I'm gonna sneak into your apartment one night with a knife. A big sharp one. And I'm gonna slice your stuff all up." She points between Uno's legs. "Down there, *pendejo*."

Chico and Raul glance at each other trying not to laugh.

"That ain't a threat, Uno. It's a promise."

Uno looks up, says, "I'm tryin' to tell you, Sofe, you saw what happened to my little bro—"

"That was an accident and you know it! You were pissed about him hitting them home runs. I know how your dumb ass thinks. I swear to God, though, you mess with Danny again, I'm carvin' you up like a pumpkin."

Sofia waves for Carmen to follow and the two of them continue skating off down the road.

"Damn," Chico says, once they're out of earshot.

"Sofe don't play, man," Raul says.

"She got bad thoughts," Chico says.

"*Real* bad."

Uno doesn't say anything. He just sits there, hands in his pockets now, watching Sofia and Carmen turn into the entrance of Las Palmas Park, out of sight.

Del Mar Fair

1

A few days later, Danny stands with Sofia on the sidewalk in front of the apartment complex watching Chico clunk down Potomac in his brother's old Impala. Hubcaps spinning rust, windshield spidered on the passenger side. Sofia finally pulled Danny off his cot by . . . well, literally pulling him off his cot. "You been in here long enough," she said, throwing a fresh pair of jeans his way. One of his collar shirts and some socks. His Vans. "You goin' with me and my girls to the fair. Twenty minutes."

Danny didn't ask questions. He got up, changed in the bathroom, threw some water on his face and in his hair. Found her waiting for him in the living room when he stepped out.

· · ·

Carmen shoots out over the hill behind Chico, whips her beat-up Ford Festiva around Chico as he pulls to the curb, leaves a little rubber on the sidewalk right in front of Danny's retreating feet.

Raul swings the passenger-side door open, starts free-styling over the syncopated beat Lolo lays down by slapping at Raul's headrest. Carmen rolls down her window, waves at Sofia and Danny.

Chico leans out of his Impala behind them, shouts: "You gonna have to squeeze in the Matchbox, Sofe. I'm seven deep in here."

"You know I got my girl," Carmen yells back at Chico.

Sofia goes to her window and gives Carmen a little hug. Danny stands back, waves when Carmen waves.

"Look at your cuz," Carmen says. "He look all nice tonight. Girls gonna want to gobble him up."

Danny smiles, but he knows she's just trying to make him feel good. He digs his nails into his forearm as he listens to a little more small talk between Sofia and her friends. Then on the sly he peeks down at his collar shirt. His Vans. He looks at Raul and Lolo. T-shirt and jeans. Timberlands. He needs to get new clothes.

The passenger-side door of the Impala swings open and Uno flings an empty Colt 45 bottle onto the lawn of a neighboring house. Danny watches the bottle roll into a dying bush and disappear. His stomach drops when he turns back to Uno and their eyes lock.

Danny looks away, digs nails deeper into skin.

In the middle of Raul's flow, Lolo mixes into his beat a whack to the back of his boy's head. Raul stops mid-lyric, spins around rubbing the sting out. "Yo, what's that about, *flaco*?"

"You got one bug on your head," Lolo says with a straight face. "I smash for you."

"Yo, you best watch your back."

"I kill bug, *gordo*. You no believe me?"

Raul turns to Carmen, points to his head: "There was somethin' on my head, Carm?"

"I ain't gettin' wrapped up in y'all's games," she says.

"Was one spider," Lolo shouts.

Raul turns back to Lolo. *"Aplacate, flaco!"*

Before Lolo can respond, Raul and everybody else turns to the road. Danny's uncle Ray is speeding down the hill in his Bronco. He screeches to a stop in the middle of the street, cranks his parking brake and flings open his door. He jumps out, still dressed in his dirty construction boots and construction pants.

He walks right up on Danny, takes him by the chin and looks over the stitches in his face. "How this really happen, D?" Ray looks into the Festiva, scans faces. "I don't like what I'm hearin'."

Danny's unable to move his face. All he can do is stare back at his uncle. But inside he's falling apart. The last thing he wants is for his uncle to draw more attention to him.

Ray pulls Danny by his face up to the driver's side of the Impala. Scans mugs. "You," he says, pointing over Chico to Uno, "get out the car."

Uno looks at his boys, confused. He turns back to Ray, "Wha'chu mean, 'Get out'?"

"Callate el hocico! What I just tell you?"

"Yo, I ain't gotta do nothin'—"

"What I tell you?" Ray shouts. "Get out the car!"

Uno gets out of the car.

Chico makes a move to get out of the car, too, but Uncle Ray points a finger in his face. Shakes his head.

Chico freezes.

Ray pulls Danny around the Impala to Uno's side. He stares at Uno for a few seconds, then turns to Danny. "How this happen to you, D? I'm not talkin' 'bout what Sofe and you told Tommy, neither. This *pinche pendejo* raise a hand on you?"

Danny sneaks a sideways glance at Sofia.

Sofia looks down.

He goes back to his uncle.

"Say the word, D. That's all I need. I'll handle it from there."

Sofia clears her throat. "Uncle Ray, you know D ain't gonna say nothin'—"

"This don't concern you, Sofe," Ray says without taking his eyes off Uno. "This between me, D, and this punk-ass *pendejo*." He spits on the ground, stares at Uno, fire burning in the whites of his eyes.

Uno lowers his gaze.

Danny stares at his uncle. The bulging veins in his forehead are the same veins he used to see in his dad's forehead. The same crazed eyes.

"Go on, D. Say the word."

Danny doesn't say anything. He watches Uno look through the windshield at Chico. Watches Chico shrug.

"Fuck it," Ray says. "Nod to me, D."

Danny takes another sideways glance at Uno. Goes back to his uncle.

"Nod to me, D. People need to know what happens when they step to family."

Danny stares at his uncle.

"Nod, D."

Danny watches Uno go to get back in the car and Uncle Ray slams his fist on the roof of the Impala, shouting: "Don't you fucking move!"

Uno freezes.

"This my big brother's kid right here. He ain't 'round right now, but *I* am. And I swear to God, they gonna have to take my ass to jail. Nobody raises a hand on my big brother's kid." Ray turns his crazy eyes back on Danny. "They gonna have to take my ass to jail, D. Just nod to me."

"It happened in the game," Danny blurts out.

Everybody turns to look at him.

Sofia drops her bag. Uno tilts his head to the side, furrows his brow. Raul and Lolo look at each other. Chico lets his hand drop from the steering wheel.

"I was runnin' for the garage," Danny says in a loud voice. "Like Sofe told me I had to do. Those are the rules. And we ran into each other."

Sofia picks up her bag, touches Danny on the elbow.

Ray wipes his brow, looks at Uno. Goes back to Danny.

"It was my fault," Danny says.

The girls in the back of the Impala let out a collective deep breath, lean back in their seats. Rene follows their lead. Lolo and Raul continue craning their necks from the Festiva.

Uncle Ray lets go of Danny's chin and nods. He looks at Uno and nods some more. Then he pulls Danny away from everybody, toward his Bronco. Slaps a hand on his shoulder and smiles. "You did right, D-man. Couple stitches ain't so bad if you got everybody's respect now."

Danny nods.

"Nobody gonna step to you no more. Watch."

Danny nods.

Ray squeezes Danny's shoulder, then turns to his Bronco. Everybody watches him climb in, release the brake, flip a quick bitch and speed back up the hill, out of sight.

A buzz quickly starts up in both cars. Sofia smiles at Danny. She walks up, takes him by the hand and leads him toward the Festiva. "Um, what was *that* all about?"

"What?" Danny says quietly.

"*What?* You *talked*. That's the first time you've said more than two words since you got here. What happened?"

Danny shrugs.

She shakes her head, continues smiling at him. "Who cares, right? Point is, you're gonna be okay now. For real. I don't know how it is up in Leucadia, but down here it's better when you deal with stuff on your own."

Danny nods.

When they reach the Festiva, Raul jumps out of the front seat and folds it back. Danny and Sofia slip past into the back. As Danny climbs in, Raul pats him on the shoulder. Carmen touches his right hand. Lolo gives him a little head nod.

Sofia climbs in behind Danny. She puts her arm around his shoulder as Raul flips the seat back up, sits down and slams the tinny door closed.

Carmen starts the car. As she pulls back onto the street, follows Chico's Impala, Raul spins around, says: "I ain't gonna lie, Sofe. Your uncle 'bout the baddest dude in the 'hood."

"Had Uno shittin' bricks," Carmen says, tuning her radio to a hip-hop station, turning up the volume.

"Turned *ese negro totalmente blanco*," Raul says over the music.

Lolo pops open another forty and pulls a swig. He hands the bottle up to Raul, who takes a swig of his own. Raul hands it to Carmen, who sneaks a quick sip and hands it back to Lolo. Lolo offers the bottle to Sofia, but she waves him off, pulls a big sipper out of her bag, shouting over the music: "I mixed up some juice!"

Lolo nods. He goes to put the bottle back up to his own lips, but at the last second he pauses.

He turns to Danny. Holds out the bottle.

Danny takes it, looks at the label, looks back at Lolo. Lolo nods. Danny tips the fresh bottle back, swallows some of the sour-tasting malt liquor—his first-ever sip of alcohol. He cringes at the aftertaste, feels the cool liquid move through his middle.

He hands the bottle back to Lolo and wipes his mouth with the back of his hand.

"Shit!" Carmen shouts as she runs a red to keep pace with Chico's Impala. She shakes her head, says, "*Pinche* Chico," and pulls a cigarette from her pack.

Raul takes a lighter from his pocket, flicks it on and lights Carmen up. He shouts: "You see the look in Uno's eyes, though?" Everybody laughs and he says: "I thought my boy was gonna piss himself."

Danny listens to everybody replay the Uno–Uncle Ray face-off again. Listens to Carmen talk with her lungs half full of smoke. Listens to Sofia giggling between sips of spiked juice. Listens to Lolo's broken English and Raul's booming voice. And at the same time he stares out the window. At National City. He watches the faces of broken-down apartment complexes flash by. Houses with bars on every window. Graffiti on garage doors. A few of them boarded up, weeds as high as mailboxes, like nobody lives there anymore.

Their Festiva clunks down a dark side street and pulls up to a four-way stop. To the right, the last few rays of sun are falling red over an ugly water tower. At the foot of it, a group of Mexican men are sitting around in wife-beaters, smoking and drinking. One of them looks up as the Festiva passes.

Danny scans his face, and for a second he thinks it might be his dad. But the longer he stares the more he realizes how stupid that sounds. His dad's in Mexico. Still, he and the guy stay looking at each other all the way until Carmen pulls through the intersection and merges onto the freeway on-ramp.

2

Danny learns the home run derby girl's name while squeezed between Flaca and Sofia on the giant Ferris wheel.

Their car is circling back down to earth one final time when Flaca points toward a small food court crowd, leans over Danny and says: "See ol' girl over there, Sofe? Brown corduroy skirt and white top? Long black hair?"

"Who?"

"New girl."

"Liberty?" Sofia says. She takes a sip of juice and passes the bottle to Flaca.

Liberty, Danny thinks.

Flaca adjusts the straw, shrugs. "I guess. I don't know her name." She sips, hands to Danny.

Danny takes a long sip and then holds the bottle in his lap, listening.

"What about her?" Sofia says.

"Well, I ain't tryin' to talk about nobody. But I heard she be slingin' booty in the Gaslamp."

"What?"

"Most weekends, I heard. She's a trick, Sofe. *Una puta.*"

"Oh, please. Who told you *that*?" Sofia swipes the bottle out of Danny's lap, gives him a funny look. "Guess you cool with drinkin' now, eh, cuz?"

Danny smiles, shrugs.

Flaca clears her throat. "I got my sources, Sofe. But can you imagine? Sixteen and already droppin' her drawers for *billetes.*"

"And here you is seventeen," Sofia shoots back, "and you droppin' yours for *free.*"

The girls bend over laughing on either side of Danny as the conductor unhooks their seat belts and holds their car still so they can climb out.

Danny waits for the girls to go first, then jumps out after them. But even on solid ground, he still sort of feels like he's floating on the Ferris wheel. Feet dangling over the rest of the fair. And there's a low buzzing moving through his head.

Sofia turns to look at Danny.

He gives her a bigger smile this time. Then he turns his attention to the food court. Looks for the girl in the brown corduroy skirt again. The white top. Liberty.

3

Outside the modernist art exhibition, Danny learns the little boy Liberty was watching the day of the Derby was either (a) her son or (b) her cousin.

The guys are posted on or around the benches outside the makeshift gallery, sipping juice and trying to count on their fingers how many girls in their year have a kid or are currently pregnant.

"It's hers, Chee," Uno hollers from an adjacent bench. "Why you think she always with little big head?"

"Oh, what," Chico fires back, "you never had to babysit somebody?" He shakes his head, pulls another hit of jungle juice through a straw, hands off to Raul. "Trust me, Uno, that's her aunt's kid."

"Her *adopted* aunt, you mean? You know they ain't even blood, right?"

"What that means, Uno? Adopted family can't have each other's back?"

Uno scoffs. "How you know anything about new girl, Chee? She ain't been here but a few months. Never seen *y'all* two talkin'."

"Liberty's aunt goes to the same church as my auntie Rosa. And she says back in Mexico—"

"Hold up!" Uno interrupts. "Your Auntie *Rosa*? Now I *know* you lyin'. That old broad too fat to go to church."

Some of the guys break up a little.

"Oh, I see," Chico says, nodding, "you wanna talk about people's weight now."

"She obese, Chee. I ain't makin' shit up."

Chico throws his hands in the air. Raul gives the juice to Lolo, who takes a long swig and moves it over to Rene. Rene holds the cup in front of his face for a few seconds without putting the straw to his lips.

"I don't talk about *tu padre*," Chico says. "The fact he all stooped over when he walks. *Viejo con el bastón*. That don't got nothin' to do with if Liberty got a kid or not."

"You got principles," Raul says.

"I ain't even gonna bring it up," Chico says, turning to Raul. "Ain't that right, Rah-rah?"

"You the bigger man," Raul says.

Chico turns to Uno. "That's right. I'm the bigger man, dawg."

Uno sips a little juice, says: "That's cool 'cause we already cleared up who the bigger *woman*."

Everybody laughs and points at Chico. Rene finally sips the juice and passes it back to Raul.

Uno looks over at Danny, catches him laughing. Gives him a little nod. "Guess the shit run in the family, Chee." Uno taps sippers with Raul.

"You cold, man," Raul says.

Danny listens to the fellas as they slowly circle back to the matter at hand: Liberty. But before they have a chance to revisit the kid controversy, the girls reemerge from the gallery raving about a particular painter's work. They all go on and on about how women are so much more cultured than men. And the guys just sit there, rolling their eyes and shaking their heads. Drinking their juice.

After a while Sofia walks up to Danny holding out a full sipper. "Looking for this?" she says.

Danny takes the handoff and pulls through the straw.

Sofia empties the second half of a Pepsi can into a plant and takes the sipper back from Danny. She unscrews the cap, pours some juice into the Pepsi can and hands the can to Danny. "Take it slow, cuz."

"I will," Danny says under his breath.

As they tap drinks and take another sip each, Danny starts thinking about Liberty again. He decides it isn't really her kid. She must have been babysitting.

4

Danny overhears Guita and Raquel's conversation as they're all feeding carrots and celery sticks to a pack of baby goats and sheep. Learns Liberty has just arrived here from Rosarito, Mexico.

"The girl can't barely even speak English," Guita says, holding out a carrot, then dropping it to the ground when one of the goats gets too close with its teeth.

"Is she legal?" Raquel says.

"Her real dad's American. White. I guess he's a lawyer or something. She wrote him mad letters from Mexico and he made the arrangements."

Danny pets a nappy-headed sheep nearby and thinks about the letters he sends *his* dad. It's weird that he and Liberty have been doing the same thing from opposite countries. And it's weird that she doesn't speak English and he doesn't speak Spanish. How would they ever communicate? It's almost like she's his exact opposite.

"But she doesn't *live* with her dad." Raquel holds a carrot out for a baby goat.

"No, I know. He has another family in L.A. He got Lib in the country, set her up with a place to live and sends her money every month. But that's it."

Guita takes a stick of celery from her feed bag, tentatively pushes it out toward one of the goats.

Raquel grabs Guita's hand, makes her keep still while the goat nibbles at the celery, lips all over both their fingers. They let out little squeals and crack up.

A few people turn to look at them.

Danny sips from his Pepsi can, watching them. If only he can find his dad in Ensenada once he lands there. Everything will be okay if he can just find him.

"She's too pretty," Raquel says. "That's the only real reason I got a problem with her."

"Nah, but she's nice, girl."

"Yeah?"

"Yeah, we talk sometimes. In Spanish, like I said."

Guita and Raquel hand a goat and a sheep a few more carrots and celery sticks and then drop their empty feed bag in the trash and head out of the petting zoo together.

Danny stays put for a while. He feels the warmth of alcohol coating his insides. Watches a little girl, dressed in a blue polka-dot dress, cautiously approach a small sheep. Watches her reach out, touch its soft, bushy back and then spin around to look at her mom and dad. Her smiling dad fumbles through a backpack and pulls out a digital camera.

The girl giggles and turns to pet the sheep again.

Her dad aims the camera and takes her picture.

Danny reaches up to touch the stitches in the back of his head.

Dear Dad:

Everything is working out so perfectly down here. I almost can't believe it. I've made friends with all the guys. Sofe's friends. We hang out at the movies and at the baseball field, sometimes we cruise to the mall. Tonight they dragged me to the Del Mar Fair. And at one point, in the middle of the petting zoo, I thought of you. I was feeding celery to one of the animals, and I thought: Man, I bet my dad used to do this all the time, considering he worked at the Wild Animal Park.

Anyway, I wanted to tell you about my new girlfriend, Liberty. She's tall and beautiful and has this amazingly straight hair that hangs to the middle of her back. And it's so shiny, Dad. She must brush it all the time. She has lighter skin than you and I, but her eyes are big and brown and darker than anything you've ever seen. It makes her look mysterious. Everybody says she could be a model. If she wanted to. But she doesn't. She's too modest.

Thing is, Dad, she's more than just a pretty face. She's really smart, too. Even though she barely speaks English, she's way smarter than any of the white girls at my private school. And she really likes me. Just last night, while we were walking back from the park, she turned to me and said: "I don't want to scare you, Danny, but I maybe love you. Is that okay?" I said,

"Yeah, Lib, it's cool." And then we kept walking. I didn't say it back 'cause I remember you telling me one time it's best to take it slow with girls. Or else you'll wake up when you're seventeen and find yourself married with a kid. Like what happened to you and Uncle Tommy.

She wasn't mad or anything. Maybe when I'm closer to making it to the big leagues I'll say it. And I bet we'll still be together. I've been with tons of girls over the past few years, but with Lib it feels different.

Anyway, what I wanted to tell you is that Lib's from Mexico, too. Like you. And she's half white like me—it's her dad that's white. I was thinking, maybe when I come visit you I could bring Lib. And you could meet her. See how pretty she is for yourself.

5

The most significant thing Danny learns at the fair has nothing to do with Liberty. Not directly, anyway.

He learns that jungle juice makes him feel light as a feather. That it makes him feel ten feet tall. But still slick on his feet. Makes him feel like smiling and talking to anybody and everybody, at any time—though he hasn't.

Danny opens his eyes, finds himself sitting against a chain-link fence behind a cotton candy stand. He looks out over the booths in front of him, sees Uno and Chico and Raul and Rene and Lolo all shooting water balloons with BB guns to make their horses move forward. He sees Sofia and Carmen and Flaca laughing with some security guard. But there's no sign of Liberty.

During his three or four hours at the fair, Danny's drunk so much juice his stomach feels bloated and his head feels numb. He looks down, finds the Pepsi can still in hand. He goes to take another sip, but it's empty.

Sofia walks over, stands right in front of him with her hands on her hips. "You okay, cuz?"

Danny looks up at her and smiles. "Yeah."

"You gonna be sick?"

Danny shakes his head.

"You wanna join us? We're talking to the guy who's sneaking us into the concert."

Danny shakes his head. "I like it here."

"You're drunk as hell," Sofia says. She calls out to Carmen: "Get over here, Carm. My cuz is blasted."

Carmen walks over and picks up Danny's head, looks into his eyes. "Hello? Anybody home?"

Danny reaches for her hand and kisses it.

The girls laugh, and Sofia takes the can from Danny. "I think I better cut you off, cuz."

Danny laughs, too. Because when he thinks about the fact that he just kissed Carmen's hand it's hilarious. And the fact that she said "Hello? Anybody home?" is hilarious, too. *Everything* is hilarious. Sofia and her friend Carmen and the cotton candy being spun in front of them and the fact that he's leaning against a fence in the middle of a fair, drunk.

And when the girls walk back up to the security guard, Danny looks at the tops of all the rides in the distance, especially the frog ride. The one for little kids. And this time he actually laughs out loud. Because that frog ride is *hilarious*.

He watches Raul, Lolo, Chico and Rene pimp up to the pitching booth, pulling dollar bills from their pockets. *His game!* He decides to get up and join them. He hasn't pitched since he was back in Leucadia, the longest he's gone without throwing a baseball since he was ten. He'll just get up and join Sofia's friends.

But instead, Danny leans his head against the chain-link and closes his eyes. And for whatever reason, his mind goes right to the dream he's been having for the past three years. The one about the hawk family.

He's running through the canyon by his old apartment, all by himself, and he comes up on a big tree. Two beautiful hawks are perched on one of the thick branches. He's tired from running so he decides to sit down and watch the hawks for a while. Then he spots a little baby hawk, sees that the adult hawks are feeding it. They're a family. It makes him feel incredibly happy for some reason and he just watches them for hours. But eventually he leans his head back against the tree and closes his eyes for a second so he can rest. But he must've been really tired because he doesn't wake up until the next morning. He rubs his eyes and looks up into the tree but the hawks are gone. The whole family. He stands up and looks for them harder. Searches all through the branches. Even runs out into the field and scans the sky. But it's no use. They're gone. And he feels so sad, he goes back to the tree and gets in the same position he was in the night before. He tries to fall back to sleep. Thinks maybe if he can wake up all over again they'll magically reappear.

But he isn't tired anymore. He tries taking long drawn-out breaths and counting sheep, but nothing happens. He's still wide awake. And the hawks are still gone.

Put Your Money
Where Your Mouth Is

1

Uno nudges Raul toward the carney, says: "Go on, big boy. Show 'em what you got." He watches his boy pull two bucks from his pocket, derby money, and hand it over. Watches him get three baseballs in return and set them on the stand.

The rest of the guys gather behind Raul and urge him on. Chico claps, says: "Show me the heat, Rah-rah."

"Put your weight behind it," Rene says, turning to Uno for reinforcement.

"Go 'head, *bola de pan*!" Lolo shouts.

As Raul steps to the makeshift mound, Uno instinctively blows into his fist. He's the one who spotted the pitching booth. Where you get clocked by a speed gun, like in the big leagues. And now that everybody's pulling out money, he wants to show them what's up. He blows into his fist again, stretches his shoulder across his body.

Raul grips one of the baseballs in his meaty right hand. He looks back at Lolo, then goes into a stiff windup and fires at the tarp. Speed gun reads: 54 MPH.

He shakes his head as he reaches for the second ball.

The sky is dark now. Over Raul's shoulder, Uno notices the fair rides spinning ugly neon lights into the cloudless sky. Hears all the different carnival tunes swirling together behind the pitching booth. He blows into his fist again.

Raul goes into his windup, fires his second ball. Speed gun reads: 53.

Uno nudges Raul from behind. "Come on, man. Pretend you eatin' a burrito. You do *that* shit fast."

Chico laughs, says: "Make like you chasin' after a bean and cheese."

"This shit's rigged," Raul says over his shoulder.

"Same gun they use in the big leagues," the carney says, folding his tattoo-covered arms. "Even had a professional ump in here to calibrate it."

"Whatever," Raul says.

The fellas all laugh as Raul reaches for his last ball. He goes right into his windup and heaves the ball with a deep guttural groan. The ball is a good two feet over the fake catcher's head, but the digital numbers spin anyway. Speed gun reads: 56.

2

Uno and Chico pat Raul on the back as he quickly blends into the group. Chico says, "Man, fifty-six. Ain't so sure that would get it done in tee-ball, Rah."

"You think you could do better?" Raul snaps back.

"I *know* I could do better," Chico says, reaching into his pocket and handing a wadded-up two bucks to the carney.

"Is easy to beat fifty-six," Lolo says.

Raul scoffs. "Yo, why don't you put your money where your mouth is?"

Lolo pulls out a few bills and bets Raul that Chico will beat his high. Uno pulls out five ones and asks in on that same action. Rene backs Raul.

Chico takes his three baseballs and sets two on the stand. He turns around and looks at the guys. "Better than fifty-six, right?"

"Fifty-six," Uno says.

Chico heaves his first pitch out of a stretch. Speed gun reads: 56.

There's a little rumbling out of the fellas behind him, but he doesn't turn around. He reaches for the second baseball, goes into a full windup this time and fires it at the tarp. Speed gun reads: 56.

The rumbling builds. "What if it's tie?" Lolo says.

"Money don't change hands," Uno says. He blows into his fist.

A small crowd gathers behind. A couple people passing stop to check out what's going on. They crane their necks around Lolo, Rene, Raul and Uno to see what the commotion's about.

Chico reaches for his last baseball and spends a few seconds rubbing it down with his hands. He shakes it up in his hands like you would a pair of dice. Like he's about to roll instead of throw. He extends his hands out to Carmen. She wiggles her fingers over the ball like she's casting a spell. The rest of the girls giggle.

Chico goes into his windup and whips the ball at the tarp. Speed gun reads: 58.

Chico spins around and points at Raul. "That's right, boy! Got your ass!" He pulls his white T-shirt sleeve up and flexes, slaps five with Uno.

The crowd behind the guys cheers.

Money exchanges hands.

3

Uno steps out of the group, hands the carney his two bucks and takes back his baseballs. New bets are placed. A few more people slow as they pass the pitching booth. A group of white teenagers wearing soccer sweatshirts stops to watch.

Uno looks back at the onlookers, feels the weight of the crowd in his blood. Nothing hypes him up more than when people are watching him. Especially white people. In every other part of life they run shit, just like his old man always says, but not when it comes to sports. You just have to look at the games on TV. Almost everybody is dark. Black, Mexican, Dominican, whatever. But barely anybody is white. He takes the first baseball and winds up, fires at the tarp. Speed gun reads: 64.

As everybody reacts, he reaches for his second ball, winds up and fires again. Speed gun reads: 66.

The small crowd of people behind him emits oohs and aahs. His blood flows quicker. He's only thrown two pitches and he's *already* blown away Raul and Chico.

The carney nods, shouts: "Not bad, kid."

But Uno's not satisfied. He wings his third ball so hard his flat-billed Raiders cap falls off his head, tumbles to the pavement. Speed gun reads: 69.

The crowd that has gathered reacts with hooting and clapping. One of the soccer girls shouts: "Sweet pitch!"

Uno reaches down and picks up his cap, pulls it slightly crooked on his dome.

Chico and Raul pat him on the back, give him daps. Money changes hands again. Raul pushes Lolo toward the pitching booth, and new bets are placed.

4

Sofia, Flaca and Bee make their way closer to the pitching booth, stand beside Carmen. They all go up on their toes to better see the action. Liberty and Raquel slip in front of a group of kids with their parents. Guita slides past behind them.

Sofia spots a swaying Danny and pulls him over to her crew. Danny sits down in the middle of everybody.

Lolo tosses his first pitch. Speed gun reads: 54. Everybody laughs as he walks halfway up to the gun and flips it off.

He picks up his second ball, backs up about ten feet behind the makeshift rubber. He gets a running start this time, heaves the baseball as hard as he can. Speed gun reads: 55.

Lolo throws his hands in the air and points accusingly at the carney. "This game ain't fair, man. I want my money back."

"Take a hike, buddy!" the carney shouts, pushing off the wall. He puts the two bucks in his bulging money clip and picks up a couple loose baseballs.

Lolo starts toward the carney, but Uno and Chico hold him back. He points and curses over their shoulders: "Gimme my money, *pinche puto!*"

"Get outta my face!"

Lolo surges forward, but Uno wraps him up. "I come back with a gun! Then what!"

The carney steps forward, shouts: "You're done, man." He

turns to Uno, says, "Get that kid out of here, man. He ain't throwin' no more pitches at my booth."

"He only got one more, though," Raul says. "He'll calm down. You can't let him throw his last ball? If he calms down?"

The carney shakes his head. "Nuh-uh. He steps back on my rubber, I'll have security here in two seconds. Threatening me like that. He's through."

Uno and Chico manage to calm Lolo until some white guy in the crowd yells out, "You're just mad 'cause you suck!"

Everybody laughs.

Lolo whips around and makes a move for a pack of frat guys near the back of the small crowd.

But Uno corrals him again, tells him to calm down.

Lolo stands there, staring at the group of frat guys, still puffed up, brows furrowed. Amateur tattoos twitching.

"What about his last ball?" Flaca yells at the carney.

"*He* ain't throwin' it!"

"Somebody else could throw it?" Raul says.

"Long as it ain't the last guy," the carney says. "I mean it, he's through."

"Who gots Lo's last ball?" Raul says, spinning to his guys.

"How we gonna work the bets?" Chico says. "We throw 'em out, right? He didn't get a full three balls."

"We throw 'em out," Uno says.

"But who gonna throw Lo's last pitch?" Raul says again.

5

Chico walks over to Sofia, Flaca and Carmen. He smiles at them, then reaches down for Danny's arm and pulls him up. "What about Sofe's cousin?" he says, looking at his guys.

"Nah, he can't pitch," Sofia says. "He's totally bombed. Look at him."

Danny is swaying back and forth with his eyes halfway closed. One of the buttons undone on his collar shirt.

"Let him pitch," Uno says. "He all right."

Chico pulls him over to the makeshift mound, says: "What's the over-under on him?"

Uno studies Danny's black eye. From his fist. A wave of regret passes through him.

"No," Sofia says, taking Danny's other arm. "He's too drunk."

"Let the kid pitch!" somebody yells.

"It's only one ball," Chico says. "It's not gonna hurt him any."

Everybody looks to Uno. He looks at Danny again, then back to Sofia and Chico, says: "He can throw one."

Chico pumps his fist and smiles. Sofia lets go of her cousin's arm.

"I got five says he throws under fifty," Chico says.

"I'll take that bet," Raul says. "You kidding me? You saw him hit. He's got natural talent."

"You're crazy," Chico says quietly. "He's smashed."

"I'm with Chico," Uno says. "He ain't throwin' over fifty. No way."

"So nobody's with me?" Raul says. "I can't get one backer?"

Everybody goes quiet. Even the crowd. They all stand there staring at Danny with blank faces.

Suddenly Liberty steps through the crowd holding out a five-dollar bill. "I bet him," she says, pointing at Danny.

She hands her money to Chico and glances at Danny. Then she blends back into the crowd again.

"It's on," Chico says, nudging Danny toward the pitching mound and the lone baseball on the stand.

6

Uno listens to the crowd noise grow as Sofia's cousin grips the baseball in his hand. He watches the kid turn around and look at her. Watches her mouth back: "Hard as you can, cuz."

Danny sways a little, turns to the tarp and goes into a halfhearted windup. He throws the ball at the fake catcher and then stumbles forward a little. Grabs the stand to regain his balance.

Uno and the rest of the crowd go dead silent.

He watches Danny turn to look at his cousin again, then Liberty. Both girls' eyes are wide with shock.

Uno turns to the carney, who is staring at the speed gun in disbelief, scratching his head. Uno looks at the number: 85.

Finally Flaca speaks up, says what's running through everybody's head: "What the fuck?"

A buzz of voices slowly builds in the crowd. Someone shouts, "Give him three more!" Others echo the same sentiment.

People crowd closer to the action as Uno takes two bucks out of his pocket and pays the carney for another round of balls.

The fellas behind Danny don't bet this time. They just stand there quiet, staring at Danny as he reaches for the first ball. Uno doesn't say anything, either. He swallows and stares.

Danny sways on the mound a second. Uno watches him glance over his shoulder at Liberty, then back at the fake catcher. He studies the kid. Surfer-ass clothes and skinny as hell. How's he throw so hard? Uno watches him go into another halfhearted windup and unleash another seemingly effortless fastball. Speed gun reads: 86.

Everybody stares at the number in shock, including Uno. Butterflies pass through his stomach. He can't believe what he's seeing. He looks at Sofia's cousin again. The kid swaying back and forth on the makeshift mound. Picking up the second baseball and rubbing it in his hands. Who is this guy? It's like he's some kind of freak.

The carney walks up to the gun, messes with a few of the settings. He turns back to Danny, says: "Jesus Christ, kid. That's the fastest pitch I had here all summer."

Sofia shouts, "That's right, cuz! Do 'em another one!"

Danny takes the next ball and steps up to the rubber. He winds up and throws a looping curveball this time. The pitch is headed straight for the fake batter's head until it snaps at the last second, spins right into the strike zone. Speed gun reads: 72.

"Holy shit," Chico says to Uno. "Dude's up there throwing curves."

"Shit is crazy," Uno says, never taking his eyes off Danny.

"Last ball!" the carney announces. "Hard as you can, kid. Give us a fastball."

Danny glances behind him again. He turns back to the tarp. He goes into his windup and flings the last ball at the fake catcher. Speed gun reads: 92.

The crowd goes nuts behind Danny. Chico and Raul slap him on the back and Sofia musses his hair. Flaca gives him a kiss on the cheek.

Uno watches the carney approach Danny, tell him, "That's the fastest reading I ever had, man. And I been working here six summers. You pitch somewhere?"

Uno watches Danny shrug and turn away from the guy. Then Sofia and her girls sweep Danny off toward the concert area. Uno can't believe what he's just seen. Danny pitches even better than he hits. This skinny, GQ kid.

Uno feels Chico tapping him on the shoulder, but he doesn't turn away from Sofe's cousin until the girls lead him over to the ticket counter, out of sight.

Mexican WhiteBoy

1

A few days after the fair, Danny takes his mitt and a bucket of baseballs to Las Palmas Park. The baseball field where his dad played Little League.

He spends a few minutes staring out over the field, trying to picture his old man on the mound. He never said if he was good, just that he pitched. That he'd come here all the time after his own dad died. Most of the time alone. Danny recalls the framed picture his mom kept in the living room for years. Even after they split. A skinny version of his dad in a Little League uniform, smiling. This very field in the background.

Field has definitely taken a turn for the worse, Danny thinks. He slides down the small ice plant cliff, jumps the short fence and walks onto the overgrown infield. Positioning himself in front of the decaying pitching rubber, he goes into his high-kick windup, fires a fastball across a rotting home plate.

He looks around the field. The weeds growing in the base paths. The giant patch of brown grass in left. The broken-down fence in right. Graffiti all over both dugouts and the bleachers.

He plucks the next ball out of his bucket, winds up and delivers. When he's fired all the baseballs at the backstop, he jogs toward the plate with the empty bucket and scoops all the loose balls off the ground. Then he hustles back out to the mound and does the whole thing over again.

He works on each pitch in his arsenal a bucket at a time. Same routine he had in Leucadia, after the team was done with the field. Starts with a bucket of fastballs, followed by a bucket of curves, a bucket of sliders, a bucket of changeups. Then he starts over again with his fastball. After several rounds of pure pitching, Danny starts thinking about his control. Why'd he perform so poorly at tryouts last year? He never goes too long without asking himself this question. Picturing all the wild pitches he threw. Why'd it happen? Out here he's putting each ball anywhere he wants. He's painting black on either side of the plate with four different pitches. At the fair, too, when he was drunk. His control was perfect.

Why's it that when he's in front of the Leucadia Prep guys he tenses up? He always comes back to this question, but he can never find the answer.

He remembers the time his mom took him to have his eyes checked. It was a complex appointment. On the one hand, if it came back that his eyes were bad it would explain why he was so erratic on the mound. Why one tryout pitch would zip right down the middle for a strike and the next would soar behind the hitter's back. Back in Little League he'd amaze all his teammates with his pitching, the parents in the stands, the coaches. His dad. But then his family split at the seams. And he, Julia, and his mom moved a bunch of times. Now when he toed a rubber in front of the team, he had no idea where his next pitch would end up.

On the other hand, Danny wasn't even sure he'd *wear* glasses if they were prescribed. In the waiting room he slipped on a pair of sample specs and checked himself in the mirror. He looked soft with four eyes. Looked like a sissy. And a Lopez boy wasn't supposed to look like no sissy. What would his dad have said?

It was bad enough he was at a private high school, wore a preppy uniform and made the honor roll every semester. Could he really take it a step further and don a pair of Coke-bottle glasses?

Danny never actually had to make that call. He covered both eyes for the doc, one at a time, read letters off the chart, and was diagnosed with perfect vision: 20-20.

After an hour or so of pitching solo, Sofia's sister, Veronica, and her boyfriend, Jesus, pull up in a revamped Mustang. Veronica pops her head out of the rolled-down window and shouts: "Come on, Danny, we're all going to Gram's for dinner!"

Danny looks up at the Mustang.

Veronica waves him on.

He picks up his bucket, collects a few loose baseballs and climbs the ice plant slope toward the Mustang.

2

After Danny and his entire family finish their huge feast, everyone's in a Mexican coma—which, according to Uncle Ray, is directly related to the Mexican minute. The women are buzzing around the table, collecting dirty dishes, glasses, silverware, wrapping what's left of the mutilated turkey in Saran Wrap and making fun of the men.

Sofia waves Danny into the backyard. Outside, she looks at him with a sly smile and says: "Guess what I just heard from Carmen."

"What?" Danny says.

"That new girl, Liberty, thinks you're cute. Carmen talked to Guita about it last night at the movies. And Carmen called me this morning. Plus she bet on you at the fair. Out of nowhere. She never talks to nobody."

Danny feels the blood rush into the tips of his fingers and toes. He looks down at his Vans, a little dirt on the tip of his shoe from dragging it after each pitch.

"I know you like her, cuz."

Danny looks at his cousin.

"Your cousin knows these things. Trust me."

Danny's just about to say something back when Uncle Ray walks through the sliding glass door followed by his two tough-looking buddies. The bigger one puts both hands on his stomach and says: "Damn, I could barely move, I'm so stuffed."

"Told you, boy," Ray says. "My moms hooks it up." He pulls a cigarette from his pack, puts it to his lips. Hands the pack to his smaller buddy and pulls a lighter from his pocket. He looks up at Danny and Sofia, says: "You guys up to no good out here?"

"Just talkin'," Sofia says.

"'Bout what?"

"Danny's girlfriend."

Uncle Ray pulls his cigarette from his mouth, stares at Danny. A smile breaks over his face. "You already got yourself a little girl down here, D-man? You just like your old man."

"No," Danny says, looking at Sofia.

"She don't barely speak English, though."

"A border broad, eh? How *you* gonna talk to her, D-man?" Uncle Ray cracks up with his boys a little, then introduces them as Rico and Tim.

Everybody stands there in silence for a while until Sofia says: "Anyway, I gotta go help clean up." She punches Danny in the arm and goes back inside.

Uncle Ray stares at Danny for a sec, says: "Wha'chu guys do then, D-man? She don't speak no English. You don't speak no Spanish. You just talk with your hands? Do sign language?"

Danny digs into his arm with his fingernails until a sharp pain hits his brain.

"Wish I couldn't talk to my old lady," Rico says.

"I hear that," Tim says, laughing.

As Rico and Tim go back and forth a bit, Ray pulls Danny to the side, says: "What I don't get, D, is why your old man never taught you Spanish."

Danny shrugs. Digs in again.

"I think maybe he didn't want you to be a Mexican. You know he gots a big-ass chip on his shoulder 'bout that, right? He gets pissed off about how Mexicans get treated. Maybe he didn't want it to happen to you."

Danny digs into his arm some more until Uncle Ray notices and smacks his hand away. "Wha'chu doin', D-man?" He holds Danny's arm and takes a look. Sees the new markings, the old scars. He looks Danny in the eyes for a few seconds with a serious face, lets go his arm. But he doesn't say anything. Instead he stares at the fence that separates Grandma's small backyard from the neighbor's, pulls another drag. "Well, I know this," he finally says. "Your pops loves you, D. More than you could ever know. Right now you 'bout all he's got."

Danny nods.

"You remember that."

Danny nods.

Uncle Ray shakes his head and drops his cig, stomps out the red tip with one of his Timberlands. "Hang in there, D-man. He comin' back."

Danny looks up at his uncle. "When?"

"When the time's right. You just keep writing them letters. They mean a lot to my brother."

3

A while later, Danny's sitting in his grandma's living room, watching a Padres game with the rest of his family. But he's not really watching. He's thinking about the fact that he doesn't speak Spanish. He only speaks English. And it really starts to make him angry. He wishes his dad had never even married a white woman. Then he'd have grown up down here like everybody else in his family. In National City. He imagines how much different his life would be. How much better.

"Yo, D!" Ray suddenly shouts from across the room. "Yo, you could help me write this letter to my old lady?"

"Which old lady you talking 'bout *now*?" Uncle Tommy calls out from the couch.

Tim and Rico crack up.

"Lucy."

"Lucy *Gonzales*?" Tommy says, slipping an arm around Cecilia's back. Slipping his free hand between his full stomach and loosened belt. "You mean that *heina* still talks to your cheatin' ass?"

"*Shit*. After I write her this letter, big brother, she gonna do more than just talk. D, you could help me?"

Danny nods.

Ray gets up from the couch, goes over to Gram's sewing table and scoops up a pad of paper and a pen. He hands them to Danny, explains the gist of how he wants the letter to go, and Danny starts writing.

This isn't the first letter Danny's written for his uncle, and he already knows how it'll play out. His well-thought-out words will work like magic on this woman, Lucy, and Uncle Ray will call him a couple days later to explain that he got him laid. Again.

But halfway through the letter, just as he gets to the part where he compares their roller-coaster romance to the rise and fall of a North County tide, Danny realizes that in writing this letter, consisting merely of lines of poetry he's memorized from English textbooks, he's not actually getting closer to his favorite uncle, but further away.

"Mr. Smart Boy," his uncle Ray will tell him over the phone.

Danny will switch the receiver from one ear to the other, secretly wishing his uncle had called him Mr. Bad Boy instead.

"I owe you big-time, D."

"You don't owe me anything, Uncle Ray."

There will be a slight pause and then his uncle will say: "Yo, that's *three* times you helped me. Know what? I'm gonna take your ass to a Padres game, D. For real. You know they got that new stadium, right? I'm gonna get us some prime seats, right behind home plate. How's that sound?"

"Cool!" Danny will say back, fully aware that there won't be any Padres game, and that because he's forced his uncle to make a promise he'll never keep, he couldn't possibly *get* further away.

It all hits him as he stares at a half-finished love letter. No matter how many words he defines or love letters he composes or pieces of junk mail he reads aloud to his grandma while she waters spider plants potted in old Folgers coffee cans, he'll still be a hundred miles away from who he's supposed to be.

He's Mexican, because his family's Mexican, but he's not really *Mexican*. His skin is dark like his grandma's sweet coffee, but his insides are as pale as the cream she mixes in.

Danny holds the pencil above the paper, thinking: I'm a white boy among Mexicans, and a Mexican among white boys.

He digs his fingernails into his arm. Looks up to see if anybody's watching him. They aren't.

Sometimes he'll just watch his family interact in the living room. The half-Spanish jokes and the bottle of tequila being passed around with a shot glass and salt. The laughing and carrying on. Always eating the best food and playing the coolest games and telling the funniest stories. His uncles always sending the smallest kid at the party to get them a cold sixer out of the fridge and then sneaking him the first sip when Grandma isn't looking. But even when she turns around suddenly, catches them red-handed and shouts, "*Ray! Mijo*, what are you *doing*?" everybody just falls over laughing. Including Grandma.

And it makes him so happy just watching. Doesn't even matter that he's not really involved. Because what he's doing is getting a sneak peek inside his dad's life.

Danny looks up at his uncles and cousins from the table, pencil dangling in his right hand. Ray is standing up now, telling a story about the construction site he's currently working at in Point Loma. How some fat Mexican dude, straight off a border crossing, fell into a small ditch and couldn't get out. They threw him a rope, and everybody had to pull. All ten of them. And still they could barely pull him out. And everybody's laughing. Including Danny. Because nobody's better at telling a story than his uncle Ray. Nobody.

But then Rico shouts something in Spanish. Everybody laughs even harder. Uncle Tommy yells something back in Spanish.

And all Danny can do is go back to his uncle's letter.

Call from
San Francisco

1

A couple mornings later Sofia walks into the living room, where Danny's eating a bowl of cornflakes. She cups the phone and mouths: "Your *madre*."

The three previous times his mom has called, Danny's waved Sofia off, told her to say he wasn't around. But this time Danny rolls his eyes and takes the phone. He puts the receiver to his ear, mumbles: "Hello?"

"Oh, Danny boy. It's so good to finally hear your voice. How are you, hon? Good, I hope. We miss you so much up here. Me and Julia and Randy. You might not believe me about Randy, being that he's only met you once, but just last night he turned to me at dinner, swear to God—we were at this real nice Chinese place near the marina, the best General

Tso's chicken ever! Anyway, he said: 'So, how's my boy Danny making out in National City? He getting along okay with his aunt and uncle?' It moved me, hon. Because you and Julia are my life and here's this beautiful, well-established man who wants to *share* that with me. I said, 'Well, I don't know because he never seems to be there when I call. Either that or he's mad at me and purposely ducking my calls.' I hope you're not mad at your mom, Danny boy. Anyway, how are *you*, pumpkin?"

Danny stares at his cornflakes, literally growing soggy in front of his eyes. "Good," he mumbles.

"That's what I like to hear. Make sure you help out around the house, hon. And Randy, bless his heart, he's gonna start sending down money for *you*, too. He already gives Tommy a couple hundred a month, which I'm pretty sure you're aware of. But he thinks you should have some kicking-around money. Pretty nice gesture, right? He doesn't *have* to do it. Anyway, look for a letter from him, Danny boy. Every other week. First one should be there by Saturday, I would think."

"Okay."

"Things couldn't be better up here, if you wanna know the truth. San Francisco is such a gorgeous city. My God. The fog rolling through the hills, Fisherman's Wharf, Chinatown, the amazing shopping, all the different restaurants. And the culture, hon. You realize real quick how little San Diego has in the way of culture. The problem with San Diego is that all the races live in different pockets of the city. The blacks are in the southeast or in Oceanside. The Mexicans are by the border. Or else they're working in somebody's kitchen or yard. That always got me about San Diego. Mexicans are treated as such second-class citizens. But it's not like that in San Francisco. Here, everybody lives together. By the way, I've started taking two classes. Intermediate yoga and classical photography. Randy says I'm a natural with lighting. And your sister's taking *three* different dance classes. Randy's taking us out to Alcatraz today. I've *always* wanted to go out there. Those prisoners back in history, being shipped out there. It's so interesting to think about, isn't it? God, Danny boy, I think this man might be the one. I mean it, honey. I think this might be *it* for your crazy mom."

Danny doesn't say anything.

"Okay, hon, gotta run. Randy's out hailing a cab. *Hailing a cab*—can you imagine, baby? Can you picture your mom and sister running around this famous city? Okay, you take care down there, and say hi to everybody. We love you, Danny boy."

The phone clicks dead in his ear and Danny sets it on the table. He looks at it for a few seconds, trying to imagine what San Francisco might look like. Trying to imagine his mom and his sister and Randy all piling into a cab. He pushes his bowl of soggy flakes away and leans back in his chair. How could his mom do this to his dad? He wants nothing to do with her ever again. He doesn't care if he has to sleep on a cot the rest of his high school career. He's not going back with her. He reaches out for his bowl and takes the spoon, resumes eating the soggy flakes so he'll have energy when he works out today.

Senior Explains
Poverty

1

"All right, lemme put it to you another way," Senior says, holding an index finger in the air. He snaps. Looks Uno right in the eyes. "Say you ain't from round here. Say you just some random Jack who got lost on your way to Mexico. You jump the gun, turn off the freeway into National City. That's the only way you could know how you livin', son. Your boys from down the block? They can't tell you nuthin'. Your moms? Nah. But an outsider, Uno. Wouldn't need to hear no words neither. The answers would be in his eyes."

On the walk home from the barbecue joint, Uno asked his old man what would happen if he couldn't raise all the money. The whole five hundred. Would he still be able to move to Oxnard? Uno watched his dad stop cold. Watched him spit into a gutter and turn to him, fire building in the whites of his eyes.

Senior took Uno by the arm, veered him into Sweetwater High's parking lot. Up the ramp. Into the football bleachers. And that's where they've been for the past forty-five minutes. Senior talking. Uno listening.

"Get too close to somethin'," Senior says, pointing at his eyes, "it ain't no longer possible to *see*. An outsider, though, lookin' in on shit with virgin eyes. That's the person who could shed a light on your reality. I mean, I done lived here with your mom, a Mexican woman, for years. So I understand the cultural background and historical symbolic stuff. You follow?"

"I think so," Uno says. In his head he tries to connect the dots. He brought up Oxnard and Senior's talking about an outsider. But they have to relate somehow.

"But a true outsider," Senior continues, "he drives past the Lincoln Acres picnic table area, sees old Indian-lookin' women sittin' huddled in the shade, crochetin'. Hardly a word passing between them. The outsider sees bus after bus, filled to the capacity with factory workers, faces like the worn-out leather on your baseball mitt. On they way to minimum-wage jobs. He rolls past an alley full of weeds after school, sees a pack of *los ratas* tape firecrackers to the back of a stray cat—then pop! pop! pop! they scatter away in they rags, laughin'. The outsider passes the run-down taquerias and liquor stores that line Highland Ave like old, broken-down Aztec warriors. Standing at the edge of the street with they arms folded."

Uno nods. He's no longer sure what these things have to do with Oxnard, but he's still listening. He's never thought of his Mexican neighborhood like this. He looks out over his high school. Wonders if he's gonna go through his entire life without paying attention.

"It's people who wander into your city, Uno. They the only ones who could see your life for what it is. National City, boy. Ain't but a forgotten slice of America's finest city. And you know what's on the tip of all y'all's tongues? Each and every one of y'all?"

Uno turns back to his dad. Shrugs.

"Money, baby."

Uno nods. What his dad's saying is totally true.

"Ain't just you, son. It's every fool down here. If it ain't money they talkin' specifically, it's some pseudonym of money. Some materialization of the concept. Maybe they usin' a different word. Like *dividends. Dough. Funds. Scratch.* The Mexican cats call it *dinero.* Or *billetes* or *scrilla.* Back in the day we used to call it paper. 'Yo, you wanna get down with homegirl you gots to have paper, son.' 'I got paper.' 'Not *that* kind of paper, you don't.' Or maybe they talkin' *around* money. They talkin' food stamps or government cheese. Supplemental housing. Unemployment checks. Disability. Welfare. Or maybe they so beaten down from a lack of funds, they don't have no talk left in 'em at all. But even these folks, Uno. They *thinkin'* 'bout money. Ain't that right?"

Uno nods, riveted. That's *exactly* right, he thinks. Even the people who don't talk about money are thinking about it. Because everybody's poor. Every one of his friends. Their families.

Senior takes a roll of breath mints out of the pocket of his khakis, unwraps it and pops one in his mouth. He wads the wrapper up and shoves it back in his pocket. "Take a look around you, son. Everywhere—it's the same goddamn thing. Some old union cat and his wife are sittin' at the kitchen table right this second, balancin' they checkbook. Scannin' overdue bills, highlightin' dates shit gets turned off.

"Across the way some little Mexican girl's openin' up a fashion magazine. The one she keep hidden under the bed. She turnin' to page a hundred and fifty-one. Pullin' out a secret stash of cash and countin': 'Ten, twenty, thirty, forty, fifty, fifty-five, fifty-six, fifty-seven, fifty-eight.' She's restackin' them bills over and over, in order of value, but it still ain't enough to get her hair done. Not like the little white girl in the magazine. The actress. She flippin' to that dog-eared magazine page again, studyin' the picture. Lookin' at herself in the mirror, runnin' a couple fingers through her nappy-ass hair.

"Your little stepbrother Manny. He at the Arby's down the street mopping a soda spill near the patio exit. The new owner just enrolled in a program where they send you partially retarded cats to work part time. He gets a tax break from the state. Gets cheap labor and a write-up in the local paper. Looks like a hero. Your little bro's mopping away until he spots an abandoned quarter, reaches down for it. When some white broad walks by with a pipin'-hot meal deal he holds the quarter out and tells her: 'Excuse me, miss? Who lost this quarter, miss?'

"But the woman just shakin' her head, Uno. She hurryin' past. Know why? 'Cause she scared of this little retarded Mexican with a mop."

Uno searches his head for connection. His brother doesn't work at Arby's. Is he just saying that as a figure of speech?

Senior slaps the bleacher, says: "And here I am with my firstborn. Just gave the boy a ten-spot. So he could go get hisself some lunch tomorrow. 'Something with vegetables,' I tell him. 'Gotta fuel a young mind with the right nutrients. Can't fly a rocket ship to the moon with the same juice you pump into a lawn mower.' But he ain't even hear me. My own son. Shades drawn on his daddy. And why? 'Cause he programmed to hear what rich white folks tell him in the media.

And he thinkin', 'Nah, Dad, I watch sports and BET and rap videos.' But who you think program that bullshit, Uno? Ain't no Miguel from down the block, Jack."

Uno straightens up a little, says, "The media?"

"The *white* media."

Uno nods his head.

"Gotta figure out what you is, baby. A jet rocket? Or a lawn mower? You ever heard of a self-fulfillment prophecy, Uno?"

Uno looks to the clouds for a sec, then turns back to his dad and shakes his head.

"It's when a person thinks of hisself in a certain way until it comes true. You ask me, that's the same thing as jumpin' off a bridge, takin' your own life."

"I wouldn't never jump off no bridge, Pop."

"Better not, boy. Not even in a metaphor way. That's a deadly sin in *two* books. God's and *mine*." Senior breaks a smile, first one of the day.

Uno nods, looks out over his high school football field again. He knows deep down he would never kill himself. He likes being alive. Even if he knows the things that happen to him aren't always good. It doesn't matter. He wants to be alive. And not only that, he wants to see who he is. Like somebody from the outside can.

"Look, I set the number high, Uno. Five hundred bones gets your ass to Oxnard. But I did that shit for a reason. Everybody in National City wishes they had more. But wishes don't pay the bills, do they? You wanna pay the bills, you gotta get out there and work. Who *you* gonna be, son? A wisher? Or a worker?"

"A worker."

Senior nods. "That's good, boy. Now get out there and work. Don't just talk about it, *be* about it."

Senior grabs Uno's head, gets him in a playful headlock. "You gonna be all right, boy," he says. "Watch."

Uno laughs as he slips his old man's grip. He looks up at him and nods. How does his pop know all this stuff about life? He didn't *used* to be like this. Is it 'cause he spends so much time going to church now? Is it the biographies? Or is it living up in Oxnard with his new family? He wishes his moms would take the time to talk to Senior. So she could see it for herself. She doesn't know anything about who he is *now*.

When Senior gets up, Uno gets up, too. And both set off in the direction of Uno's apartment.

2

A few days later, Uno's sitting on the curb outside his place picking at the web of his beat-up mitt. It's been almost three weeks since his old man told him he needed five hundred bucks, and he *still* doesn't know how he's gonna come up with it. At least not before the end of the summer. He *wants* to work, it's just nobody will hire him.

He looks up, watches a few little Mexican kids huddle around a dead possum a few yards down the sidewalk. Watches the kid without a shirt poke at the little corpse with a stick and his boys back up, laughing.

Uno goes back to his mitt. He put in applications at a mess of places, but nobody's called him back. Not one restaurant, one clothing store, one shoe shop. Not even the coffee shop outside the mall that always has the "Now Hiring" sign taped to the door. What's up with that? The pot at last Saturday's derby was crazy fat, over thirty bones. Kids were coming out of the woodwork with their two bucks. And when it was his turn to pick up the bat he rose to the occasion. Hit ten dongs, his personal record. Too bad Sofe's cousin hit fifteen. Six that cleared *two* houses.

Uno shakes his head, pulls his hand out of his mitt to scratch the back of his head. What's *up* with that kid? Uno wonders again.

He stands up, brushes the dirt off the back of his jeans, then spots Sofia wandering out of her apartment complex lugging a bulging backpack.

Uno and his boys can always make out Sofia by her walk. It's the perfect mix of fading tomboy and budding diva. When they were all kids, she was one of the guys. Talked as much head as anyone, threw down if somebody got in her face. But over the past few years she started hanging out more with the girls. And the less time she's spent with dudes, the more time dudes have spent noticing her.

3

He breaks into a slight jog to catch up. Halfway up the hill he yells out: "Hey! Yo, Sofe!"

Sofia turns around, waits on him.

"Sofe," Uno says, a little out of breath. He slows to a walk. "Where you goin', girl?"

"Me and Carmen are goin' bladin'," she says, pointing to her pack. "What's up with you?"

Uno shakes his head. "Nah, Sofe, I'm tryin' to figure out how to make some money. My pop got me on some deadline shit, man."

"Yeah?"

Uno slaps his mitt with his right hand. "But how I'm supposed to get a job if don't nobody call me back?"

Sofia reaches down to adjust one of her flip-flop straps. She slips her foot out, slips it back in. "I heard Foot Locker's hiring."

"Tried 'em already."

"What about the coffee shop?"

"Ain't got one call, Sofe. And you know why, right?"

"No, but I'm sure you're about to tell me."

"It's 'cause my ass is half black. It ain't right."

"That's not true, Uno."

"Seems like it. I been out droppin' applications for a week straight. Nothin'."

Sofia looks up the hill, says: "Wanna walk with me?"

Uno nods and they continue up the hill together. At the top they veer into Las Palmas Park and cut across the empty parking lot to the walking trail. Sofia tosses out a couple more ideas, but nothing sticks. She switches her backpack from one shoulder to the other. Uno tucks his mitt under his arm and picks up a couple of rocks. He lobs one of them into a tree.

As they approach the potholed road that leads to the baseball field, Sofia points and says, "How much you wanna bet my cousin's down there right now?"

Uno looks at her strangely. "He go to this place?"

"Every day."

"Stop lyin'. Why?"

"I swear. He works on his pitching. He's so good for a reason. He's totally obsessed about baseball."

"Yeah?"

Sofia nods and then stops walking. "Hey, you wanna go check him out for a sec?"

4

The two of them march down the hill with the broken-up concrete, toward the ice plant bank. When they round a group of bushes near the right-field fence, they find Danny firing a fastball toward home plate. Watch him reach into his bucket for another baseball and go right back into his windup.

They sit on the hill together, behind Danny, out of sight. Uno sets down his last rock, says: "He do this shit every day?"

"Every day."

"Damn."

"Right?"

They watch Danny in silence for a few more minutes, then Uno clears his throat. "Yo, Sofe."

"What's up?"

"I meant to tell you, man. I apologize, you know. For jumping your boy a few weeks back. I just . . . you feel me? It messed with my head seeing my brother's face all bloody like that."

Sofia nods without taking her eyes off the baseball field. "Especially when my cuz kept hittin' 'em over the roof, right?"

"Nah, Sofe. That didn't have nothin'—"

Sofia faces him. "Come on, Uno. You act like I don't know your dumb ass."

Uno looks at her for a sec, a blank look in his eyes. Then he picks the rock back up and flips it over in his hand. "Look, the shit didn't exactly put me in a good mood, all right?"

"That's what I thought."

"I'm tryin' to reach a certain number, man. And I was countin' on them derby pots. Then along comes Sofe's damn cousin, out of nowhere. Jackin' tennis balls out like it wasn't nothin'. I was like, 'Who the hell is *this* cat?'"

Sofia puts her hand on Uno's and then takes it off. "I know, Uno, but he's *family*."

Uno nods. "I got you, Sofe. I'm sayin', for real, I'm sorry."

Sofia nods. They both watch Danny fire another fastball and then walk toward home plate with his bucket to collect balls.

Uno tries to imagine being out here alone. Every single day. No friends or anything. And then he thinks back on something his dad once said. About how studying the Bible taught him to love himself. Taught him to look inward for companionship. Taught him to actually look forward to spending time alone with himself. He turns to Sofia, says: "Yo, Sofe, you ever think about goin' to church?"

Sofia turns to him with a look of surprise. "Me?"

"Yeah. You believe in that stuff?"

"Oh, man, I don't know. I mean, I definitely believe there's something out there. I don't know what, but something. Or else—I don't know."

"What?"

Sofia sits there for a second before answering. "I don't know. It's just, sometimes I wonder if there's even a point. We wake up every day, go to school, do homework, eat dinner, talk to our friends, go to sleep, and then wake up and do it all over again. It's like this story my teacher was telling us. About the guy who spends all day rolling a boulder up a hill and then, when he gets to the top, he just lets it roll back down. That myth or whatever. I mean, what kind of shit is that? What's the point?"

Uno nods, turns back to the field.

After a long silence Sofia says: "Why'd you ask me that, anyway?"

Uno shrugs. "I don't know. It just popped in my head."

Sofia shrugs, too, and they both go quiet again.

5

Uno watches Danny step back onto the mound. But the kid doesn't go right into his windup this time. He looks up, watches a big bird that's circling in the sky. Stands like that for a long time. Neck all craned upward, ball hanging limp in his right hand. Eventually Danny turns his attention back to the plate, but he doesn't go into his windup. He just stares at the backstop. Or the plate. His body frozen like a statue.

"What's he doin'?" Uno says.

"You got me," Sofia says. "Do you think it's kind of weird he comes here all alone?"

"Seems like it'd be boring. Especially 'cause he ain't got no catcher."

"My dad thinks he's antisocial. And he says it has something to do with his own dad leavin' so suddenly because of all this stuff that happened."

"What's weird is how he don't barely talk. And when he does you can't even hear his ass."

Sofia turns to face Uno. "Yeah, except when he saved your ass from my uncle Ray. He shouted that shit out, right?"

Uno smiles. He picks up a stick, breaks it in half. Rubs the two ends together. "What happened to his dad?"

"Long story," she says, shaking her head. She turns back to the field.

They both go quiet for the next couple minutes. They watch Danny resume pulling baseballs from his bucket. Watch him go into his high-kick windup and fire pitch after pitch at the backstop. Finally Sofia breaks the silence. "I'm sorry about Manny bein' gone."

"Yeah."

"Do you at least get to see him?"

Uno tosses the sticks back into the grass. He doesn't

answer. He looks over his shoulder and spots a Mexican dude with a Padres cap watching Danny from on top of the hill, his arms folded. He nudges Sofia, says: "Yo, Sofe, you know that guy?"

Sofia turns to look where Uno's pointing. "Nuh-uh," she says. "Why?"

"I thought I seen him watchin' your cuz pitch at the fair, man."

Sofia shrugs. She looks at her watch and gets up, says: "I should go meet Carmen. She's probably waitin' on me."

Uno gets up, too, and they both climb back up the hill toward the main park road. The sun's almost directly over their heads, and the air is warm and dry. Uno notices the big bird is still circling in the sky.

"We're supposed to meet over there," Sofia says, pointing to the tennis courts.

"Cool," Uno says.

They give each other a quick hug and wave their good-byes, and then Sofia heads down the narrow path, toward the tennis courts. Uno continues down the road a ways, in the opposite direction. But as soon as Sofia's out of sight he spins around, heads back toward the baseball field.

Uno Interrupts
Danny's Workout

1

Danny tosses his mitt down next to the mound, takes a seat on a patch of dying grass.

After every ten buckets of balls he makes himself do a couple sets of sit-ups and push-ups. A few nights ago he came up with a theory. Maybe one of the reasons he was mentally weak at the Leucadia Prep tryout was because he was *physically* weak. Maybe the two are directly related. Even if it's just a confidence thing. Sure, he could throw a lot harder than anybody his age, but that wasn't because he was strong. It was because he had long arms. Because he'd stumbled into the perfect pitching form for his particular build. Truth is, he could only do about eight pull-ups in gym class.

That's when it hit him. If you think you're strong

physically, you'll probably be stronger mentally. And though he doesn't have access to a weight room, or even a set of dumbbells or a pull-up bar, he figures a bunch of sit-ups and push-ups will probably do the job.

He lies on his back on the grass, folds his arms and starts in on another set of crunches. This is his first time doing any type of strength training. And even though it's only been a few days, he already feels more cut. He's been checking his abs and arms in the mirror before going to bed, and something's definitely happening. Is it really possible to change the makeup of his body in only two weeks? Maybe not. But if he *thinks* he can, what difference does it make? If he *thinks* he's stronger, he *is* stronger.

Danny flips over and starts in on some push-ups. But after five, out of the corner of his eye, he spots somebody sliding down the ice plant slope. A black dude in jeans and a white T-shirt. Shaved head.

Danny cuts short his set and sits up. It's Uno. He watches the guy rip down the hill, mitt in hand, and land perfectly on his feet.

2

Uno looks up, gives Danny a head nod.

Danny nods back, picks up his own mitt and hops to his feet. Watches Uno unhook the rusted latch on the gate and step through, relatch behind him. Watches him stroll out onto the field, looking over both shoulders. As he nears the mound Uno shoves his hands in his jeans pockets and clears his throat, says: "Hey, man."

Danny says "Hey" under his breath and studies his mitt.

Uno looks around at the field and shakes his head. "Know when's the last time I played ball here?" he says.

Danny shakes his head, pulls the baseball out of his mitt and grips it in his right hand for a sec. Then he drops the ball back into his mitt.

"I was twelve, man. Little League semifinals. I played catcher. Even made the all-star team that year."

Danny looks up the hill. Nobody else is around. He wonders what would happen if there was another fight right here, with no one to break it up. What would he do?

Uno shakes his head, staring in the direction of the backstop. "Yeah, man. Caught a foul tip off the mask." He looks at Danny. "But it spun the shit around on my face, right? Must've been mad loose or somethin'. And the metal wire of the mask broke my damn nose. It didn't hurt that bad at first, but I flipped when I saw blood streamin' down my shirt. I was twelve, man. I didn't know if I was hurt real bad or somethin'. So I pulled off the mask and held my hands to my face and fell my ass on the ground."

Danny looks down at the mound, kicks at a clump of brown grass, looks back at Uno. Why is Uno telling him this story? He pulls the ball from his mitt again. What's the point?

"Both coaches ran on the field to check my shit. The ump called time. But then my old man comes out of the stands, too. Yellin' his head off. This is back when he was doin' mad drugs. I knew it was his voice right away, man. At first I thought he was yellin' at the ump or somethin'. But it turned out he was yellin' at *me*. 'Get up, you little punk-ass bitch! Get your ass up! Ain't no son of mine gonna lay there cryin'!' I was shocked, man. But I stood my ass up."

Danny stares at Uno.

"I was like, Damn, what's this dude's trip? But he kept on yellin', even after I got up. And then my moms yells from the stands, 'Don't yell at my son!' And my pop turns to her and yells back, 'You shut the fuck up, bitch!' I tried to put the catcher's mask back on, but the coach from the other team stopped me. And my own coach took my face and looked at my nose and told me I was hurt. I still tried to put the mask on 'cause I barely even heard what he was sayin', man. 'Cause I was trippin' on my old man. But they didn't let me. Instead my coach walked me back to that dugout right there."

Uno points to the dugout on the first-base side. He laughs a little under his breath, says: "I remember all my friends was starin' at my dumb ass, man."

Uno pulls a baseball from Danny's bucket, snaps it in and out of his glove a couple times and says: "Anyway, that was the last time I played organized baseball. I quit the next day. Didn't even go to the championship game, man. Or play in the all-star game. I was through."

"That's messed up," Danny says, surprising even himself. The words just popped out of his mouth. English words, but for some reason it doesn't matter.

Uno studies Danny for a sec, then says: "Like I told you, dawg, the old man was on mad substances back then. He all changed now. A cool guy. But sometimes when I walk out on this field, man, I remember that shit. The look on his face and how scared I was."

3

Uno digs his foot into the side of the mound, goes into a pretend windup and throws a pretend pitch at the backstop. Then he lobs the ball back into the bucket. "Anyway, you can keep on with your workout, man. I ain't mean to interrupt nobody."

Danny grips the ball in his mitt, thinks about what he's gonna say this time. "You can work in if you want."

"Yeah?"

"I'm just throwing at the backstop."

Uno smiles, says: "Hey, man, I thought you barely talked."

Danny shrugs.

Uno laughs. "Anyway, maybe I could catch a few. Then you ain't gotta chase 'em down."

Danny shrugs.

"Cool, man." Uno starts toward the plate. He turns around midway and says, as he backpedals: "Yo, but don't throw no crazy hard ones. Like you did at the fair. I don't got enough padding on my mitt."

Danny steps back up onto the mound and tries to take in what's happening. He's about to pitch to Uno. To the black dude who gave him stitches. He wipes his sweaty hand on his pants and digs the toe of his Vans into the hard dirt. This guy gave him stitches. And even though he's over it, even though he'd like to pretend it didn't even happen, he knows he can't. At some point he's gotta fight back. Stand up for himself. That's what his dad would tell him. And his uncle Ray. They'd *make* him fight back.

"Go 'head," Uno says, setting up behind the plate. He slaps his mitt, sets a target.

Danny goes into his windup and lobs a pitch across the plate.

Uno catches it, stands up and fires it back. "See? It's better when you don't gotta go chasin' it."

Danny watches Uno squat behind the plate again. Pictures the guy's fist coming at him. The back of his head hitting the dirt. The doctor's hands in his face while he stitched

111

him up. He reaches up behind his head, fingers where the stitches used to be. There's still a lump. And he realizes he's mad that it happened. He's pissed off.

Danny grits his teeth, goes into his windup and fires a rocket at Uno, the hardest pitch he can possibly throw.

When it hits Uno's open mitt it sounds like a gunshot, and Uno literally flips over backward. He sits up quick, flings the mitt and ball away and holds his left hand. He looks up at Danny, on his knees, the pain all over his face, and shouts: "What the hell, dawg? I said not to throw it hard! Jesus!"

Danny stares back without a word. He doesn't care what happens next. He feels a little bit of rage rise up through his middle. Let the guy come out to the mound.

"Goddamn, man!" Uno shouts, looking down at his hand. "You almost broke my shit!"

Danny stays silent and stares. He feels physically stronger from the sit-ups and push-ups. Mentally, too.

Uno stares back at him for a few seconds, holding his hand, shaking it out and then holding it again. And then a slight smile comes over his face. He even lets out a little laugh. "Okay," he says, getting up, going over to get his mitt, the errant ball. "All right, D. I got you. It's cool."

He tosses the ball back to Danny and lets that be the end of it. Still shaking out his hand, he sets back up behind the plate. Smiles again. "I deserved that shit. Go 'head with another one if you want to."

4

Danny goes right back into his windup, throws a mellow curve this time.

Uno snags it, tosses back.

They go on like this for a few more pitches, then Uno walks the ball halfway to the mound and says: "Yo, I been thinkin' 'bout somethin', D. You interested in makin' a little money?" He tosses the ball back.

Danny snatches it out of the air and shrugs. He thinks about his trip to Mexico. The plane ticket.

"It'd be cool, man. I swear."

Danny shrugs again.

"How 'bout I explain the details when you done workin' out?" Uno turns and walks back behind the plate, sets up.

The wind has picked up. The trees are swaying behind the backstop. Danny peeks into the sky, but he knows the hawk is long gone. Sometimes he plays a little trick on his mind. When he sees a hawk soaring around in the sky, he pretends it's been sent all the way from Mexico by his dad. To look after him. And then it goes back to Mexico to report what it sees. He knows it's just kid stuff, but he does it anyway. He just wishes the hawk hadn't already left so it could've seen what he did. Because he finally punched somebody back. The first time in his life. Sure, it was weeks after the fact. And it was with a baseball instead of a fist. But he's pretty sure Uno knows what's up now. And how cool would it be if his dad did, too?

Danny looks over his shoulder at the hill. Nobody else around. Just him and Uno. He winds up and lobs another curve over the plate.

Uno snags it, tosses back.

The Workouts,
the Hustles,
the Drive-in Theater

1

A week later Danny and Uno are walking home from another all-day Las Palmas workout session, their seventh straight. Danny's arm is sore, but it's a good sore. The kind that tells him he's been working hard. What's surprising to him is that Uno is working just as hard. Joins in on every set of sit-ups, every set of push-ups, every set of sprints, catches every pitch. Never even complains. Danny trips out sometimes, looking at Uno crouched behind the plate, holding out his target. Who would've guessed that this was how things would play out?

"Got some good news for you, D," Uno says as they walk down the hill, side by side.

Danny turns to look at Uno.

"We meetin' up with this cat Carmelo tomorrow after his summer league workout. I sort of know him 'cause Lo's brother does all his ink. He plays second base for Morse High. Batted three-twenty last year, made second team all-league."

Danny nods, switches the bucket of baseballs from his right hand to his left.

"Like I been tellin' you all along, man. Key's to play on a dude's ego. Let 'em hit you around a little when y'all warmin' up. Before the money's on the table. For all he know, you just another punk Mexican kid from National City. One of *my* boys. Trust me, he gonna be laughin' at you."

Danny nods.

As the sun drops under the horizon the National City sky grows dark and colorless. Ugly almost. And though the wind is cool for a summer evening, both Danny's and Uno's shirts are soaked in sweat. Danny circles his right arm a couple times to stretch his shoulder. Sore for sure, but he doesn't care. He likes this feeling.

It's been a full week since Uno approached him with his big moneymaking idea on the infield grass. What if they hustled guys around San Diego using Danny's pitching prowess? Danny shrugged and Uno took it as a yes. Which it was. And ever since, during each break they take during their workout, Uno excitedly reviews the way these hustles will go down.

They'll show up at a high school when the school team is wrapping up a summer practice. They'll cruise out onto the field, harmlessly toss a ball back and forth without saying much. Soon as the coach takes off, Uno will make small talk. He'll find out who's the best hitter on the squad, dare him to step into the batter's box against Danny. At first Danny will let the guy spray a couple hits around. But he'll also whip one or two by, give him a hint of what's to come. After a little more warm-up, Uno will bet the guy he can't put one in play before Danny strikes him out. They'll put the money in the hat, just like they do at the derby, winner takes pot.

For 50 percent of Danny's payout, Uno's offering an on-call practice catcher, 24/7. Anytime Danny feels like climbing the Las Palmas mound he can call Uno, and Uno will drop whatever he's doing and meet him at the run-down park. Plus Uno will do all the research, find out all the teams' practice schedules. He'll do the haggling and be the strong arm if anybody acts crazy. In fact, Danny is never even to speak. Not a word. "Ain't exactly a stretch, right, money?" Uno told him just this morning during their first break.

Danny frowned, said: "I talk."

"I know that, dawg, but *they* don't. You not talkin' is gonna be part of our image. Be the buzz on the street, money. Watch. People be sayin': 'Yo, you hear about that stud mute pitcher and his handsome-ass businessman catcher?'"

They both laughed and Uno stepped off the mound, headed back to his spot behind the plate, where he set up yet another target.

2

As they continue down the street, Danny peeks at Uno out of the corner of his eye. Will he actually be able to come through for this guy? Sofia explained how bad Uno needs money, how he wants to go live with his dad. It hit home with Danny. But what happens if he can't strike this Carmelo guy out? If he goes wild again, like at the Leucadia Prep tryout? What if he makes Uno *lose* money and Uno can never get up to his dad's?

Uno scoops up a stray rock and skips it toward the gutter.

Danny watches the rock ricochet off the sidewalk and into the street. He wonders if Uno will still wanna work out with him if he doesn't come through.

"Hey, D," Uno says. "You see that big Mexican dude up on the hill today?"

Danny looks at Uno. "Yeah."

"You know that cat? Seems to be everywhere you go."

Danny looks forward again. "He's a scout. He used to watch this guy Kyle Sorenson at my school."

Uno stops cold. "Oh, shit, man. That makes sense. He scoutin' your ass, too, D."

Danny shrugs.

"I thought homey was a molester or some shit." Uno laughs, shakes his head. "He tryin' to see what round they gotta draft you by, D."

Danny shrugs. Can that be possible? Is the guy who scouted Kyle now scouting him?

As they pull up to Uncle Tommy's apartment building, they find Sofia sitting on the sidewalk smoking a cigarette. She stands up, ashes into the street, says: "You two? Together *again*? Yo, this is gettin' mad weird." She turns to Uno. "Better not be corruptin' my cuz. You remember what I told you about that pumpkin."

Uno walks up on her. "Gimme that," he says, swiping the cigarette from her mouth and pulling a drag.

"Go get ready, Danny," Sofia says, taking her cigarette back. "Movie starts in forty-five minutes. Carmen's swinging by in twenty."

Uno cocks his head. "What up, girl? Your boy can't get no invite? This movie's only for full-on Mexicans? They can't let nobody in if he got a drop of brother?"

Sofia laughs. "Carm's car is already full. Get Chico to go

or something. Come on, Uno, use your resources. You ain't as dumb as you look, right?"

As the two of them continue going back and forth, Danny slips by. Heads into his uncle's apartment to shower up, already thinking about the hustle he and Uno are gonna do. Hoping he doesn't let anybody down.

3

"Oh my God!" Carmen shouts, reaching for Sofia's hand. "Why you even going in there, *tonta*?" She turns to Sofia. "Why she's going in there, Sofe?"

Sofia grabs Carmen's arm, cringing. Her eyes glued to the big screen.

"I can't even watch," Angela says, covering her eyes with her hands.

On the giant screen, a pretty black girl walks into a dark barn only to be snatched by some mummy-looking person and immediately hacked to pieces. The girls all scream in unison, piercing Danny's ears again.

He's crammed in the backseat of Carmen's Festiva with Angela and Bee. Sofia and Carmen are in the front. All the girls have a cell phone in hand, occasionally sending or receiving texts between murders, their mesmerized faces made bright by the horror flick showing on National City's rundown drive-in screen.

The movie's about a big group of high school kids who get trapped in a house and barn in the middle of nowhere. The girls are absolutely riveted, but Danny's finding it hard to pay attention. All the murders seem too fake. Every time somebody's killed and the girls scream he just feels like laughing. The girls are so into it.

The giant screen has a tear in the upper right-hand corner. It must be super old, Danny thinks. He wonders if his dad ever watched a movie on this screen. And whose car would he have been in? And did he ever take Danny's mom?

Sometimes it hits Danny how little he knows his dad—even back when they lived under the same roof. His dad hardly ever spoke. After work he'd sink into the far end of the couch with the remote and his smoke box. He'd roll a joint and start toking away. After a while his eyes would sag and he'd laugh at whatever was on TV. Then he'd go to bed early.

Danny's watching a door creak open on the big screen, like everybody else, but he's thinking about this one time when he stayed home from school with an ear infection. His dad was off work that day and watching him.

He remembers how they were sitting on opposite ends of the couch, in front of the TV. His dad flipping through channels. Their old cat curled up in the corner of the living room, on a square of sunlight. Remembers watching his dad blow out his smoke long and steady. Remembers thinking it looked like a magic carpet. And because *he* was a little high, too, from the secondhand, he started wondering what it would be like to ride a magic carpet. Where would he go? Who would he take? Would his dad wanna come? But then he got another sharp pain in his ear, and he realized the only place he'd wanna take a magic carpet was away from the smoke.

Of course, at that point he already knew enough about being high to know not to mess up his dad's high, so he snuck into the bathroom, flung open the window and took a few deep breaths. Then he slumped down in the tub, wrapped his skinny little arms around his skinny little knees and waited.

After an hour or so his dad knocked on the door.

"I'm in here," Danny said, quickly spinning his head toward the door. "I'm goin' pee."

But his dad walked in anyway, found his boy lying in the tub with all his clothes on. "Why you in the tub?" he said.

"I don't know," Danny said.

His dad stood there staring at him for a while, a strange look on his face.

"I was gonna take a shower," Danny said, "but I got tired. And then I just sat in here. And my ear started hurting. I liked that old movie we were watching."

His dad motioned for Danny to follow him back into the living room, so Danny climbed out of the tub. He cracked open a couple windows and turned on the fan. When they both sat back down on the couch his dad dotted out his joint and put away his smoke box. Then he picked up the remote and tossed it over to Danny. "Go 'head," he said. "Whatever you want."

But Danny only wanted to watch what his *dad* wanted to watch. So when he picked up the remote and started flipping, he concentrated on his dad's face. He moved from one channel to the next looking not for the best show but for the best expression on his dad's face.

4

All the girls scream again, pulling Danny out of his head. Carmen pounds the dash.

The screen goes black for intermission and they grab for each other's arms. "You saw *mi novio* get a knife in the back like that?" Bee says, pulling on Sofia's hair. "I wanted to run in there and save him."

"Why's everybody so dumb in movies?" Sofia says.

"Yeah, like anybody'd really just walk right in some psycho dude's barn," Carmen says.

"Right?" Angela says, pulling lipstick and a mirror from her bag.

Sofia opens her phone, reads a text. She looks at Carmen with a big grin and then turns to Danny. "Cuz, if I give you money, will you go get us popcorn? We need somethin' to keep us calm during the second half."

Danny nods. He waits for Sofia to pull a couple crinkled dollars out of her wallet and hand them over.

"Go to *that* line, though," Sofia says, pointing to the far snack stand behind them. "It's way better."

Danny feels the girls' eyes on his back as he climbs over the seat and slips out of the Festiva. He walks toward the far snack stand wondering what his cousin's up to. He saw the way she looked at Carmen. It doesn't take long to find out. He spots Liberty getting out of an old Camry, heading for the same line.

Danny turns right back around, toward the Festiva, but then he stops himself. He stands frozen for a second, fingering Sofia's money in his pocket. He should just go back to the car, he thinks. Or maybe he should suck it up and talk to her, like his uncle Ray would. But how's he gonna talk to a girl who only speaks Spanish? Besides, every guy she meets probably wants to talk to her. She's probably tired of guys coming up to her.

Come on, he thinks. She's just a girl. A person like anybody else. Go talk to her. His dad would just go talk to her. He spins around, marches right up to the far snack stand and joins the line, one person behind Liberty.

When he looks at her long black hair, a knot rises in his stomach. What the heck is he gonna say to this girl? He doesn't even know what to say to girls who speak English. He only knows how to play baseball. He notices she's wearing cool-looking overalls and a white tank top. There's a black hair thing around her left wrist, and she's playing with a button above her back pocket. Even her thin little elbows look pretty.

Danny feels something happening inside his head. Almost like when he sat too close to his dad when he was smoking. That's *exactly* what it's like, he thinks. The magic carpet. He takes a deep breath, tries to calm himself down.

Liberty looks back at him, smiles, quickly cuts away.

Danny's chest fills with her smile. He breathes it in. Feels it spreading into his shoulders, his arms, his fingertips. He just has to come up with something to say. But what? Maybe he could compliment her clothes. Or her shiny silver earrings. Or he could make a joke about the movie. Maybe he could ask her a question about school or Mexico. Or maybe he could ask her if she wants popcorn, too.

The older couple in front of Liberty get back their change and leave with two big pretzels. Liberty steps up to the cashier, points to the popcorn machine.

Uncle Ray would probably compliment her clothes, Danny thinks. He hears his uncle's voice in his head: "Hey, girl, that's a nice blouse you got on." "Girl, I could sit here and watch you walk in that skirt all day." That's probably the best thing, he thinks. A compliment. He rehearses the line in his head. Hey, I really like your overalls. Your overalls are really nice. You look pretty in those overalls. I like to watch you walk in those overalls. Does he know how to say it in Spanish? He digs his nails into the inside of his arm until the pain shoots up into his brain, looks at the marks he's left.

Liberty gets back her change and turns around with two things of popcorn and a giant Coke. She gives him another smile, one that slices up all the organs in his stomach. He looks right in her eyes and feels a sharp pain in his middle, like when you look in the eyes of a little baby. He looks down at his Vans. Back up at her. But as she walks past he can't seem to pull the overalls line out of his throat. He doesn't have it in Spanish or English. All he can manage is a shy little wave.

She waves back at him and hurries off.

The person in front of Danny leaves with her food and the cashier asks him what he wants. He orders popcorn and watches the girl fill his tub. He turns around, watches Liberty climb back into the old Camry, out of sight.

When he gets back his change and his tub of popcorn, he heads back to Carmen's Festiva.

Sofia's leaning against the car with her arms crossed when Danny returns. Carmen sticks her head out of the passenger-side window. "Well?" she says.

Danny shrugs.

"You at least talk to her?"

"Not really," Danny mumbles.

"*What?*" Sofia says, opening the door and pulling up the seat. "We had it all set up, cuz."

Carmen laughs, says: "You cute as hell, honey, but you ain't got *no* game."

Sofia laughs. "Not even a little bit."

Danny hands the tub of popcorn to his cousin and climbs into the backseat.

"You got *negative* game," Carmen says.

"Don't worry, though," Sofia says, still laughing, "we'll work on it. Trust me, by the end of the summer you gonna know how to talk to girls."

Danny Overhears Sofia
and Uncle Tommy

1

A couple nights later, just before bed, Danny overhears Sofia asking Uncle Tommy: "Did he always have such a bad temper?"

They're both in the kitchen. Tommy's fumbling with his lunch box, and Sofia's mixing tap water into a pitcher with concentrated frozen orange juice. Danny stops cold when he sees them. He backs out of the kitchen, out of sight, and listens at the door.

"I guess," Tommy says. "He and Ray both got in a lot of trouble when we were kids. Some pretty violent stuff. Fights and assaults. Definitely wasn't the first time."

There's a short pause and then Sofia says: "You think he'd ever do it again?"

"I don't think so," Tommy says. "We talked about it last time I went to see him. He seems changed. But you never know, I guess."

Sofia says: "You think Danny will be like that, too? When he gets married?"

"I don't think so," Tommy says. "Nah, Danny's got a different way about him. He takes after Wendy."

"They say when you're exposed to it, though, it's more likely."

"Guess you never know for sure."

There's a little pause and then Danny hears Sofia say: "For some reason I was thinkin' about it. I was remembering how scared Aunt Wendy looked when she came to stay with us that weekend. The way her face was. And how she acted."

"It was a bad time, Sofe. Real bad. Much as I love my big brother, I can't say he didn't deserve this."

When they don't say any more about the subject, Danny sneaks away from the door and lies on his cot in Sofia's room. When she peeks her head in a couple minutes later, he pretends he's already asleep.

Morse High Hustle

1

Carmelo Esposito is tall and lean, with extremely broad shoulders. Easily as broad as Danny's. He has green eyes and light skin, a swing so sweet that every time he makes contact off Danny during warm-ups his boys in foul territory yell out: "Butter!"

Danny looks in at Uno's thinly padded target and goes into his windup. He throws a fastball that bounces in the dirt. Shakes his head as he gets the toss back from Uno.

He looks in again, spins a soft curve toward home plate and Carmelo jumps on it, lines the pitch into deep right. The ball one-hops the fence and caroms back toward the infield. One of Carmelo's teammates hustles after it.

Danny gets a new baseball from Uno, toes the rubber. He eyes his target again, goes into his windup and flings a fastball

126

that's way too high. But Carmelo takes a powerful cut anyway, launches Danny's pitch over the centerfield fence.

Again the cries from foul territory: "Butter!"

One of Carmelo's teammates starts laughing and goes down on one knee.

Danny glances at him, then shifts his attention back to the rubber. Uno wanted him to take it easy while they warmed up so the hits don't bother him. What bothers him is his lack of location. He feels incredibly wild. Has no idea where any of his pitches are going. It's the exact same feeling he had during tryouts, and he doesn't understand what's going on. He's throwing with the exact same mechanics he does every day with Uno. The same leg kick, same release point, same follow-through. It doesn't make sense.

"Come on, Melo," a guy sitting on the dugout says, "leave the poor kid alone. Let's go eat."

Uno stands up, shouts toward the mound: "Yo, you gotta keep the ball down, D. What I tell you yesterday 'bout keepin' your pitches down?"

He winks at Danny.

Danny nods, toes the dirt in front of the rubber again. Digs in.

Uno flips up the mask he borrowed from Morse High's catcher and takes a couple steps toward the hill. "What's wrong with the mound? You makin' excuses, man? Don't make excuses, just keep the ball down. It ain't like you goin' against some great hitter."

"Say what?" Carmelo says, stepping out of the batter's box.

Uno continues staring out at Danny. "It's not the mound, D. Listen to what I'm tellin' you, it's your mechanics."

Carmelo lowers his bat, says: "Right, I'm not a great hitter. I've only crushed three out of the last four over the fence. One-hopped the other. Yeah, dude, I totally suck."

Uno turns to Carmelo. "Money, I ain't tryin' to disrespect

you or nothin'. I'm just sayin'. I bet my boy D keeps the ball down he'd probably strike your ass out."

Carmelo laughs, says: "Oh, okay, dude." He rips apart the Velcro on his batting glove, pulls it tighter. "You're a funny guy, man. How much you willin' to put down?"

Uno reaches into his pocket and pulls out a crisp twenty-dollar bill. "This twenty says my boy strikes you out before you can hit one out the infield."

Carmelo laughs again, looks at the twenty Uno's holding. He looks toward the mound, at Danny, then turns to one of his boys, shouts: "JJ, lemme get a twenty, man. These dudes want me to take their money."

JJ approaches home plate pulling out his wallet. He hands a twenty to Carmelo, says: "This is highway robbery, Melo. Like taking candy from a baby."

"Candy from a baby," Carmelo repeats. "But if that's how they wanna play it. Screw McDonald's. Dude, we'll go to a *restaurant* for lunch. What do you say, J?"

"Sounds good to me."

Uno shoves both twenties into his hat, the way he would at a Potomac Street home run derby, and sets the hat a safe distance from the plate. He pulls his borrowed mask down and squats behind the plate.

2

Carmelo steps back into the batter's box, takes a couple easy practice swings and looks to Danny.

Danny tucks his glove under his arm and rubs the ball in his hands. He's gotta find his control. The fact that he can put a baseball anywhere he wants when he's alone tells him the problem's in his head. It's psychological. But how would he know how to fix psychological?

He takes a couple deep breaths and looks around the field. It's well-groomed but small. A hitter's park. The day is clear and warm. In the distance, a guy in a red vest on a jackhammer is breaking up a patch of street. A flock of pigeons floats over the outfield in the shape of an arrow. But not a perfect arrow, he thinks. More like a boomerang.

He digs at the dirt in front of the rubber some more with his Vans. He can't let Uno down. He needs a strikeout. But not just any strikeout. Nobody's out here calling balls and strikes. Nobody's gonna ring the guy up if he paints the corners. He has to get him to swing and miss. Three times.

He glances down the left-field line, spots the Mexican scout with the Padres cap standing there with his arms crossed. He can't believe it. The guy seems to know *everywhere* he's gonna be at all times. More than half the days they're working out at Las Palmas the scout shows up on the hill. Stays for a few minutes and then leaves. At first Danny wondered if Uno was right, that the guy was checking out his skills. But why would he leave so fast? Maybe that's how some scouts work.

He turns back to the plate, grips the ball and looks in at Uno's sign. Nods. He goes into his windup and fires a hard fastball. But the ball gets away from him and soars over Uno's head, hits the backstop on the fly.

Uno hustles after it, tosses the ball back to Danny.

Carmelo shakes his head, watches Uno squat back down behind the plate with his thin fielder's glove.

Danny circles the mound, his insides tensing up. That was the worst pitch he's thrown all summer. Above the guy's head. What the hell's going on? He steps back up on the mound, shakes off the fastball, nods at the curve, goes into his windup and spins the ball toward the plate. But his curve breaks early and right into the dirt a foot in front of the plate.

Uno scoops it up after the second bounce. Tosses it back.

Danny shakes off another fastball and nods at the curve. He delivers again. This one breaks even earlier and Uno has to lunge to his right to snag it off the short hop.

"We're gonna be here all day," Carmelo's boy yells from the side.

"He's scared," another guys shouts.

Uno hustles out to the mound, hand-delivers the ball back to Danny. "What's wrong, D?"

Danny shrugs. He looks at Uno's confused face, then looks down at the mound.

"What should we do?" Uno says. "You're all over the place. Wanna stick with fastballs?"

Danny nods.

"You okay, man?"

Danny nods again, kicks his heel into the rubber. He looks at the scout. He's totally blowing his chance.

Uno hustles back behind the plate and puts down the sign for a fastball.

Just put it over the plate, Danny tells himself as he goes back into his windup. Just put it over the plate. Doesn't matter how fast, just put it over the plate. Just put it over the plate. He delivers a very average fastball, a good 15 MPH under his usual speed, but it's in striking distance of the plate.

Carmelo steps forward and takes a quick swing. He lines the pitch into deep left field. The ball lands a few feet in front of the warning track, takes a couple bounces and caroms off the wall.

Danny looks down the left-field line for the scout, but he's gone. He turns back to the plate but doesn't look up.

3

Carmelo's teammates laugh as he flips the bat over his shoulder and yells: "Let's go eat, J."

JJ pulls both twenties from Uno's baseball cap and all the Morse High guys pack up their stuff and file out of the gate in waves, still laughing and making jokes. The catcher holds his hand out for his mask and Uno hands it over.

Danny and Uno stand together watching the guys flee the scene. Uno picks up his cap and pulls it low on his forehead. He sticks the remaining baseballs in Danny's bucket, walks over to the gate and waits. When Danny catches up to him, he says: "What happened, man?"

Danny shakes his head. "Sorry."

"You ain't gotta be sorry," Uno says. "Just tell me what happened."

"I lost control." He looks up at Uno.

"I know, but why?"

Danny shrugs.

"You throw 'em perfect every day at Las Palmas. Hardly ever throw a bad one."

Danny looks at his feet.

Uno goes silent for a while, staring at Danny. Then he says: "Man, I ain't never gonna make it to Oxnard. Shit ain't meant to be." He pulls his phone from his pocket, flips it open to check the time.

Danny looks up at Uno.

"Listen, we better go grab the bus." He heads out the gate without another word.

Danny catches up, and the two of them walk in silence to the bus stop.

Don't Worry,
They're Asleep

1

Danny hears the front door of the apartment creak open, watches Uncle Tommy and Cecilia stumble in reeking of cigarettes and tequila. Tommy's long-sleeved flannel is untucked and wrinkled and he's trying to press his puckered lips against Cecilia's neck. "Come here, *mi amor*. One little kiss, baby."

Cecilia, dressed in a low-cut red and blue sundress, is playfully pushing him away, whispering: "Tommy, the kids!"

Tommy looks toward the couch, where Danny and Sofia look asleep. Sofia really *is,* her body curled up at the far end of the couch, breaths slow and heavy. But Danny's wide awake. Through half-closed eyes he's watching Uncle Tommy and Cecilia's drunk dance. The TV light flickering through the otherwise dark apartment. The sound of the late-night talk show host's voice and the rise and fall of the show's laugh track streaming over his and Sofia's limp bodies.

Earlier tonight, the four of them sat at the dinner table, ate homemade chicken enchiladas and rice and beans and talked about the big construction job Tommy'd just landed in Nevada for the fall. It would be two months on the road, but it was almost double the money Tommy was used to seeing for any San Diego job. He and Cecilia were so excited about the extra money they decided to go out dancing to celebrate.

Once they left, Sofia talked to Danny about everything from Tommy's job to her strange love-hate relationship with Uno. But as soon as she fell asleep, Danny's thoughts drifted to baseball. He obsessively reviewed his failure against Carmelo. Why did he always seem to mess up when the pressure was on? And in such a specific way. He lost his control. Not his speed or the movement on his breaking ball or the drop in his sinker. His *control*. What did that mean? Why couldn't he just fire the ball over the plate, the way he did when it was only him and Uno?

He was deep in thought about his failures at Morse High until his uncle and Cecilia walked in.

Tommy reaches for his wife again. "But you smell so nice, *mi amor*. At least lemme smell you."

Cecilia giggles, holding on to the door frame. She extends her neck, but when Tommy's lips get close she pulls back, giggles some more.

Tommy pulls her toward him, bites her shoulder.

She lets out a little squeal and pushes his face away. "The kids," she whispers again. "They're right *there*."

Tommy doesn't even look this time. He stays with his lady, pulls her all the way into the apartment and shuts the door. *"Mi amor,"* he whines, leaning her against the end table, kissing her on the mouth this time. They hold their kiss for a few seconds, Cecilia running her fingers through Tommy's thick brown hair.

When they separate, Tommy says, "I love you, baby."

Cecilia sets down her handbag and pulls Tommy in close. "I love you, too," she says. "And I'm gonna miss you when you're gone." She kisses Tommy's forehead and nose, both cheeks.

"I'll drive back every other weekend. And maybe you can visit me." He kisses her neck, reaches a hand up for his wife's chest.

She moves his hand away, whispers: "Baby, the kids!"

"Come on," Tommy says back, kissing her freshly manicured fingers, one at a time. "Don't worry, baby, they're asleep."

Cecilia glances Danny's way again. Then she pushes off the end table and takes Tommy by the hand, leads him through the hall and into their bedroom, where she pulls the door shut behind them.

Danny glances at Sofia. Still out cold.

He goes back to meditating on his wild pitches for a bit, both against Carmelo and at last year's tryouts. But after a while his head starts spinning. He let Uno down. Cost the guy twenty bucks. He feels overwhelmed with guilt and sick to his stomach, digs his nails into his arm and looks at the marks he leaves.

He has to stop thinking. Shuts his eyes, decides to try to sleep. He has to sleep. But when sleep doesn't come right away, he starts thinking again.

He hops off the couch and grabs his keys, pulls on his jacket. Opens the front door, steps out, closes it behind him. Starts across the apartment complex parking lot toward the dull lights of the all-night liquor store, where he can at least get a soda and read a baseball magazine.

Dear Dad:

Things couldn't be going better. Me and my best friend, Uno, made this traveling San Diego all-star team. It's totally prestigious. He plays catcher and I, of course, pitch. We've won every game we've played so far by at least six runs. We've flown to great places like Arizona and Las Vegas and Orange County and even Texas. Have you ever been to Texas? We stayed in a hotel surrounded by cactuses. Uno picked one and put it in water, and now we take it everywhere we go. It's our good-luck charm.

To be honest, I'm not in National City as much as I'd like to be. But whenever I'm here I make sure I hang out at the places you've mentioned. I mostly go with Sofia or Uno or Liberty. By the way, she's really amazing, Dad. Liberty, I mean. And smart. We talk about everything. Last night she told me she's gonna go to college wherever I get drafted. She wants to make it work no matter what happens. Like I told you before, she's from Mexico, so you'll totally get along with her. Sometimes we talk about going out to see you. She's so excited to get to know you.

Anyway, I hope you're liking Ensenada. I bet it's perfect there. The weather and

the beach and the jobs. I'd love to see
what it's like for myself. I was thinking,
maybe if I really like it, when I play in
the big leagues I can spend my off-seasons
there. You know? Like a second home. I bet
I'd have enough money. And Liberty can
come. And maybe we could all go out to
dinner sometimes.

Uno Gets
Another Drunken
Tongue-Lashing

1

Ernesto steps through the bedroom door and stands over Uno, fists clenched. "And next time you don't put the trash out I throw your black ass out *with* it, you hear?"

Uno plops down on his futon bed and looks at his bedroom rug—the last gift he got from his grandma. The shaggy red and green and white, like the Mexican flag. The shapeless stain in the upper right-hand corner from the time Manny dropped a full cup of Kool-Aid.

Uno's still got on all his clothes, his scuffed Timberlands. Still got a dose of Hennessey cruising through his veins from the party he just left.

"I'm the man of the house!" Ernesto yells. "You ain't nothin' in here! You do what *I* say!"

Uno nods, stays with the rug stain. He keeps his mouth shut whenever he smells tequila on his stepdad's breath. Knows that when Ernesto's been drinking tequila he's liable to swing an open hand. 'Course it ain't the open hand he's scared of, it's what he might do in *response* to the open hand. So instead of killing this man and getting locked up for real, he nods and nods and nods and nods.

"Who you think you are?" Ernesto shouts. "You don't pay bills! *I* do! You isn't the breadwinner here! *I* am! *Me!*" Ernesto pounds his chest. His breath is forty proof, his flannel shirt untucked, bushy hair falling in his eyes as he shouts. "And don't you say shit back to me, boy! Not *shit!*"

Uno nods at the stain on the rug.

His stepdad stands over him a few seconds longer. Gritting his teeth. Seething. Pointing a stiff index finger. Then he storms off.

Uno's mom rushes into Uno's room as soon as Ernesto leaves, a couple tears running down her flushed cheeks. She puts a hand on her son's shoulder, says in a hushed voice: "Just do what he says, Uno. You know how he gets sometimes, *mijo.*"

Uno nods, tries to make things out of the shape of the stain. A bear on a bike. An upside-down anchor for a boat. A cannon blast. A guy smacking a tennis ball at the derby.

"It's not hard to do what he says. I don't get it. You could just avoid all this."

Uno nods.

His mom tries to give him a hug, but he slips her arms like a running back, scoots over to his window and pulls it open.

"Don't walk away, Uno," his mom says. "*Uno!* I'm telling you how to make it better. Wait."

But Uno's already got his right leg out. And he's pulling

his left through and leaping down onto the sidewalk and walking away with his hands in his pockets. He's sort of laughing, too, as he moves away from his place. He doesn't know why, but the shit's funny to him. They can't touch him anymore. His stepdad especially. He's invisible now. A talking mannequin. A ghost. Because he's already moved away in his head. To Oxnard with his *real* dad. And so as he's walking away from his yelling mom, he's laughing. Like he's watching a funny movie. And he's imagining what it'll be like when he never ever has to go back there again.

He takes a look over his shoulder, sees his mom hanging halfway out the window, still calling after him, waking the neighbors. But he can hardly even hear her now. And the whole thing seems like a cartoon. Maybe *that's* why he's laughing. He looks ahead again, doesn't really care where he's going. Or where he's coming from. He's just another black kid on the street now. A black kid concentrating on the Hennessey warming his chest. The Hennessey making his fingertips and toes tingle. His mind able to see everything like it's a cartoon.

2

Uno can't believe his eyes when he walks into his favorite liquor store. It's Danny, dressed in khakis and a nice shirt, like he's going out or something. He's standing by himself reading a magazine. He hasn't seen the kid since they went to Morse High a few days back—not one call for a Las Palmas workout or anything. He walks right up on Danny's blind side, shouts in his ear: "Yo!"

Danny spins around wide-eyed.

Uno bends over laughing. "What up, D? Couldn't sleep or somethin'?"

"Yeah," Danny says, closing his magazine and setting it back on the rack. He buries his hands in his pockets.

Uno thinks about how strange his boy is, going everywhere solo. Barely ever talking. Mexican as anybody else in the 'hood but dressed like some kind of skater dude. Doesn't seem to make much sense. Uno picks up a *Sports Illustrated,* flips to some random page. "Where you been, D? You straight-up went MIA."

Danny looks at the unfinished liquor store floor, scratches his ear. He opens his mouth like he's gonna say something, but then he closes it and looks to the floor again.

Uno forces a little laugh, says: "Yo, I was at this little house party in Chula with Chico. Mad women, D. Latinas, black bitties, even a couple loopy white broads. You'd have loved it, man. I ain't gonna lie, though, I'm still pretty faded from the Hennessey."

Danny looks up at him.

Uno peeks over Danny's shoulder at the store. A few old Mexican dudes staring through cracked glass at the beer selection. A hunched crazy-looking woman walking a box of cat food to the counter. The young Mexican cashier behind thick, bulletproof glass watching a mini TV. He thinks, Man, I'm over this entire neighborhood.

He pulls his cell from his jeans, flips it open and checks the time. "Sofe's dad let you out the house this late, D? It's almost two in the mornin'."

Danny shrugs, pulls his hands from his pockets and links them behind his back. Starts digging his nails into his arm on the down low, as if nobody can see him.

Uno doesn't know why Danny does that, or what it means, but he smacks his shoulder to get him to stop.

"Wha'chu readin', anyway?" he says, sticking the *SI* back and pulling the mag Danny was looking at. He reads the title out loud: "*Street and Smith's College and High School Baseball Preview*." He looks up, says: "You in here, D?"

Danny shakes his head and points to Kyle's smiling face on the cover. "He's from my school."

Uno flips to the story, reads the title: "'Is Kyle Sorenson the best baseball prospect in the country?' Damn, dude must be all that."

Danny nods.

Uno scans the rest of the article in silence, Danny looking over his shoulder. When he reaches the end he looks up at Danny, says: "Yo, your boy's 'bout to get *paid*."

"Yeah," Danny says, nodding. Then he pulls his wallet from his back pocket, takes out a twenty and holds it out for Uno.

"What's this for?"

"I owe you."

Uno waves him off. "For *what*? Nah, put that shit away, D."

Danny holds the twenty limp at his side.

"I'd make the same bet if I could do it all over. You just had bad karma that night. Shit happens. You just gotta get your karma right, man. Besides, I got me a little busboy job at El Torito. Started yesterday. Six bucks an hour plus tips. I'm cool, man. Have the cash in no time."

The two of them stare at each other for a sec, then Uno says, "Hey, wha'chu doin' right now? You gotta get back to the house right away?"

Danny shakes his head.

"Wanna check this place I know by the train tracks?"

Danny glances out the window, at his uncle's apartment complex, then back at Uno. He shrugs.

3

After navigating a few quiet side streets and narrow alleys, Uno leads Danny to a line of graffiti-laced train tracks cutting through a wide valley of jagged dirt hills. They slide down the face of the steep bank one at a time, walk along the rusting tracks. The sky is starless and dark, but the trash along the tracks is impossible to miss. Uno kicks through empty fast-food bags as he walks, steps on faded soda cans, discarded cigarette cartons.

After a few minutes he stops in front of a bridge that runs over a dried-up marsh and reaches down for a couple rocks. He looks up at a railroad crossing sign, scans the tracks. When he spots the line he spray-painted black back in the day, he stands behind it and fires the first rock at the sign. Barely misses.

"This is my spot," he says, turning to Danny. He fingers the second rock and hops up on the track, balances himself on one foot. "Usually come by myself so I could think about shit. Get my head straight. But a couple times I brought Manny. 'Fore my moms put him in that mental house."

Danny picks up a rock of his own, tosses it from one hand to the other as he listens.

"One day I made up this karma game. First you make a wish about some shit you want to come true. Like passin' algebra or havin' some honey give up the booty or me graduatin' high school on time. Whatever. Then you stand behind this line with a handful of rocks and you get five throws at the sign. Hit three out of five and it's supposed to come true to life."

Danny looks at the line, then at the sign.

Uno reaches down and picks out five rocks, says: "It's legit, D. Hundred percent guaranteed." He shifts all the rocks except one to his left hand and toes the line. "Here, I'll show you. This is on me gettin' outta damn National City, movin' to Oxnard." He winds up and throws the first one: misses. Throws the second one: hits, the cracking sound echoing down the tracks. Throws the third: misses. Throws the fourth: barely nicks it. "Don't matter how square you hit it, by the way," he says, turning to Danny. "You just gotta hit it." He throws the fifth: hits.

Danny nods, mumbles: "Got it."

Uno pounds his chest and points into the dark sky. "I'm good as gone, D. Yesterday's news."

Danny fingers the rock in his hand.

"Go 'head," Uno says, picking up a few rocks. He tosses them to Danny. "First you gotta figure out what's it gonna be on."

Uno watches Danny turn his eyes to the dull sliver of moon in the sky to think. He scans the kid's gear again. The skater button-down shirt. The khakis. Vans. If he saw this private school cat at *his* school, he'd walk right on by. Think he was just some damn skateboarder or something. A kid he'd have nothing in common with. Who would've guessed a kid dressed like this could throw a baseball harder than anybody he's ever seen? Maybe even harder than some big leaguers.

Danny looks at Uno and shrugs.

"Come on," Uno says. "Could be anything."

Danny looks toward the black line spray-painted on the tracks. But he still doesn't say anything. Then, just as Uno's about to offer up some ideas, he blurts out: "Seeing my dad . . . in Mexico."

Uno nods. "Yeah, man. That's cool."

"I'm gonna buy a ticket to Mexico. Stay with my dad."

"All right, D. That works. Hit three out of five and you be breakin' out the passport."

Danny turns to the sign. He fires the first one: hits dead center. He fires the second one: hits dead center. Fires the third: dead center. The fourth: dead center. The fifth: dead center.

4

Uno walks up to the sign, stares at the battered metal, shakes his head. He turns back to Danny. "Yo, money, you just hit the exact damn spot five straight times. That's some freak-factor shit."

Danny shrugs, steps off the tracks.

"Your old man probably straightenin' up the pad as we speak!" Uno shakes his head again, looks back at the sign. He turns to Danny. "What's the deal with Mex, anyway?"

Danny looks at the ground, shrugs.

"Come on, D. You gotta know *somethin'*. What'd the old man tell you before he left? What's your crazy-ass uncle say?"

Danny shrugs.

"He got a lady down there? A job? He born there?"

Danny stares at the tracks a sec, looks up at Uno and says: "I don't know." He reaches his arms around his back, like he does. But this time Uno snatches Danny's left arm, looks at all the old scars, the deep bruises. He looks up at Danny, confused. He doesn't get it. Kid seems like he's got so much going for him. What's wrong?

Uno lets go of Danny's arm without a word and sits down on the tracks. Looks across the bridge. In the distance he can make out the big recycling plant where his stepdad works. Where all Chico's uncles work. "My old man left when I was a kid, yo. Don't even really know the guy if you wanna break it down. But for the past couple years he been comin' down here to see me, you know? And now he says he wants me to move in with him. And I wanna do it, D. I could start fresh up there. Quit gettin' in trouble and get my grades up. Maybe even play catcher on the high school squad."

Uno picks up a rock, flings it down the track a ways. "Anyway, D. That's some shit you just did. Five straight. All in the same spot. You the opposite of my bro, Manny. He never hit the sign once. Couple times he threw the damn rock *backwards*."

They both smile. Danny looks up at Uno and then looks down the tracks toward the bridge.

Uno picks up a rock, says: "Lemme ask you somethin', D. Why you think you got such good aim here, and when we at Las Palmas, and then you was kinda *off* the other day with Carmelo?"

Danny sits down on the track across from Uno, shrugs.

"Was the mound different? Dude intimidated you? What's your theory?"

Danny runs a hand down his face. Doesn't say anything.

"Is somethin' botherin' you in your head?"

Danny turns and stares Uno right in the eyes. Holds his stare and doesn't blink. "That's the thing," he says. "I have no idea."

Uno notices something different in Danny's eyes and looks down at the rocks between the tracks. He lets out a laugh, says: "Damn, D. You one confused-ass Mexican." Uno looks up at him with a smile.

But Danny doesn't see it. He's too busy looking down at his Vans and shaking his head.

They're both quiet for a few minutes. Uno watches Danny for a second, thinking maybe *he's* the reason for what happened at Morse High. He knows Danny'd make out better with a *real* catcher. To be straight, he doesn't know the first thing about calling pitches for a guy with Danny's talent. He hasn't played real baseball, on a team, since he was a little kid. Doesn't even have a real catcher's mitt. He knows Danny deserves better.

They're both quiet for a few more minutes, then Uno says: "Know what I always wanted to do, D? Watch the sun come up over that recycling plant over there. From right here on these tracks. My old man says he did it once and it was mad cool."

Danny doesn't say anything.

"One day I'm gonna do it."

They both turn toward the bridge when they hear a faint train whistle in the distance. Uno pops up, says: "D, follow me." He hustles for the foot of the bridge, starts sliding down the bank toward the dried marsh. When he looks back, he finds Danny right there behind him.

5

"Grab a post," Uno shouts over the growing sound of the on-coming train. "Hold tight, man. Trust me."

Now directly underneath the bridge, Uno takes hold of one of the wooden pillars. Hugs it. Danny hugs the one next to him. Their arms wrapped around their own thick column of wood. And suddenly the powerful train is roaring by over their heads, rumbling over the tracks, its whistle blowing again. The sound of the train deafening. Uno shakes with the power, watches Danny shake, too. Their lips trembling. Teeth chattering. The power of the train's massive weight vibrating through their arms and legs and stomachs and deep into their chests.

Uno watches Danny close his eyes and lower his head. He does the same. Holds tight and feels the train above him and in the wood and in every part of his body, and he breathes in the power and opens his eyes to check on his boy. And when the last car finally passes overhead, he lets go and shouts, "Hell yeah, boy! That's some *power*!"

Danny opens his eyes, lets go. He looks at his hands.

Uno glances up at the tracks, shakes his arms out and stretches his neck. "Trains got crazy power," he says. "Sometimes I think about that shit when someone steps to me in a fight. I think how I stood under this bridge and held on to this pole and took all that train power into my body. And then it ain't really me that's fightin' no more. It's the power of the train coming outta my body. And ain't nobody gonna mess with that kind of power, right?"

Danny stares back at Uno, nodding.

"I could never be as strong as a train," Uno says. "So why pretend, right? Sometimes when I'm down here and there's a train, I wonder if that's the kind of power that God gots. And I pretend it ain't just train power I'm takin' in, but maybe it's some bigger shit. Somethin' spiritual, maybe."

Danny puts his hands back on the pillar, looks up at the tracks above.

"My pops is into God, man. Jesus up in heaven and all that. And maybe he's right. But sometimes I think maybe God's down here. In regular everyday stuff. Like the power of a train."

They're both quiet for a sec, and then Uno laughs hard, says: "Check me out, D. Gettin' all deep down here at three in the mornin'."

"Maybe you're right," Danny says under his breath, looking at his hands.

"You think so?" Uno says.

Danny shrugs.

Uno shakes his head, laughs a little more and starts to climb back up to the bridge. When he's almost at the top he looks back, finds Danny right behind him.

Danny's Return
to the Mound

1

A week later Danny finds himself following Uno again, this time onto a ghetto-looking field somewhere in Logan Heights. They set their stuff near the dugout, take a seat on the brown grass in foul territory and look over the setting. Danny notes the holes in the dugout chain-link, the nonexistent center-field wall, the brown home plate. He tries to imagine the faces of the Leucadia Prep guys if they had to set foot on the fields Danny's been on this summer.

Uno loosens the laces of his Timberlands one at a time, slips them off.

Danny turns around when a couple big black dudes walk through the gate behind them, laughing. Three Mexican girls follow close behind. "What up, Uno?" the first guy says, giving Uno a quick pound.

"What up, C?" Uno says.

The guy turns to Danny. "This the cat you was talkin' 'bout? Come on, dawg, he out here in Vans."

"Nah, he could pitch, though," Uno says. "You don't think I'd throw paper down if I was backin' a cripple-ass horse, right?"

"I see, it's part of y'all skeeze." The guy laughs, turns to his buddy. "This my boy Uno. We was up in juvi together when we was fifteen. Uno, this Marzel."

The two give daps and Uno says, "Cory, D. D, Cory." More daps. Then Cory and Marzel continue to the other side of the field. Danny glances at the girls, who are still hovering by the gate. They're all staring at him.

"Cory's good peoples," Uno says as he pulls a pair of old Nikes out of his bag, slips them on. "He was in juvi for sellin' to an undercover. Spent a year in a group home in Lemon Grove after that. Told me his boy can hit like a mother, but he's a little shaky when it comes to character."

Danny nods.

As the girls walk by, the prettiest one pats Danny on the head and smiles. Uno holds his hands up at her, says: "What up, baby girl? Daddy can't get no love? I ain't handsome, too?"

The girls laugh and continue toward the far dugout, next to Cory and Marzel, and duck inside.

Uno unzips his bag, reaches a hand inside. "Got a surprise for you, D. You know how I been busin' tables, right? Check it, dawg. I made an investment. Now you could throw it as hard as you want." Uno pulls out a brand-new catcher's mitt, slips his left hand in and flexes the leather. Punches the pocket a couple times.

"Thought you were saving for Oxnard," Danny says.

"I been gettin' tips, though. My choice, D. And since next year I might wanna try out for the squad, I gotta buy one eventually, right?"

Danny nods.

"Anyway, we win this thirty-dollar pot, the mitt basically pays for itself. And don't worry 'bout no double or nothin'. These fools ain't got a penny more than thirty. Trust me. Now, you ready to go show some fools what a Mexican could do in a pair of Vans?"

Danny tosses a baseball into Uno's new mitt and they both stand up.

2

As Marzel steps into the batter's box, Danny digs into the loose dirt in front of the beat-up pitching rubber. He glances at Cory, who's checking his cell. The girls, who are all talking to each other and laughing. He checks Uno's hat behind home plate, filled with sixty bucks. He knows he can't let Uno down this time. It's not even an option. He has to win back the money he lost last time.

Danny eyes Uno's brand-new mitt, nods at fastball and goes into his windup. He fires the first pitch at the outside part of the plate, but the ball gets away from him, ends up a good two feet outside. Uno lunges for the ball but misses, has to chase the errant pitch all the way to the backstop. He gathers the ball, tosses back.

Danny snags it out of the air and walks around the mound rubbing it down. He feels uncertainty climbing into his throat again. That old familiar feeling. This can't be happening again. The whole reason Uno wanted to hit up some guys off the street is so Danny wouldn't get nervous. And here he is again, first pitch way out of the strike zone. Danny steps back on the mound and eyes the target, nods at another fastball and goes into his windup. He fires his second pitch, but the ball gets away again. This one is headed right for Marzel's left shoulder, but luckily he dives out of the way in time.

Uno lunges to his left, barely snags the pitch on the fly.

Marzel gets up slowly, eyeing Danny. He looks back at Cory, then takes a few steps toward the mound, points a finger. "You throw inside like that again, I'm gonna break this bat on your face."

Uno hustles in front of the guy, slows his forward progress. "Chill, baby. He ain't throwed it like that on purpose. Pitch got away from him, that's all."

Marzel stops, dusts off his shirt and says: "Better check your boy, G."

"I got 'im, I got 'im." Uno turns the guy back toward the plate and heads out to the mound himself. He pulls his mitt off and smiles. "Yo, D. I just figured somethin' out. You tryin' too hard, man. Like I do at the derby sometimes. 'Member what I said down at the tracks? 'Bout the power of a train? It's in here now, D." He lightly punches Danny in the chest a couple times. "It ain't about you no more."

Danny nods, pulls in a deep breath. Over Uno's shoulder he sees Marzel talking to Cory, pointing his finger.

"It ain't about you," Uno says again. "It's bigger than your dumb ass. It's about your right arm, man. Your talent."

Danny nods.

Uno puts his mitt back on, punches the new leather. "Look at this thing, D. Brand-new. You gonna help me break this shit in or what?" He laughs and heads back to the plate.

After Uno sets up and Marzel steps back into the box, Danny looks in at Uno's sign. Another fastball. He nods. Takes a deep breath and pictures the train over his head and then pictures nothing at all. He goes blank during his windup, like he does when it's just him and Uno at Las Palmas. Or at the train tracks. He lets go. And this time when he fires his fastball it rips right past a late-swinging Marzel and straight into Uno's new mitt.

"Strike one!" Uno calls out, tossing the ball back.

Marzel turns to look at Cory, who shrugs.

Danny snags the ball out of the air. He looks in at Uno's fastball sign with a blank mind and nods again. Winds up and fires. The ball rips right past a late-swinging Marzel again. Marzel slams his bat into the ground.

"Strike two!" Uno calls out, tossing it back.

"Come on, Zel," Cory shouts from the side. "Put some wood on it."

Uno pumps his fist at Danny, crouches behind the plate and puts down another fastball sign.

Danny's completely blank when he nods this time. There's nothing in his head but quiet space. He winds up, fires, watches a third straight fastball speed right past the incredibly slow swing of the bat. Uno doesn't even have to move his mitt.

"Strike three!" Uno calls out, and hustles to the mound to push Danny, smack him in the back of the head. "It ain't about you, D. It's your talent. Just gotta get out the way, boy."

Danny smiles, nods. It feels good to get out of the way. To watch a hitter swing late and slam his bat in frustration.

They step off the mound together. Danny heads to Uno's bag, while Uno heads for his hat and the money.

Danny's not over there for two minutes before the three girls walk over and start talking to him in Spanish. When he shrugs they giggle. "He doesn't even speak Spanish," one of them says. "Told you he was a halfie. You could tell 'cause how he dresses."

"Why don't you speak no Spanish?" another says.

Danny shrugs.

"*Tu Mexicano*, though, right?" the first one says.

Danny nods.

Marzel storms the scene looking pissed and says, "Gia, wha'chu doin', girl?"

"We was just askin' him a question, Zel," she says. "Chill. God."

Marzel turns to Danny, shoves him, says: "First you throw at my head, then you gonna talk to my girl like that?" He pushes Danny again.

Danny slips his left hand out of his mitt, takes a couple steps back.

Gia yells at Marzel to back off, but he continues forward, shoves Danny again. "You ain't disrepectin' me like that, dawg. You don't know where I come from." He rears back to throw a punch, but out of nowhere Uno steps in and blasts the guy from the side. Puts him flat on his back and then stands over him, glaring down.

"Now what's up?" Uno shouts.

Marzel looks up at Uno, touches his bloody lip and holds his fingers in front of his eyes. He stands up slow, swings wildly at Uno, but Uno ducks it, lands two quick and powerful body blows, doubles Marzel over.

Uno glares. "Ain't nobody touch my boy Danny like that!"

Danny looks at Uno standing there with his fists clenched.

Cory hustles onto the scene, steps in front of Marzel. He looks back at Uno, says: "You guys get outta here! Go! Go!"

Uno mad-dogs Marzel a few more seconds, then grabs Danny by the arm and they both hustle for their stuff and leave the field.

A ways down the street Uno turns to Danny, says: "Know that punch I just threw, D? That wasn't me, man. Was the train. Same thing as when you pitch."

Danny looks back as they run for a bus that's pulling up to the stop, opening its doors. He can't see the field anymore, but he imagines Cory still holding Marzel back. The girls huddled off to the side.

Dear Dad:

Look who your son's become. He's the ace of the best traveling team in the state. The kid the coach hands the ball to when it matters most. Whenever your son steps onto a mound, Dad, the rest of his team stops and watches. They wanna see what he does next. Scouts hang on his every movement.

Ever since you first taught me how to throw a baseball, Dad, in the alley behind the boarded-up Laundromat off Twenty-third St, this is who I was destined to become. A superstar pitcher. I couldn't have chosen another path if I'd tried. When I'm in the classroom at school I'm just a regular kid. I got a certain score on a certain test just like all twenty-five of the other scholarship kids. We blend together like sheep. When I step on this mound, though, Dad, I'm special. I stand above the rest of the kids in the school. The rest of the players in the state. I pitch down to them. Something I've learned—when you're a great pitcher, a mound is your throne. A baseball cap is your crown. You give orders. Make laws. Rule people.

When you think about it, Dad, it's amazing I ever step down from that hill of dirt.

Senior Reads
Danny's Mind

1

Several hustles go the exact same way. Danny blows away whoever he's facing with almost exclusively fastballs. And every pitch hits Uno's glove wherever he sets it. His control problem has basically gone out the window. The trick, Danny's found, is clearing his mind. Just like Uno said. Getting out of the way. Letting his talent do the work.

At Sweetwater High he struck out a Mexican dude named Rafael. At Chula Vista he whiffed a tall white guy named Gary Sutterfield. At San Diego High he overpowered a muscle-head black kid named Ernest. Uno lays down his signs, and then Danny shuts off his mind and deals. Nobody has even touched him in four hustles. And the money is starting to add up. On the trips back home Uno talks about

Oxnard and Danny thinks about Ensenada, Mexico. He's even started researching plane tickets.

But after today's hustle he's ended up at Tony's Barbecue with Uno and Uno's dad.

Uno's dad takes a small break from his lecture to pour house barbecue sauce all over his ribs and corn bread. Uno takes the bottle after him and does the same. Danny studies the similarities in their faces. The thick nose, the droopy eyes, the strong cheekbones and powerful chin. The only real difference is that Uno's face is younger, a little lighter because his mom's Mexican. When Uno recaps the bottle, Danny reaches for it, aims over his own plate of ribs and corn bread.

"All right, an example then," Senior continues, turning to his son. "Take last Sunday. I caught some Mexican kid breakin' in my place. Caught 'im red-handed. Me and my wife and my baby was walkin' back home from church, and there he was, 'bout eighteen, nineteen years old, climbing in through my damn bathroom window."

Uno drops his fork. "You playin', Pop. Really?"

"That's my word, Uno. Right after church, middle of the day. But I'm sayin', it's an example of how man is capable of change. The *old* me would of put this skinny kid in an emergency room. Asked questions later. But I ain't react like that no more. Today I got control, got a perspective."

"That's different, though," Uno says, his mouth full of baked beans. "He was comin' into your place. Tryin' to take your stuff."

"*Is* it different?" Senior says. He turns his glare at Danny. "Think about it. Does it *really* make a difference?"

Senior continues staring, and Danny feels like something's expected of him. He shakes his head and looks down at his plate. When he looks up again, Senior's back to his own food. Uno's sipping Coke through a straw. Danny picks up a rib and tears off some meat. As he chews he tries to imagine what it'd be like to find somebody climbing into his mom's apartment in Leucadia. What would he do? How would he feel about the robber?

2

Earlier in the day, Danny and Uno completed their latest successful hustle and cleared another thirty bucks. This one wasn't even on a real baseball diamond, it was on a patch of open lawn in Balboa Park, where they challenged some rich Mormon kid. Uno'd heard through the grapevine that there was a traveling team from Utah practicing in front of the Aerospace Museum.

And amazingly, the Padres scout was there for a bit, too. He showed up in his same getup: jeans, a plain collar shirt and his Padres hat. This time Uno yelled out to him: "Hey, man. You really work for the Pads?" The guy nodded and slipped his hands in his pockets. He watched a few more pitches and then took off like he always did.

On the bus ride home Uno went on and on about how easily Danny had handled the Mormon. Three straight hard fastballs, right down the pipe. Guy didn't have a prayer. The only problem, Uno explained, was that Danny was making things look too easy. So easy that the Mormon, like the last two guys, had refused to go double or nothing, even when Uno said all he had to do was foul-tip a pitch to win his money back.

They went silent for a few seconds on the bus, and then Uno asked Danny if he wanted to have lunch with him and his dad at their favorite barbecue joint. Danny quickly accepted.

3

Senior slaps his palm on the table, says: "People is people! Don't matter if it's a convict or a preacher man." He takes a big bite of corn bread and chews through, swallows. "Five, maybe six years ago, I wouldn't have thought twice about it. I'd have beat that kid within an inch of his life. But that's the point, see. I wasn't thinkin' back then. I was just *doin'*. And where was I learnin' what to do? On the street. From the thugs comin' up in front of me in southeast San Diego. Now I slow down, make decisions based on well-thought-out justifications."

"What'd you do then?" Uno says, lifting a couple sweet potato fries to his mouth.

"First thing I did was tackle him to the ground and put his ass in a headlock. No matter how your heart is for people, you still gotta apprehend somebody tryin' to climb in your damn bathroom window." Senior laughs a deep laugh, wipes his face. "I tackled him and yelled: 'You gonna come 'round *my* property, scare *my* family? Boy, you caught me on this a few years back I'd have snapped your neck already!' Then I looked at my wife, my baby. And I smiled at 'em and said: 'It's okay, now. This boy here's one of God's children, too. Just like us. And I'm gonna show you.' Then I pulled the boy to his feet and we all went in the house together."

"You took him in the *house*?" Uno says.

"That's right. Made him sit right next to me on the couch. Kid was shook, too. Wouldn't look nobody in the eyes, not even my new li'l puppy. Tried to make a run for it at one point. But I just grabbed him by the hood of his sweatshirt, pulled him right back to the couch and kept talkin' to him. I told him about my past, bangin' and sellin' and snatchin' people's shit. Told him how I served time, lost my marriage, lost my son. Lost my damn sense of who I *was*."

Danny watches Senior and Uno stare into each other's eyes for a few seconds. Senior shakes his head, says: "I told that kid I didn't want nothin' more, Uno, than to make it right with my firstborn. With my boy. And that's what made me fly straight. So I moved from San Diego up to Oxnard, got a job with the city, met my second wife and turned my life around. Told him it took me a long-ass time to learn the honorable path. But I *did*. And he could, too. And then you know what happened? He opened up to me, man. Said he'd knocked up one of his little girlfriends, one he didn't hardly even know. And he was scared. Didn't neither of them have no job or money, and she was dead set on havin' the baby. So for the past week he'd been stealin'. Much as he could. Outta houses and off people in the street. He said he didn't even think he wasn't stealin' for the money no more; he was stealin' to get caught. So somebody'd put him away and he wouldn't have to think about what to do about no baby. I turned to my wife and my baby and told 'em, 'You see that? Behind every act, good or bad, there's a reason. People don't just go out and do things by unfounded chance. They do things based on some aspect of they personal psychology. They unconscious.'"

Uno looks down at his plate, works his fork, lost in thought. Danny picks up the barbecue sauce, pours a little more on his ribs, looks up at Senior.

"I took hold of the kid's face," Senior says. "Made him look into my eyes. And I told him: 'I forgive you, son. You hear what I'm tellin' you? My whole family, my wife, my baby and me, we forgive you. You hear me? We forgive you.' Then I reached for my wallet and pulled out all the cash I had. Fifty-somethin' bones. I told my wife to get her purse and do the same. She had a little over twenty. I handed a wad of bills to this kid and told him a famous quote: '"Never to suffer would never to have been blessed."' Told him: 'That's Edgar Allan Poe who wrote that, son, and he wasn't lyin' when he said it. Edgar Allan Poe was a world-famous poet, and he told it to me in one of his books. Now I'm tellin' it to you.'"

Uno and Danny both nod as they eat and listen to Senior.

"The boy cried and cried when I told him that, see. And then he leaped up and off the couch and shook hands with me and apologized, over and over and over, for tryin' to break in the house. He hugged my wife and touched one of my baby's little socks and shook my hand again and then he jogged out the house and kept on joggin' till he was completely out of sight."

"Wait, Pop," Uno said, dropping his fork and wiping his face with a napkin. "I don't get it. The guy tries to rob you, and you give 'im all your money? It ain't like you got a bunch of extra cash to be throwin' around, right?"

Senior laughs a little and shakes his head. "Money ain't nothin' but a rabbit in a hat, Uno. It's an illusion. A trick up Uncle Sam's sleeve. Advertisers make it out to be this big thing in America so we'll buy their fancy cars and their big-ass sailboats and their high-end radio equipment, but it's just paper. No different than the napkin you holdin' in your hand, Uno. You see what I'm sayin'?"

Uno puts down his napkin. "But people need money to *live*, Pop."

"Do they? They need food and water and shelter, sure. And they work a job for those things. But do they really need the money in they pockets?"

Uno looks hard at Senior, then turns to Danny. "You the fancy private-school cat, D. Wha'chu think?"

Danny looks at Uno, goes back to Senior. He's not sure what's expected of him and he quickly cuts back to Uno.

Senior smiles. "That's all right, Danny," he says. "You ain't gotta say nothin' 'bout this. You just listenin', right? Maybe this is the part of your life where you *supposed* to be listenin'. To the world. To grown folks. To biographies and good movies, even the winds. Nature. The talkin' part, man, that shit can come later on. Too many people rush into that part. They talk before they know what they wanna say."

Danny looks down at his food, trying to process what he's hearing. Either Uno's dad is some kind of modern-day philosopher or he's totally nuts. He can't tell which it is. But just in case, he's trying to make meaning out of what he's hearing. He picks up his fork, moves his beans around.

Senior turns back to Uno. "When I looked into that young man's eyes, son, you know what I saw? I saw a little piece of God. It was hidden, all right. Buried under a lifetime of hurt. But it was there. *That's* who I gave the money to."

Uno shakes his head. He picks up a rib but doesn't make a move to eat. Danny watches Uno out of the corner of his eye.

"A little piece of God," Senior repeats, leaning back in his chair and crossing his arms. "Just like I got a little piece. And you got a little piece, Uno. And you, too, Danny. Listen, I can see in your eyes somethin' be botherin' you. Somethin' confusin' inside, right? Real deep. I see it."

Danny looks back at Senior straight-faced, nodding. But inside everything's all jumbled up. More than ever. How does this guy *know*? How can he tell that Danny never stops thinking about his dad? Where he is. What he's doing out there. Why he doesn't answer his letters or call on the phone. And is he ever coming back?

"It don't matter, though," Senior says. He glances at Uno, who's sitting completely still, watching, untouched rib still in his right hand. Senior turns back to Danny, points a finger directly at his chest. "You got a piece of God in you, too, son. I can feel it. Matter a fact, you got the biggest piece I seen in forever. I'm tellin' you."

Uno's dad continues staring at him, and Danny keeps nodding respectfully, but inside he feels overwhelmed. Inside he's battling a giant lump that's quietly climbed into his throat. The weightlessness that's taken over his stomach. How can this older black man from Oxnard, a person he doesn't even know, his best friend's dad, how can he be the first person he's ever met who understands that Danny's heart is broken?

Uno's Own Vision
of a Future

1

Uno winces as he takes in another warm-up fastball from Danny, another shot of pain that shoots up his arm. Lately it seems like Danny's throwing harder than ever. His numbers would be off the charts on that speed gun they use at the fair. Which is great. Except it's killing his hand.

He leans forward onto his knees and tosses the ball back. Watches Carmelo tighten both his batting gloves, one at a time. Pick up his bat and flex his fingers around the grip. Uno smiles behind his borrowed face mask, thinks: This cat ain't got no idea. He facin' a different Danny this time.

On the bus ride over to Morse High, Uno tried to explain the art of double or nothing to Danny. Again. "Dude's gotta think he has a legit chance," he said. "Even as he's striking out. It's just like Vegas, man. They let fools feel just good enough so they keep throwin' down paper. Get it?"

Danny nodded, but Uno knew it wasn't sinking in.

Since the last Carmelo hustle—the only time they've actually lost money in eight hustles—Danny's been lights out. Sometimes Uno can't believe the talent he's witnessing. It's like playing a video game when you know all the cheat codes. He lays down the sign for fastball, sets his target and the ball pops his mitt perfect. Doesn't have to move a muscle. Lays down the sign for a curve and preps for something freakish. A pitch that drops right out of the air. Like gravity gives it a sec to play around in the air before sucking it back down to the dirt. But Uno's favorite is when he calls for a change-up after two straight fastballs. The batter will be so far in front on his swing he'll stumble across the plate, fall flat on his face. Sometimes it makes Uno laugh so hard he can hardly toss the ball back out to the mound.

Uno knows he's lucky. Being this close to greatness. Being an actual part of it. He knows Danny's gonna go off and do amazing things in the future. Get written up in all the papers, all the magazines. Get drafted by a big-league squad and sign a sick contract. And when they show a close-up of him on TV, Uno will be able to point at him and shout: "Yo, that's my boy, right there! Nah, for real! I used to be his catcher back when we was kids!"

At the same time, Danny can't just destroy a guy on three straight strikes and expect him to go double or nothing. As the bus pulled up to their stop, Uno tried to put it another way. "Think about it, D. The art of hustlin' is preservin' a sucker's hope. Throw a couple in the dirt. Let him foul off a couple high ones. You ain't gotta use your *best* stuff to get these punks out. Right?"

Danny nodded again, but Uno could see there was still a disconnect.

2

After Uno tosses the last warm-up baseball back to Danny, Carmelo steps to the plate. "Can't believe you guys wanna give me more money," he says, digging his right toe into the dirt and tapping the plate with his bat. His boys in foul territory are hardly even paying attention this time. It's a foregone conclusion to them. One kid has JJ in a headlock. The other two are trying to throw pieces of concrete from the dugout over the left-field fence and into the street.

"It's all right there in my hat," Uno says. "Forty more bones for you. Too bad you 'bout to get got."

Carmelo laughs, spits over the plate. "You're a comedian, dude."

"We'll see who laughin' in a couple minutes."

"Whatever, dude."

Uno points at Danny, lays down the sign for fastball.

Danny goes right into his windup, fires a heater past a late-swinging Carmelo that nearly rips Uno's catcher's mitt off. Uno cringes as another dose of pain shoots up from his left hand into his shoulder. "Strike one," he shouts, pulling the ball out and tossing it back to Danny. He reminds himself to catch it in the web, not on the hand. He can't take too many more fastballs on the hand like that.

Carmelo backs out of the box, looks at Uno. "Okay," he says, nodding. "He's got a little more juice this time. That's cool. I like when suckers make me earn my money."

"How 'bout suckers who *take* your money?"

"Yeah, right."

"You buyin' *my* meal this time. Me and D."

Carmelo shakes his head and looks out at Danny. He takes another practice swing, steps back in the box.

Uno puts down the sign for curveball. But he taps his

right thigh this time, hoping Danny will figure out he wants it outside the strike zone.

Danny goes into his windup, throws a wild curve that skips past Uno and rolls all the way to the backstop. Uno gives chase, a smile behind his mask. He gathers the ball, throws it back to Danny, watches him walk around the mound like he's confused. He can't believe it. They're on the same page.

"That's why he'll never make a team," Carmelo says when Uno squats behind the plate again. "He can wing it, I'll give you that. But he's too wild. He'll always be right here, with you, pitching on the street."

"Better hope one of them wild ones don't get you in the neck," Uno says. "Could make it hard to breathe."

"What?" Carmelo says, turning around.

"Nothin'." Uno sets up in a squat again, gives the sign for another curve. No thigh tap.

Danny goes into his windup, delivers a spinning pitch headed right down the pipe, but at the last second it cuts down and away from a wild-swinging Carmelo.

Uno gathers the pitch off a one-hop and stands up. "Strike two!" he shouts in Carmelo's ear, tosses the ball back to Danny.

"I can't *believe* I swung at that," Carmelo says.

"Thought you was better than that," Uno says. "Paper said you supposed to make all-league this year. Gotta know when to swing if you gonna make all-league, right?"

Carmelo doesn't answer. He balances the bat between his knees, tightens his batting glove again. His boys grow a little more attentive in foul territory, get a little louder with their encouragement. Carmelo doesn't look at them. He's too busy watching Danny dig at the dirt around the mound.

Uno grins behind his mask. He can tell by Carmelo's

posture that Danny's got him whipped. When the guy steps back into the box, Uno lays down another curve. This one's payback.

Danny winds up and spins a wicked pitch. The ball barrels right in on Carmelo's fists, but as he bails out of the box the pitch spins back over the plate. Carmelo takes an awkward half swing. Misses badly. Slams his bat into the ground.

"Strike three!" Uno shouts, rising out of his crouch. He rolls the ball back to Danny. "See! What I tell you about keepin' it down, D?" He turns toward his hat, walks over and pulls out the two twenties, goes to stick them both in his pocket.

"Hold up a sec," Carmelo calls out, reaching down for his bat. "Just . . . hold on." He turns to his boy JJ again. "You got any more cash, man? We gotta go double or nothin' with these punks. I'm not goin' out like that."

JJ reaches for his wallet and looks inside, pulls out a folded bill. "I only got one more twenty."

Carmelo turns to the rest of his teammates, pleads for financial backing. Two guys hesitantly hold out tens.

"You sure?" one of them says.

"Hell yeah, I'm sure," he shoots back. "I'm about to destroy this street *vato*." He turns to Uno, holding out the cash. "Here, dude. Okay? Your boy's going down this time."

"Cool," Uno says, stuffing a fresh forty bucks into his hat. "All you gotta do is put one in play, dawg. A little dribbler down the third-base line. *Anything*."

Before Uno gets back into his crouch, he glances toward the bleachers. They're totally empty. Not even that scout dude who's always around. Too bad, he thinks. Somebody should be here to see this. People would have to see Danny pitch to believe it.

3

Carmelo steps into the box, a look of pure concentration on his face. He means business now. No more messing around. His teammates slink back toward the dugout to watch.

"Let's roll, D," Uno says, crouching behind home plate. He points to the mound, lays down the sign for fastball. No more messing around on their end either, he thinks. Time to go with all fastballs.

Danny fires the first one right down the middle, past a late-swinging Carmelo. It pops Uno's mitt. "Strike one!"

Danny fires the second pitch right down the middle, as Carmelo swings wildly. Pops Uno's mitt. "Strike two!"

Danny delivers his third fastball with such crazy velocity that Uno, who doesn't even have time to shift his weight to the balls of his feet, is literally lifted off the ground and onto his ass. He pulls the ball out of his mitt, on his back, laughing. He holds it up and shouts: "Strike three!"

Uno springs to his feet and goes for the money hat, shoves all the wrinkled bills into his pocket. He spins around half expecting trouble from Carmelo's camp, but all he finds is Carmelo arguing with JJ.

Carmelo turns to Uno, says: "Dude, we aren't done. JJ's going to the ATM for more money. We're going again."

Uno looks out at the mound—Danny shrugs at him. He turns back to Carmelo. "Long as you got funds, yo. We'll stay out here all day."

"Go!" Carmelo shouts at JJ, and JJ takes off running out of the gate, toward the bank across the street. Carmelo picks up his bat and takes a few practice swings by himself. He's gone quiet. His three teammates squat near the dugout, talking to each other in low voices, occasionally looking up at Danny.

Uno doesn't like the way things look.

4

When JJ comes running back, holding the money in his hand, he goes right up to Uno. "Here you go, dude. Eighty bucks. Now pull out yours."

Uno takes the money from JJ, counts it out again. Eighty. He pulls out the wad in his pocket, counts all the bills together. One-sixty. Shoves the money in his hat and turns to Carmelo. "You sure you up to this, money? Lot of paper on the line."

"Get your ass behind the plate, dude."

Uno walks out to the mound first, stops in front of Danny. "Listen," he says, "there's gonna be a little friction after you strike 'im out this time."

Danny looks back at Uno, confused.

"After the last strike, I'm goin' straight for the money. You take off for the bus stop and I'll meet you there."

"But what if—"

"I'll handle it. Trust me. You just concentrate on these three pitches. Then hop the centerfield fence and get to the bus stop." Uno gives Danny a quick pound and makes for the plate. But he stops suddenly, turns back around. "You promise you're gonna do what I said, right? Head for the bus stop? I'm gonna be pissed off if you hang around here."

Danny nods.

Uno stares at him for a couple seconds, then heads for the plate.

Carmelo is oddly silent as he steps back into the batter's box. Uno glances over at the guy's teammates. They're all squatting by the dugout still. JJ is standing between them and the money hat, his arms crossed.

Uno lays down the first sign: fastball.

Danny goes into his windup, fires the first pitch right past a hard-swinging Carmelo. "Strike one."

Uno watches Carmelo step out of the box and slam his bat into the dirt. He looks at Carmelo's teammates again. Still squatting together, but they're no longer talking. Just watching.

Uno lays down the second sign: fastball.

Danny kicks and delivers his hardest fastball of the day. The ball rips right past Carmelo again, pops Uno's mitt. Uno cringes as the pain from catching it on the heel of his hand runs up his shoulder again, into his neck. He tosses the ball back to Danny, takes off his mitt and shakes out his hand. Looks at Carmelo's teammates.

Carmelo squats outside of the box, looks out at Danny. He takes a couple deep breaths and glances at JJ. Then he steps back into the box.

Uno checks out JJ, too. He's a couple feet closer to the money hat now. Uno stands up and shouts, "Yo, back away from that shit, dawg!"

JJ holds his hands out, acts like he doesn't know what Uno's talking about. He takes a couple steps back, looks at the other guys. Looks at Carmelo.

Uno crouches again, lays down his sign: change-up. He glances back at JJ, the other three guys. Turns back to the mound.

Danny goes into his windup, delivers the pitch with the same exact mechanics as his fastball, but his change-up comes out molasses-slow.

Carmelo is so far out in front of the pitch he steps and swings awkwardly before the ball is halfway to the plate. He misses badly, spins himself and goes down on one knee.

"Strike three," Uno calls out, flipping off his mask and turning to the money hat. But JJ's already there, pulling the money out and shoving it in his pocket. The other guys have stood up and are walking toward JJ with their bags. Uno sprints over to JJ, shouting: "Let go the money, bitch!"

JJ tosses aside Uno's empty hat and turns to take off, but Uno's already on him. He shoves JJ to the ground and reaches for his pocket. But one of the other guys slugs him in the back of the head. Uno spins around, narrowly avoids a wild right from another kid and punches the kid who hit him in the jaw. The guy goes down hard but quickly gets back to his feet. Two other guys wrap Uno up.

"Get off!" Uno hears Danny shout from behind him. But Carmelo's there, too. Uno turns to watch Carmelo shove Danny to the ground and kick him in the ribs.

Uno breaks free and pounces on Carmelo. He gets him in a tight headlock, tries to choke the life out of him. But the other guys pull Uno off, hold his arms while Carmelo punches him twice in the stomach, doubles him over. JJ and the other kid start working over Danny on the ground.

Uno tries to wrestle free, but he can't get away. He shouts at Danny to run, watches Carmelo rear back and throw a punch right at his face, but he ducks it and the punch grazes the face of Carmelo's own guy. Uno wrestles free and pounces on one of the guys on Danny. He swings a vicious right and hits him on the side of the face, sends him sprawling onto the ground. Blood starts coming from the guy's nose.

But there are too many of them and soon Uno and Danny are both being held and pummeled. They take a few blows each and then, out of nowhere, the big Mexican scout rushes through the gate and dives at the Morse High kids. He takes three of them to the ground at one time. Grabs two of their heads and slams them together. They both spin around, one of them falling to the grass.

Uno pulls Danny up. He goes for JJ, pins him to the ground and rips the money from his pocket. He gets up and narrowly avoids a wild left from Carmelo.

The Mexican scout pins two kids against each other with one hand, barks at Uno and Danny: "Leave now! Go!"

5

Uno snatches up his bag and they both tear off through the gate, toward the bus. When they make it over the little hill, the field temporarily out of sight, Uno spots their bus pulling up to the stop. "Let's go," he yells at Danny, and they sprint to the opposite sidewalk, bob and weave through the thick traffic on the main road, and pound on the bus door as it's shutting.

The driver reopens, and they climb the stairs onto the bus.

They shuffle toward the back and sit in two different rows, both breathing hard, putting their fingers to their wounds, checking for blood. Uno turns to Danny, shouts: "What the fuck you doin', D? What I tell you to do after the third strike?"

"I know, but—"

"What the fuck I tell you?" he shouts, smacking Danny in the back of the head.

Danny looks back at him, confused. "To go for the bus."

"Then why didn't you do it?" Uno slams his catcher's mitt against his seat and shakes his head.

An older Mexican lady interrupts her knitting long enough to turn around and give Uno a dirty look.

Uno stares out the window. He could slap Danny in the face for not listening. He told him three times: take off for the bus after the last pitch. He runs a hand down his face and takes another deep breath, turns to Danny. "Look, man, you okay?"

"Yeah."

Uno stays staring at Danny. "It's just . . . I can't let you get hurt, D. I can't."

"But I'm okay."

"It wasn't for that Mexican dude who's scouting you we'd have got it bad. Both of us, man. There was too many of 'em." Uno slips his mitt in his bag, zips up. "You gotta understand somethin', D. You goin' places. You gonna be somebody."

Danny pulls off his mitt, lays it in his lap. "So are you, Uno."

Uno shakes his head. "Nah, it's different. This is what I got and I know it. Even when I move up to Oxnard, D. I'm still gonna be right here on these streets. It's too deep. But it's cool. You, though, D. Man, you're on some different shit."

Danny doesn't say anything.

The bus driver sounds his horn as he moves the bus through traffic. Uno pulls in a couple more deep breaths. Rubs the sore spot on the back of his head and checks his fingers for blood. Nothing. He pulls the cash from his pocket and counts in his head. Ten, twenty, thirty, forty, sixty, eighty, a hundred, hundred twenty, hundred forty, hundred sixty. A hundred sixty bucks. "Take this for a sec," he says, extending the money to Danny.

Danny takes the money in his hands.

"You ever held that much before?"

Danny shakes his head.

Uno takes back half the money, slips it in his pocket. With the tips he's made from the restaurant he has just under five hundred now. Almost enough to give his old man a deposit for Oxnard. He watches Danny slip his own share of the money in his pocket. Watches him touch a red spot on his face. And a strange feeling comes over him. This is probably

174

one of the best days of his life. It's true. He's sitting on the bus with his boy D, riding back home to National City, but he knows there's something else out there. Oxnard. With his old man. And they just hustled some real punks. And it's such a beautiful day out. Not a cloud in the sky. For some reason it all hits him really hard and he shouts, "You gonna make it, D! I swear to God you is! Watch! You gonna be somethin' special." He reaches a fist out to his boy.

Danny's face lights up as he gives Uno daps.

The old lady turns back around, gives Uno another nasty look. When she goes back to her mittens this time, Danny and Uno look at each other and laugh. Quietly, though, so she can't hear them.

Outside his window, Uno watches another poverty-riddled pocket of San Diego flash by. Graffiti decorates the street-side windows of every taqueria, every Mexican bodega and barbershop. Short Indian-looking women scurry into the intersection whenever a streetlight turns red to hawk giant sunflowers, bunches of roses, bags of hand-picked oranges, gum. At the street corner nearest the bus, an old scruffy-looking Mexican man wearing a cowboy hat is being pushed in a rusted wheelbarrow by a shirtless boy. The man has no legs, and when he smiles in the direction of the bus Uno sees he has only a single crooked tooth.

For the first time in his life, Uno feels removed from all of this. He feels a million miles away, in fact. Like he and Danny are up in the clouds somewhere. Floating above the thick traffic and the women selling oranges and the old guy in the wheelbarrow. All the trash and graffiti. He touches his sore right cheek, checks for blood that isn't there. Maybe he has a future, too. Not like Danny's. But something. He's going up to Oxnard. And he's gonna try to change, like his old man did. He never thought he could do it before. But something about today has changed his mind. Something about sitting here with his boy D. On this bus. During his last summer in National City. For the first time in his life he thinks maybe he understands what his dad's been trying to tell him all this time. About how people can change. He gets it now. He understands.

The Green Lollipop

1

Danny watches Uno pop open two cans of Tecate. He takes one on the handoff and then they both push off Carmen's mom's kitchen counter.

"To your pitching," Uno says, holding up his can. "And my dope-ass target." The two touch aluminum and drink.

Danny cringes as the cold beer washes past his tastebuds, down his throat. It's only his third time drinking beer—all this summer—and he doubts he'll ever *like* the taste. He wipes his mouth, watches Uno chug his entire Tecate and crack himself a new one.

It's been almost two weeks since the fight with Carmelo and his teammates, and he and Uno haven't done a hustle since. They've just been working out at Las Palmas and hitting

Saturday derbies. Laying low. A couple days ago Uno went with him to a travel agency so he could look into plane tickets to Ensenada. He found out he has more than enough to get there now. He just has to figure out his dates and go back to pay. That's all he's really thought about lately. His trip. What it'll be like to see his dad again. To talk to him. See if he still looks the same. But for some reason he hasn't bought his ticket. He keeps putting it off and doesn't know why. He almost went again tonight, but when Carmen's mom took off for the weekend with her new boyfriend, Sofia and Uno dragged him to this party.

When Uno moves off to the living room, to rejoin the truth-or-dare game Chico and Raquel started, Danny follows closely behind. They sit on two of the lawn chairs Carmen has set out next to the couch, watch Lolo pour a shot of tequila into Raquel's belly button, slurp it out and bite into a wedge of lime. He comes up with his hands above his head and everybody cheers. Raquel lowers her shirt, laughing.

"Nice work, Lo," Uno says, holding his fresh can in the air.

"You know how many germs is in a belly button?" Carmen says, looking to Sofia.

"You saying I'm dirty?" Raquel shoots back with a smile.

"It's not just you," Carmen says. "Everybody."

Lolo slaps five with Raul, picks up the tequila bottle and turns to Raquel. "I do again?"

"Nah, it's one and done," Chico says. "Go 'head, Raquel, your turn."

"Uno," she says. "Truth or dare?"

"Truth," Uno says.

"Weak-ass," Raul says, tossing a throw pillow into Uno's lap. "You goin' soft, Uno? What up?"

Uno drops his beer from his lips, shoots Raul a crazy look. "Slow your roll, Biscuit. We just warmin' up here."

"Yeah, okay."

"All right," Raquel says. "I always wondered this. *Tu hermano,* Manny. Don't get mad, but do you ever get sad he like he is?"

Everybody goes quiet and stares at Uno. Danny watches him turn his beer can so he can read it, then take another sip. "I ain't mad," he says, staring at the can again. "Yeah, when I was younger I wondered why I had a messed-up little bro, you know? Couldn't teach 'im no baseball or nothin'. Couldn't barely talk to him. But now it's different. Now I don't even care." He coughs into his fist, looks up at Raquel. "Take the other day, right? Me and Manny was ridin' the bus back to where he stays. It was mad hot and shit, and none of the windows were open. I looked around and everybody looked all pissed off. Frownin' and shit. Even me. And then I looked at my little bro, and he had this big-ass smile on his face. I said, 'Manny, man, why you smilin' for?' But he just shrugged at me and kept smilin'. Here it's the hottest day of the year, right? And we all sweatin' and Manny headin' back to the halfway house my moms stuck him in, and the dude can't stop smilin'. That's why I look out for his stupid ass all the time. I gotta make sure he stays bein' happy like that."

Uno takes another big swig of beer.

"Yeah, Manny's a cool cat," Chico says.

Everybody agrees.

"I love that boy," Raquel says.

"He's such a sweetheart," Flaca says.

"Anyway," Uno says, "it's the hostess's turn. Truth or dare, girl?"

"Dare."

"Word. Take it in the bedroom with your boy Chico and

179

don't come out for sixty seconds. What y'all do in there is your biz."

Chico leaps up from the couch and starts toward the bedroom. When he gets halfway to the door, he looks back, realizes Carmen hasn't moved. As everybody laughs and urges Carmen on, Danny turns to Sofia, catches her still staring at Uno. After a few seconds she realizes Danny's watching her and quickly joins in on her best friend. "Go in there, Carm. Don't be no chicken."

"No way," Carmen says, wagging her finger in the air. "I ain't goin' into no bedroom with nobody. Come here, Chee."

Chico walks over, and Carmen stands up. She kisses him on the mouth for a few seconds and then pushes him away, sits back down. "There. That's all he was gonna get in the bedroom. Might as well do it right here in front of everybody. I ain't no *puta* like Flaca."

Flaca swings a pillow at Carmen, smacks her in the shoulder. They both crack up.

Chico clears his throat and leans down, says: "Carm, we still got a few seconds. Lemme get one more."

Carmen turns her head, waves Chico off.

Danny laughs with everybody else as Chico closes his eyes, puckers his lips, and Carmen hides behind her hands.

And it's from this position, a little outside the circle, leaning back in his well-worn lawn chair, half-full beer in hand, that Danny watches the rest of the game unfold in front of him. He watches Raul, on a dare from Lolo, struggle through twenty-five sit-ups while Lolo holds down his Timberlands. His white T-shirt occasionally riding up, exposing the chubby brown rolls of his stomach. He watches Flaca, on a dare from Raul, saunter over to Raquel, take her face in her hands and kiss her while all the guys cheer and the girls laugh. He watches Sofia, on a dare from Raul, pull up Uno's black Dickies shirt and leave a dark brown hickey on his already dark stomach. He listens to Flaca, on a truth from Sofia, talk about the scar on her stomach, the result of some big operation she had as a kid, the one that made it so she'll probably never be able to have babies. She laughs and tells everybody it's like having built-in birth control. Doesn't need no stupid pill or condoms. And then, when the game moves on, her laughter slowly dies and her face grows serious and she stares at the rug. He listens to Sofia, on a truth from Carmen, talk about how she doesn't miss her real mom because she hardly even knew the woman. She took off for good when she was three and then supposedly overdosed six years later. Cecilia might as well be her real mom, she says. That's how close they are.

And then, as if they've had it planned like this all along, they all move in on Danny at once.

2

Raquel's the one who starts it. "Danny, truth or dare?" She turns to Sofia. "I'm sorry, honey, but I gotta go at your boy. He lookin' *way* too comfortable over there."

"Get him," Sofia says.

"Turth or dare?" Raquel repeats.

Danny looks to Sofia, then back to Raquel. "Truth," he says with a shrug.

"So, what's the story? You in love with Liberty or not?"

Danny stares back at her, eyes bugged. He opens his mouth to say something, but nothing comes out.

"What do you think?" Sofia says. "My cuz is head over heels for that girl."

"Then when you gonna talk to her already?" Carmen says. "Pretty girl like her gonna get snatched up you wait too long. Trust me."

Danny turns to Carmen.

"My man's takin' his time," Raul says. "Right, D?"

Danny turns to Raul.

"Yo, I been hearin' stories about them hustles," Chico says. "You strikin' fools out all over the city, right?"

"Yeah, but you guys pullin' any *billetes*?" Raul says.

Uno sits up in his lawn chair. "We straight," he says. "You know I'm a businessman, Rah-rah."

"Oh, I see," Raul says, and then he turns to Danny. "You got a sick arm on you, D. You ever think about maybe you could be an all-star when you get to the bigs?"

"Pinche puerco," Lolo says. "He goin' in the Hall of Fame."

"'Course he's gonna be an all-star," Uno says.

"D got a sick future ahead of him, man," Chico says. "Better not forget about us, *ése.*"

"He gonna play for the Pads," Carmen says.

"He gonna play for whoever steps up with the most money, girl," Uno says. "Ain't no hometown discounts. It's about finances."

Raquel reaches into the chip bowl, says: "My dad took me to a Padres game last year."

"I been to a game, too," Carmen says. "When I was little. They won like three to two in overtime."

"Extra innings," Uno corrects her.

"Whatever," Carmen says. She turns to Danny, says: "What I wanna know is what it's like at your private school. Got mad smart kids there, right?"

Danny turns to Carmen.

"Gotta wear uniforms?" Lolo says.

"All private schools got uniforms," Uno says. "Don't be ignorant, Lo."

"How come you don't speak no Spanish?" Flaca says. "I mean, you Mexican just like us, but Sofe said you don't speak a word."

"Yeah," Raquel says. "I been wonderin' about that, too. They don't let you speak Spanish at your private school?"

Everybody in the room stares at Danny. And this time nobody answers for him. Because nobody, not even Uno, knows the answer. They're all stumped. He looks up at Flaca, and just as he's about to open his mouth to say something about his white mom, the doorbell rings and Raquel and Carmen spring up off the couch and race to the door. Carmen gets there first and opens up. She sings, "Hey, guys," and steps aside.

In walk Guita and Liberty.

3

Everybody stands up to welcome Guita and Liberty. Uno gets them beers from the fridge and Carmen shoos Raul off the couch so they have a place to sit together. Sofia pushes the big bowl of chips to their side of the coffee table. Guita and Liberty thank the girls and everybody clinks cups and beer cans and settles back in, and then Raul says: "All right, Sofe, your turn. Truth or dare, girl?"

Sofia spits an ice cube back into her coffee mug of jungle juice. "Dare."

"Uh-oh," Chico says. "We got a ballplayer in the house."

Danny glances at Liberty again. She's wearing a little more makeup tonight. But not too much. Her long black hair is down and she's wearing a light green sundress and black flip-flops. There's a thin silver ring around the middle toe of her right foot. She turns and smiles at him. He smiles back. And then they both turn to Raul.

Raul taps a finger to his right temple a couple times and looks to the ceiling, plays like he's deep in thought. "Okay," he says, going back to Sofia. "I dare you to go in the bedroom with my boy Uno. Sixty seconds."

"What?" Sofia says. "Come on, Raul."

"That ain't right," Carmen says. "Give my girl somethin' normal."

"That *is* normal," Chico says.

"Uh, try *shady*."

"How's it shady?" Flaca said. "They ain't gotta do nothin' crazy. Nobody said they gotta come out married."

All the girls laugh.

"All right, all right," Raul says. "I'll switch it up."

But Sofia stands up suddenly, turns to Uno. "Let's just get it over with." She looks to Raul again. "Sixty seconds, right?"

"One full minute."

Sofia reaches for Uno's hand, pulls him out of his lawn chair. Danny watches as his cousin and best friend walk into Carmen's bedroom holding hands and close the door behind them. He turns to Liberty, who smells her beer and makes a sour face, puts it on the table next to the chip bowl.

"Who's got 'em on a stopwatch?" Chico says. "Make sure they in there a full sixty seconds."

"I got one," Raquel says, holding her watch up to her face. "Okay, forty-five seconds left." Everybody goes quiet. They stare at the closed door with curious smiles stuck to their faces, occasionally drinking. "Thirty," Raquel announces. Danny peeks at Liberty again. He can't believe how pretty she is. Her skin so smooth and her hands on her knees and her thin shoulders and her perfect lips. He wonders if he's ever noticed a girl's lips before. Liberty's lips are perfect. They make his stomach feel weird.

"Fifteen." Flaca reaches for a handful of chips, holds one

up to the light and then pops it in her mouth. Lolo picks at a scab on his elbow. Raul cracks open a new can of beer and chugs half of it down. He lets out a little burp and excuses himself. "Okay, time!" Raquel shouts. "You guys made it!"

Everybody stares at the door waiting for Sofia and Uno to emerge. But it remains shut.

"Yo!" Raul shouts through cupped hands. "Time's up!" But the door still doesn't budge. Raul looks at Chico and shrugs. Lolo yawns and stretches his arms. Raquel pulls eyedrops out of her purse and drips the clear liquid into the corners of both eyes, one at a time. Liberty reaches for a chip. She covers her mouth as she chews.

"I guess the game's over," Chico finally says. He stands up, says: "Who needs another beer?" A couple people nod.

"I got one last dare," Raquel says when Chico comes back from the kitchen. "Everybody cool with that? Then we can stop if you want."

Everybody shrugs.

"I dare Danny," she says, looking at him, "and Liberty"— she turns to Liberty—"to go somewhere together, too. Like, maybe the bathroom or the kitchen or outside or something. But don't you guys think?"

Danny and Liberty look at each other.

"Sounds about right to me," Chico says.

Raul stands up, says: "It's game *on* for you two." He walks over to the front door, pulls it open, turns around to wait for them.

Liberty stands up, giggles a little in the direction of Guita. She straightens her dress.

"Go on, Lib," Guita says.

Chico walks over to Danny, pulls him up by the arm. "Time to go outside, superstar."

Danny looks at Liberty. She gives him a shy smile.

They both step out of the circle and head toward the door Raul's holding open. Everybody in the apartment cheers as they slip out into the warm summer night. The cheering goes faint as Raul pulls the door shut behind them.

4

Danny and Liberty stand there for a second, quiet, looking everywhere except at each other. Danny slips his hands into the pockets of his khakis, then pulls them back out and leans back against the closed door. From the corner of his eye he watches Liberty look out over the apartment complex and then down at her unpainted fingernails. Suddenly, she turns to Danny and says: *"Lo siento que nos hicieran venir aquí."*

Danny's stomach drops. The shame of his ignorance hits him hard, runs all through his body, makes the hairs on his arms and legs go dead. He looks up at her, shaking his head. "I don't know what you said."

Liberty gives him a strange look back, as if she doesn't understand what *he's* said, either. She shakes her head. They continue to stare at each other, both slowly realizing the situation. Their respective shortcomings. Then Liberty smiles. Danny smiles back, says: "Maybe we should sit." He points to the run-down steps a few apartment doors down. "Sit down?"

"Yes," Liberty says with an exaggerated nod. She smiles big and says it again. "Yes."

"Sí," Danny says, waving for her to follow him.

They walk over to the staircase and sit together on the second step. Liberty's dress falls on one of Danny's Vans for a second before she moves it off. But the image of her dress on his shoe sticks in his head. Like a photograph. He can see it whether his eyes are open or closed. And for some reason this small thing makes him feel happy.

Carmen's apartment complex is located right across the street from the giant recycling plant, the one Uno pointed out from the train tracks. But looking at it from this angle, so close, up four floors, it seems totally different. It looks like an old mechanical giant. A sleeping robot. Something out of a cartoon. The signs are all rusted out and hang crooked, and the roads into the place are potholed and worn down. The huge faded red walls of the plant are covered in graffiti. Years and years' worth of taggers leaving their mark, Danny thinks. Like the entire history of the city has been written into the metal walls. A permanent record. Original. While everything inside is recycled.

Danny lowers his head and clears his throat. "My dad's from here. National City."

"Tu padre?" Liberty says. She nods.

"He's in Mexico now. Where you're from. I'm gonna go visit him in a couple weeks, at the end of summer."

She smiles, nods some more.

Danny nods, too. And then the two of them fall into silence again. Liberty pulls some of her long black hair in front of her chest, starts making tiny braids. Danny watches her out of the corner of his eye as he picks at the sole of one of his Vans. Here he is, in National City, sitting next to Liberty, so close he can smell her perfume, but they can't talk to each other. He wishes he could speak her language, and she probably wishes she could speak his language. A word he learned in school comes to mind: *irony.* This is what his teacher meant when she'd talk about that word. Liberty's come to National City to be more American. And he's come to be more Mexican.

Liberty finishes another skinny braid, her third, and lets it flop back down on her chest. She turns to Danny suddenly, says: "I say something *en Español*?"

"Sure," Danny says.

She looks across the street for a few seconds, at the recycling plant, and then faces Danny again. *"Me recuerdas de un chico mayor de donde soy yo. He tendio ganas de decirtelo desde el principio del verano. Pero a veces me da tanta vergüenza hablar en ingles que prefiero no decir nada."*

Danny smiles at her and shakes his head. "I wish I understood what you just said."

Liberty shrugs and giggles. "Is okay, no?"

"Can I say something in English now?" Danny says.

She smiles at him and shrugs.

Then it all pours out of his mouth. "I'm so happy right now. Being here with you. In National City. I came here because sometimes I feel like a fake Mexican. And I don't want to be a fake. I wanna be real. I love my dad's family. And I love the culture and the language and everything my gramma cooks and the way they live. I've always wished I was more like them. But it's twice as bad since my dad left. . . . I wish I could tell you how pretty I think you are in Spanish. But I can't. Because I never learned."

Liberty shrugs. She has no idea what he's just said. She smiles and turns back to the recycling plant, starts working on another skinny braid. But then she drops her braid and reaches into her bag. She pulls out two lollipops, a green one and a red one, and holds them up.

Danny smiles, takes the green one hoping the red ones are her favorite. They both pull off their wrappers, pop the lollipops into their mouths.

After they've been sitting there for a few more minutes, in silence, staring out at the giant recycling plant, Liberty lets her head fall against Danny's shoulder. She leaves it there a couple seconds and then straightens back up. That's it. She doesn't look at him or anything. But Danny wonders if maybe those few seconds, where her head touched his shoulder, mean *more* than words.

Soon somebody will open Carmen's apartment door and call them back in. Danny knows this. And he and Liberty will get up quietly, walk back into the apartment, retake their seats in the group. If Uno's out of the bedroom, he will make Danny have another beer and they'll tap cans. And the music will be playing and everybody will be joking around, cracking on each other, sometimes in Spanish but mostly in English. And the girls will be leaning against pillows on the couch and eating chips and gossiping. The TV will be on without sound.

But at least for now, he and Liberty are still outside. Alone. Sitting side by side on a second step. Across the street from a giant recycling plant. In National City. Eating lollipops in silence.

A Final Phone Call
from San Francisco

1

"Danny!" Sofia yells through the bathroom door. "Phone's for you!"

Danny opens the door, a towel wrapped around his middle. His hair is wet from his shower and steam is whipping out of the bathroom at a recoiling Sofia.

"*Tu mama,*" she says, cupping the cordless and waving away the steam with her free hand. She snickers at the sight of her half-naked cousin. "What were you doing in there so long, beating off?"

"No," Danny says, taking the phone, cupping the receiver in his own hand now.

Sofia tilts her head to the side, says: "You sure, cuz? It's perfectly normal, you know. I heard ninety-five percent of guys beat off and the other five percent are lyin'."

Danny looks at the ceiling and impatiently taps the door. It's been several days since Carmen's house party and tonight Danny's heading to the movies with Uno, Chico, Lolo and Raul. Chico's driving and they're sneaking in cold forties and rolled tacos from Juanita's. He's excited to cruise out with Uno and his crew again. Sofia and her girls weren't invited, though. And Danny figures that's the reason she's coming at him.

Sofia laughs, shaking her head. "Look at you, cuz. You can't even admit it. Gettin' all flustered." She spins around and walks off.

Danny closes the door and says hi to his mom. He pins the phone between his ear and shoulder and slips into his jeans. Pulls a blue short-sleeved button-down over a fresh white T-shirt. Starts tying his Vans.

His mom tells him how amazing the weather is in San Francisco now that it's near the end of summer. It's been beautiful at the beach and all along the wharf. She tells him how well Julia's doing in her dance classes, about the trip Randy took them on to the Napa Valley. She brags about the black-and-white photograph she took of Haight Street that Randy had blown up, framed, and mounted on the wall next to the dining room table. Danny rolls his eyes at pretty much everything his mom has to say.

But then there's a long awkward silence and Danny thinks he hears his mom sniffling. He sits down on the side of the tub, says: "Mom?"

She doesn't respond.

"Mom?" he says again. "You okay?"

"Yeah," she says in a strange, high-pitched voice. "I'm okay—" Her voice cuts out.

Danny transfers the phone from one ear to the other ear. "Mom?"

"I'm sorry. I'm just—there's nothing wrong. Not really. Maybe that's the problem."

"What do you mean?"

His mom doesn't answer right away. Danny can hear her blowing her nose. Then she says in a more composed voice: "This apartment's just so big, Danny. The living room alone is the size of our entire place in Leucadia. We have three bathrooms, a study, a spiral staircase. We have satellite TV with hundreds of channels. A woman comes in every afternoon to clean the place and do all the laundry. Another woman cooks for us three nights a week. But aside from them, I'm the only one who's ever here. Randy's always at work. Julia's at her dance studio. I feel so useless and alone."

Danny stares at the throw rug in front of the tub. He has no idea how to respond.

"It's a woman's dream, Danny. I know. It was *my* dream. But I honestly can't take it anymore. Me and Julia are moving back to Leucadia. And you, too. We're all moving back. I miss our life. I miss my son."

"What about Randy?"

"I talked to him a couple nights ago, told him everything I was feeling. It was eleven-thirty at night, Danny, and I had to call the man at *work* to talk to him. But he's great. He really is. This has absolutely nothing to do with Randy. You know, he's even sending down Padres tickets for you. Two so you can take a friend. Supposed to be a surprise. And he's considering finding his own place in San Diego, bless his heart."

A few seconds of dead air and she starts sobbing into the phone again, making little hiccupping sounds whenever she pulls in a breath.

Danny stands up and walks over to the sink. He looks at himself in the mirror, looks at the soap scum on the shower curtain. Then he sits down on the side of the tub again. Even after everything, he still hates to hear his mom cry. "You okay?"

"I'm just being ridiculous. . . . Listen, hang on, okay?"

Danny nods, listens to the sounds on the other end of the line: his mom setting the phone down, pulling a tissue and blowing her nose again, her shoes clicking as she walks somewhere on hardwood floors, the faucet running, then her shoes again. She picks up the phone, says, "Okay," and gives a nervous laugh. "I don't know why I'm so emotional right now."

"What *happened*?"

"I don't know, Danny. The last three years—I mean, I'm just tired. Tired of chasing after all these *men*. Every time I meet somebody new I think the same thing: 'He's the one, Wendy. You've finally found him. This is the guy who's gonna make it all better.' But no man can make it better, Danny. That's what I've figured out in this giant apartment. And it's not even their *fault*. I could meet Prince Charming and it wouldn't be any different. 'All better' isn't something you can find in a man."

Danny shoots back at her: "You were happy with Dad."

"Oh, honey, I *was*. Your dad's the only person I've ever been in love with. It's just, well, things happened that made it impossible for us to stay together."

"Like what?" Danny digs his nails into his arm. He watches himself break his own skin. He digs in even deeper, until the pain shoots up into his head.

There's a long pause and then his mom says: "We were kids, Danny. And deep down your dad is a good man."

"What happened?" he demands, determined not to let it go this time.

Another long pause. "He's a good man," she says again. "That's all you need to know, I think."

Danny doesn't say anything. He focuses on the rug in front of the tub again. The ratty tentacles of yellow material. He digs into his arm. A fresh spot.

His mom clears her throat. "It never stops, you know," she says. "Even when you get old like your mom and your dad. You're still trying to figure out who the heck you are. And what everything means. Sometimes it all gets so confusing you don't know which way to turn. Even your mom and dad, Danny. I don't think kids know that about their parents. But we're human, too."

Danny picks at the rug. He pulls out a chunk and studies the little strands, tosses them in the trash. He knows there's something he's not being told, but he doesn't want to think about it. He's not ready. He sits up, switches the phone from one ear to the other and says: "I miss my dad."

"Oh, Danny, I know you do. You've missed him every day for going on four years. And I'm sorry I ran off to San Francisco. But in a way I'm not. Maybe I needed to do it. You know? Because now I understand that even a man like Randy isn't what I've been looking for since me and your dad split. Maybe what I've been looking for was right in front of me this whole time. You and Julia, Danny. My kids. That's why I'm coming home. So I can try and make everything right."

Danny digs into his arm some more as she goes on about coming back to San Diego. How it's gonna be different. When she's gonna pick him up. And eventually she winds it down and they both say goodbye and hang up.

Danny stands up, walks out of the bathroom and through the living room to the front door. He opens it, pauses there. He turns around slowly, glances at Sofia, who's watching a movie on TV. After a minute or so he says: "Hey, Sofe, can I ask you a question?"

She turns around. "If it's about beating off, you better go ask your boyfriend."

"What happened with my mom and dad?"

Sofia stares at Danny, doesn't say anything.

Danny looks at the movie on the TV, then back to Sofia. "Did he do something to her?"

Sofia puts the remote down on the coffee table and picks up her can of Dr Pepper. But she doesn't drink from it. She just holds it. "I think he hit her, cuz. I'm sorry to tell you, but I think you got a right to know. He hit her and she came to stay with us after. And then when that thing happened at the beach he got in trouble."

"He hit her?"

Sofia nods. "You got a right to know."

Danny stands there a few more seconds, staring at her. Then he hears a voice calling his name from the street. He looks out toward the road, sees Uno hanging out of Chico's passenger-side window, waving for him to come down. He turns back to Sofia, stares at her in silence for a few more seconds. "Thanks for telling me," he says, and steps through the door, pulling it shut behind him.

Uno's Big Talk
with His Mom

1

Uno's sitting on the living room couch, staring at his mom's little static-ridden TV. He's watching an old show about this group of white teenagers living in Beverly Hills. But he's not really *watching*. He's thinking about how he's finally gonna tell his mom what's up. Soon as she gets home from the hotel he's gonna do it. Has to. She needs to know he's decided to do his last year of high school in Oxnard. Get a fresh start. Try out for the baseball team. He can't put this talk off any longer, especially now that he has the money.

He glances at the clock again: 3:45. His mom cleans her last room at 3:30 today. She'll be back any minute. Uno feels a wave of butterflies pass through his stomach. He knows she won't take the news well. Much as he gets in her way, in

Ernesto's way, she'll still cry. It'll still mess her up a little. Either that or she'll start yelling and carrying on, cursing him in Spanish, listing all the reasons he can't do it. Why his dad's no good. He knows this little talk won't turn out good, but he has to do it. Today.

He looks up at the clock again, back to the TV.

When the Beverly Hills show ends Uno gets up and walks over to the cupboard. He pulls out a tub of generic peanut butter and a package of saltines, fixes himself lunch. He eats it standing at the counter, occasionally looking up at the clock. Then he cleans up and sits back in front of the TV. A show comes on about cops busting people.

Thirty minutes later, his mom finally comes in through the front door. He stands up, helps her with the bag of toiletries she's taken from the hotel. "Hey, Ma!" he shouts after she walks into her bedroom to change. "Ma! Can I talk to you about something?"

"Hang on, Uno!" she shouts back through the door.

When she comes out she's wearing her house pants and an old sweatshirt, the same outfit she always wears around the house.

"Ma, can I talk to you?"

"Hang on," she says. "I got some news. Me and Ernesto's havin' a baby. I'm pregnant."

"What?" Uno follows his mom into the kitchen.

She pulls a roll of paper towels from the plastic bag, a hand soap. "Found out yesterday afternoon. We had an appointment. Ernesto says this is gonna set us straight, and I think he's right."

Uno stares back at his mom, trying to think. He says: "Congratulations."

His mom sets down a roll of toilet paper and gives him a big hug. Then she moves toward the fridge, pulls a package of ground beef from the freezer and sets it on a few folded paper towels. "If it's a girl, we wanna name her Silvia. After your late grandmother. But if it's a boy, Uno, get this. He's gonna be Ernesto junior. Can you imagine how happy it's gonna make Ernesto?"

"That's great, Ma."

She walks back into the living room and starts straightening the cushions, picking up old sports pages. As she cleans she tells Uno they hope the baby's a boy so Ernesto can have a son of his own, but what really matters is having a healthy baby. When Uno asks her what about Manny, she says she means a son that's not sick.

"What's that supposed to mean?" Uno says.

She avoids Uno's eyes, says: "You know what I'm talking about, Uno. We both love that boy. You know we do. But Manny's not here. Ernesto wants a son with his own blood *here*. It's nothing against you or Manny." She pulls up all the curtains in a huff. Opens a couple windows. "Anyway, didn't you have something to say?"

Uno watches her walk back into the kitchen and put the stopper in the sink, start the water. Just as he opens his mouth to talk, she says: "Uno, take out the trash, honey. And wrap that hose up outside, it's hangin' all in the street. You know Ernesto gonna yell at you about that hose. He's gonna be home in a couple hours."

Uno stands there nodding for a few seconds. He watches his mom pull out a few pots and pans for dinner. Then he turns and walks outside to deal with the hose.

Along for the Ride

1

Danny only has twelve days until his mom's supposed to come get him, and he still hasn't booked his ticket to Mexico. But he can't even think about that after what happened yesterday. He can't get even the image out of his head. The hippie guy's face, his uncle's Bronco, the blood flying everywhere. He didn't know anything about Uncle Ray until that second.

He peeks out of his grandma's bedroom window, sees Ray finally pulling into the driveway.

Ray moves across the sidewalk, toward the house, without talking to anybody. He pulls Uncle Tommy into the sitting room outside Grandma's bedroom, snaps his fingers for all the cousins to go find another place. It's the third week of

August and it's crazy hot. Everywhere Danny looks somebody's pulling clothing away from their sticky body. Wiping
forehead sweat before it runs into their eyes.

Vanessa and Sofia chase Grandma's new kitten into the
living room. Jesus sets down the remote and disappears. His
kid brother, Little Mario, tugs at his diaper and just stands
there. Nobody notices him at first until Cecilia reaches a
hand in and pulls him out.

"Somethin' I gotta tell you," Ray says, closing the door.
He slips a hand in his pocket, pulls out his smoke pack. "Happened yesterday."

Danny's crouched behind the door to his grandma's bedroom, listening. He can only see his uncles' faces through the
crack, but by this point in the summer he knows everything
that's going on throughout the house. The different laughs
coming from the yard. The women in the kitchen, making
things with their hands. The smell of fresh tortillas and chile
colorado. Mole sauce simmering in a pot on the stove. The
baseball game on TV without sound, the radio tuned to a
Spanish music station.

More importantly, though, he knows every word his uncle Ray's gonna say before he says it.

Ray breaks up a bud, rolls the weed in a Zig-Zag and licks.
He pulls a lighter from his pocket and, out of pure habit, cups
a hand over the fire.

2

Danny had just finished scrubbing the tub with Sofia when
Ray pulled up outside Tommy's apartment. He waved to
Sofia, came at Danny with some fake jabs and a left, wrestled

him into a headlock. "Let's go, D-man," he said. "You comin' shoppin' with me for tomorrow."

Outside, his Bronco was idling, music thumping. He opened the back door and let Danny in, reintroduced him to his buddies. "You met Tim and Rico," he said. He turned to them. "This my big brother's kid right here. D-man."

They said what's up and Rico led him through the whole hand-shaking thing.

He settled in the backseat with Rico. Tim and Uncle Ray were up front. These were serious-looking dudes, the kind Uncle Ray always rolled with, and Danny was excited to be along for the ride.

Rico jumped right in about how he got messed over by some woman he'd met in a bar. "Ol' girl begs me to come home with her, right? Then she turns around and throws my ass in the street. What kinda sense does that make?" He threw his hands in the air.

Uncle Ray peeped Rico in the rearview. "Come on, big Reek. Wha'chu do, man?" Ray shook his head, turned to Tim. "I know this *pendejo* had to did somethin'."

"Nah, I'm tellin' you," Rico said. "I didn't do nothin'."

Tim spun around and faced Rico. "You gonna sit there and tell lies like that? Come on, Reek."

Rico wiped a hand down his face. "Man, I was just being straight with the broad." He looked out his window, stared down a Mexican girl sitting in the passenger seat of a souped-up Civic. When the light turned green she sped ahead.

"Ol' girl asked me if I thought she was fat and I *told* her. I said, 'Baby, I like my women thick.' Told her, but if we was gonna get all technical about it, yeah, she could trim down a little in the abdominal region. I pinched a little roll of stomach fat to show her what I was talkin' about."

The Bronco erupted in laughter.

"That's what's up," Rico said with a straight face. "I ain't tryin' to play games. Ol' girl asks me a question, I'm gonna give her an answer. But then she gets all crazy on me, right? Cussin' and yellin'. And she throws my ass in the street. Don't make no kinda sense."

Uncle Ray laughed hard, pounded the steering wheel.

Tim spun halfway around and said: "D-man, you gotta understand about Reek. This *pendejo*'s always gettin' thrown outta people's house."

Danny laughed right along with everybody else. But then things turned on *him*.

"What about the kid?" Rico said. "You said he go to private school, right, Ray? Your boy ever get slick with one of them uniform-wearin' girls?"

Uncle Ray said: "Yo, leave D alone, Reek. That's my big brother's kid."

Tim took Rico's side. He put a hand on Ray's shoulder, said: "Ain't nothin' but a question, Ray." He spun around. "How old you anyway, little bro?"

But Uncle Ray said: "Yo. I ain't playin'."

Tim and Rico let up.

Ray pulled into a Mexican shopping center across town. He and Danny bought all the meats and vegetables Grandma had written down on a piece of paper, and then they piled back into the Bronco. But as Ray was pulling out of the parking lot, a blur on a bike smacked Uncle Ray's side mirror.

"The hell was that?" Rico shouted, spinning around.

Everybody peered out the back window, spotted this crazy, buffed-out hippie-looking dude sitting on a ten-speed, gazing back at the Bronco.

"Oh, hell nah!" Rico shouted.

"Who this white dude think he is?" Uncle Ray said, cranking the steering wheel around and hitting the gas.

"Hell nah!" Rico said.

Danny saw another car roll by slow. The driver turned to look.

By the time Ray had the Bronco completely spun around, the ten-speed guy had ditched his wheels and was walking right down the middle of the road, toward Uncle Ray's Bronco.

3

"Listen, brother," Uncle Ray says to Tommy. "This *pinche loco* was coming straight for the truck. Musta been on PCP or somethin'."

Danny notices that Ray's careful not to make too much eye contact with his brother as he speaks. He places the roach clip in the ashtray, lets the last embers burn out.

Tommy runs a hand down his face. "What happened?"

"I hit him, bro. Wasn't goin' fast or nothin', but I ran him over."

Tommy drops his feet off the table and sits up. "Ray, man, you can't keep—"

"I know, brother," Ray interrupts, standing up. "I'm only telling you 'cause Danny was in the car. We were just goin' out to get the meat for today. . . ." Ray turns his eyes on the brown rug, shakes his head.

"*Danny* was in the car?" Tommy says.

"I wanted to tell you—"

"You hit somebody with *Danny* in the car?"

Danny watches his uncle Ray reach for his cap.

"What he tell us 'fore he went in there?" Tommy shouts. "Said he didn't want Danny involved in *any* of this shit. None of it. You and me promised, Ray."

"I know," Ray says. "It's on me—"

"Damn right it's on you!" Tommy interrupts. He points to his own head. "You really that stupid, Ray?"

Ray pulls on his cap, adjusts the bill.

"I told Javi I'd have Sofe watch his back," Uncle Tommy says through gritted teeth. "Didn't know she had to check *you*." Tommy stands up, and suddenly the two men are nose to nose.

Danny sees the bulging vein in Tommy's neck. The tightness in his mouth. But what stands out most is how much his uncle Ray looks like his dad. A younger version. He can really see it now.

"I didn't mean for it to happen," Ray says, turning away.

"That's Javier's boy!" Tommy yells, his finger almost poking Uncle Ray in the face.

"Look," Ray says, linking his fingers on top of his head, "I brought you in here to say I messed up. I *know* I did."

"You just like him, Ray. You don't *think*."

"Where you think I *learned* all this shit from?"

"Throw everything away if that's what you want. I don't give a shit anymore. But Javi made me promise to keep Danny away from this shit." Tommy slugs the wall and Danny almost jumps out of his skin. "Goddamn it, Ray!" Tommy yells. "This shit's gonna come down on *me*!"

Tommy steps to Ray again.

Ray backs up. "I messed up," he says, reaching for his lighter. He looks up at Tommy again, slips the lighter in his pocket and leaves the room.

Danny hears him rumble through his grandma's place, fling open the door and slam it closed. Hears him do the same with the door of his Bronco, rev the engine and speed off down the road.

His uncle leaves the sitting room, too, and Danny's left

alone, behind his grandma's bedroom door. He's not surprised at what Uncle Ray left out. He was expecting it. How could he have told the truth?

Danny replays it all in his head again. The Bronco and the guy and the blood and the speeding away. He replays it the way he's replayed it, over and over, literally hundreds of times, since it happened. But this time he tries to picture his dad at the wheel instead of Uncle Ray.

4

As the big hippie guy came walking down the middle of the road toward the Bronco, Tim was up front trying to talk Uncle Ray down. "Don't do it, Ray," he kept saying. "I know you, Ray. Don't do it."

But Rico was in the back getting off on the whole thing. "Hit this *chingado*!" he yelled. "Run 'im over!"

Ray hit the gas and ran smack into the guy, a nasty thumping sound against the hood. The guy's head whipped all forward, and when Ray hit the brakes, he flew from the Bronco like a rag doll.

"That's right!" Rico yelled, pointing at the guy.

Danny sat there, stunned. He stared at the guy's body lying limp on the pavement. He looked at his uncle's wild eyes in the rearview. But what he saw was his dad's wild eyes. At the beach. In any fight with his mom.

The hippie guy somehow pulled himself off the pavement and started walking toward the Bronco again.

Everybody's face went dead serious. "What the hell?" Tim said. *"Que loco."*

When the guy made it to the driver's-side door he was

breathing hard like a wild animal. He threw a right at Uncle Ray through the open window, but Uncle Ray ducked it, grabbed the guy by the arm and pulled him halfway into the cab and he and his boys started whaling on him.

Danny's heart climbed into his throat. He couldn't believe what he was seeing. Blood was flying everywhere. It splattered all over the windshield and streaked down the steering wheel and pooled in the leather seats.

Uncle Ray held the guy in a tight headlock while Rico and Tim pounded his face and torso. Rico smacked him in the same part of the face so many times, the sound of the blows actually changed. They became muted. Tim delivered blow after blow to the guy's ribs and stomach.

And the crazy thing was that Danny's dad was there, too. Throwing punch after punch. Trying to kill the guy. His face mashed up in concentration. Danny saw him clear as day.

The guy stopped flailing and went limp and Ray released his head so they could push him back out the window, onto the pavement.

Blood was all over the place, on Danny's face. His heart slammed the inside of his chest a hundred miles an hour. And everybody yelled things out at once: "Let's go!" "Get outta here, Ray!" "Beat it!" "Come on, Ray!"

But instead of speeding off, Uncle Ray flipped the Bronco into reverse and backed up. He turned the wheel slightly and pulled forward, ran over both the guy's legs. Danny could actually hear and feel the bones crush and snap under the tires and he vomited into his own lap.

The whole thing was so much like a movie. Only it wasn't a movie. It was real. And everybody kept yelling things at the same time, making it hard to think. Danny's heart pounded in his throat and he felt light. So light he had to grip his seat, hard as he could, so he wouldn't float off somewhere.

"Go, Ray! Go!" Rico yelled, and Ray turned the Bronco around and pulled back into the street.

Danny spun around and looked through the back window. The guy was completely still and covered in red. Lying in the middle of the street. He looked like a big dog that got hit by a car. But different from that, too. Not like a dog at all, in fact. It was like nothing he'd ever seen or had ever imagined.

Uncle Ray slammed his foot on the gas and the Bronco sped down the empty road. His eyes looked psycho in the rearview mirror, full of rage. And then it was Danny's dad's eyes. Like the time at the beach with the white guy, his mom holding Julia and crying. Or on the freeway when somebody cut him off. Or at Danny's Little League game when the ump made a bad call. Or in the parking lot when somebody snuck into his spot. And then it was somebody else in the mirror entirely. Somebody Danny didn't even know.

He turned to look back at the guy as Tim and Rico yelled stuff at each other and Ray drove. National City all around them. Closing in on them. He watched the guy's body get smaller and smaller and smaller. Like when a kid lets go of a red balloon filled with helium and it climbs up into the sky, higher and higher. Or like a red car driving on the freeway when he used to stand on the bridge in Leucadia, watching. Moving further and further away with the rest of the cars.

Danny kept looking back until the guy's body became so small it disappeared completely. Until it became nothing more than a bloody image he knew would never leave his head.

A Last Las Palmas
Practice Session

1

Uno counts out loud as he and Danny finish the last couple push-ups of their third and final set. When they sit up he looks at Danny. There's been something bothering his boy the past few days. He can tell.

He clears his throat, says: "Hey, D, you wanna throw an extra round? Or you just wanna take off?"

Danny shrugs, doesn't make eye contact.

Uno studies him for a few seconds. He wonders if the kid's tired of this setup. Throwing pitches to a regular old catcher. He's known all along that this is a temporary thing, that Danny would eventually move on to bigger and better things. But he didn't realize it'd be this hard for him to say goodbye. Makes him feel kind of soft.

"Up to you," Uno says. "I'll do either one."

Danny shrugs again.

Uno picks up the bucket full of baseballs and stands in front of Danny. He decides he's not gonna say anything until Danny says something. Uno's not gonna be the one who decides this time.

Danny looks up at Uno, holds eye contact for a few long seconds and then looks away.

Something strange in Danny's eyes, Uno thinks. But he has no idea what it is. He's not a shrink. Uno looks around the ghetto Las Palmas field. At the run-down dugouts, the brown grass, the weed-infested mound. The epitome of National City, he thinks. Forgotten. Abandoned. Left to rot. Maybe he and Danny are growing apart. Maybe the kid doesn't need him anymore. They haven't done a hustle in weeks, and Sofia told him Danny's mom's coming to pick him up in a few days.

As Uno looks at the caved-in fence he runs through his summer with Danny. The losses at the derby, the punch, the speed gun at the fair, the hustles, the train tracks. But he'd have to say his favorite times have been right here. Working out on this ghetto field. Hundreds of pitches and sit-ups and push-ups. Him going off about anything and everything and Danny barely talking.

Uno smiles just thinking about it. Danny's a weird cat. Sitting there all quiet in his Vans. His skater shirt. But he's all right. He's Uno's boy.

"Hey, D," Uno finally says, breaking the silence. "Let's do another round, man. I don't really feel like goin' home yet."

Danny shrugs. Reaches into the bucket for a ball and walks up on the mound.

Uno looks at him for a sec, wondering what's wrong. If it's something he did. He sets down the bucket and walks toward the plate. Squats and holds out his target. Danny goes into his windup.

Here I Come

1

"I just feel like everybody's leaving," Sofia says, holding on to the rusty chain of her swing. "I mean, I'm happy for you. I really am. But it makes me think about my own life."

"I know what you sayin'," Uno says.

"Like why am I here, you know? And what am I supposed to be doing?"

Uno and Sofia are in the park part of Las Palmas, sitting on the swings, late at night. The playground is lit only by the full moon in the sky. The park's lights were long ago shot out by *los ratas,* and the city never got around to replacing them.

Uno picks up a rock, tosses it into a dark bush. "You got good grades, right, Sofe? You ever thought about college?"

"What do I know about college? Nobody I know's ever

been there. Nobody in *my* family, that's for sure." She pushes off, swings back and forth past a still Uno. He watches her lean her head back, her long brown hair grazing the sand on the downswing.

They're both quiet for a few minutes. Sofia swinging and Uno tossing rocks into the closest bush. Then Sofia jumps off, walks over to the jungle gym. Uno follows. She does the monkey bars, skipping two at a time. At the end she jumps down right in front of Uno.

He bends down a little and kisses her forehead. "Anyways," he says, "you'll figure it out. You smart and people like you. Maybe you could be a lawyer or somethin'."

Sofia laughs. "Could you imagine me tellin' some judge what's up about my client? Gettin' all ghetto on 'im."

"I'm just sayin'," Uno says. He watches Sofia for a few more seconds. He has an urge to kiss her forehead again, but he tells himself to chill. Picks up another rock instead, lobs it into the bush. "What's up with your cuz?" he says. "He been actin' mad weird the past couple days."

Sofia nods. "Yeah, it's this thing with his dad."

Uno reaches out and rubs Sofia's back for a sec, then he picks up another rock, twirls it in his fingers. "Thought maybe he was gettin' tired of my dumb ass."

"Nah, he loves you, Uno. Trust me."

Uno plays Sofia's words off, tosses the rock. "What up with his old man?"

Sofia looks at Uno, says: "It's a long story. A lot he doesn't know."

"Like what?"

Sofia's quiet for a second, staring at the slide. She moves toward it. "Know what's crazy, Uno?"

Uno follows her.

"A few weeks ago, Carmen and me were swingin' here and

I was watchin' this little Mexican girl play. Probably three or four years old. Had the cutest little pink dress on. And her parents totally loved her. You could tell."

"What's this got to do with D's old man?" Uno says.

"Shhh, I'm tellin' you something important, all right? I'll explain about Danny's dad in a minute."

Uno smiles, says: "All right, all right. Go on."

"And when I tell you about my uncle Javier, you can't say nothin' to Danny, okay?"

"Ain't my place."

"Exactly." Sofia puts her hands on the ladder leading up to the slide. She looks up. "Anyways, this girl climbs up the ladder real slow, right? But her parents let her do it all by herself. And the whole time she gots this huge smile on her face. And when she gets to the top of the slide, she sits there for a sec, clapping her hands and laughing. Her parents hustle around to the bottom of the slide and wait for her. And she looks down at them and says in her little-kid voice, 'Here I come.' And she slides into her parents' arms."

Uno gives Sofia a weird look, says: "What the hell you talkin' 'bout, girl?"

Sofia climbs the ladder and sits at the top. "It was like she was saying it to more than just her parents, though. She was saying it to everybody around her that day. To the whole world, even. 'Here I come.' And I kept thinking, Man, I bet I was like that when I was little, too. What's happened to me since then? We all start out believing we can do anything. Even Mexican kids that grow up here. But at some point we lose it. It totally disappears. Like me, for example. Why is that?"

Uno walks around to the front of the slide, says: "You talkin' nonsense, Sofe."

"Am I?"

"I mean, I'm tryin' to get what you mean. I think I do, but I ain't sure."

They're both quiet for a few seconds, and then Sofia claps a couple times, says: "Here I come." And she slides into Uno's waiting arms.

Uno pulls her up, kisses her on the lips.

She laughs, wipes her hands on the sides of her jeans.

Uno brushes off her backside, shaking his head. He laughs, says: "You crazy, Sofe."

"I'm just me."

"That's enough, girl. Trust me." They stare into each other's eyes for a sec and then Sofia makes a face at him.

"Now come on, Sofe," Uno says. "Tell me what's up with D's old man."

Danny and Uno
at Petco Park

1

Six days before his mom is supposed to come for him, Danny and Uno take a bus downtown, hop off at the stop in front of San Diego's Petco Park, where the Padres play. They join the line to get inside and both stare up in awe at the brick-and-stucco outside of the huge baseball stadium.

"Yo, D," Uno says. "This my first time ever goin' to a game."

Danny nods. "Me too."

"I mean, in *any* sport." Uno holds out his hands, says: "Look at me, D, I'm so excited I'm shakin'."

Inside, they race up several flights of stairs and emerge from the concourse. Their mouths drop at the sight of the pristine baseball diamond. The manicured grass and sculpted infield. The uniformed players tossing long rainbows to each other in the outfield. Taking grounders at second and short and third in the infield dirt. The pitcher standing on top of the mound like a king, looking in at his catcher, going into a warm-up windup. Uno and Danny cruise through the various bleacher sections, Danny feeling excited for the first time in more than a week. Uno talking nonstop but saying nothing. Oddly nice to Danny. Not even one crack at his expense.

They ride an elevator up to the top of the giant tower, take in the breathtaking view of Balboa Park and the downtown skyline, Coronado Island, and off in the distance the mountains. They ride the elevator back down and walk around the entire food loop, checking out the vast concession options. They sneak past a pair of gray-haired ushers and make their way right down to the home dugout, where they hang their faces over the railing to get a glimpse of their favorite players.

When the game is about to start they find their seats and stand up for the national anthem and sit down when the organ sounds and the voice of the stadium announcer booms. The first Dodger batter steps to the plate to boos and they watch the first pitch rip right past his slow bat, and everybody in the crowd cheers. The giant scoreboard lights up in bright colors.

Food vendors circulate through the narrow aisles holding up their goods and shouting.

"Peanuts here! Peanuts!"

"Popcorn!"

"Ice cold beer! Get your ice cold beer here!"

"Hot dogs! Foot-long and regular! Polish sausage! Hot dogs!"

Uno points out every subtle gesture between pitcher and catcher. Every head nod and smack of the glove. Every understated tap on the inside of a shin guard. But Danny hardly hears him. He's too busy dreaming about how it would feel to stand atop a big-league mound. To go into a windup in front of thousands of screaming fans. Wing a fastball past an all-star centerfielder and have a close-up of his face flash across a scoreboard. The baritone announcer drawing out his name for everybody in the house: *"Daaaaannnny Loooooooooppppeezzz!"* The shirtless bleacher bums hanging another *K* over the right field fence, next to a giant replica of the back of his jersey.

During the second inning the Padres score two runs. During the fourth, the Dodgers score one. During the fifth, Uno reaches into his back pocket for his wallet. He waves down the beer guy and shouts: "Yo, lemme get a couple drafts, money. Whatever you got in a light."

The guy shouts back: "Still got a couple years yet, chief. Tell you what, I'll send up the guy sellin' apple juice."

Everybody around them laughs—including Uno, who settles for a couple Cokes off the Coke guy.

They both turn back to the game. A Dodger hitter pops a pitch straight up in the infield. The third baseman and shortstop almost run into each other going for it, but at the last second the shortstop sidesteps his teammate and comes away with the catch. The crowd cheers as the San Diego infielders throw the ball around the horn. Lob it back to their pitcher.

Danny hears the voice of the hot dog guy coming their way. He nudges Uno. "Want one?"

"Wha'chu think?" Uno says, pulling out his wallet.

"I got it," Danny says, waving him off. "Keep it for Oxnard."

Uno nods at him, says: "You gonna be all right, too, D."

Danny gives him a strange look. What the heck is Uno talking about?

"I'm just sayin'," Uno says. "You a good kid. That's all that matters in the end."

Danny shoots Uno another look. He turns to the hot dog vendor, watches him kneel in front of a family of four and squirt catsup onto five dogs, one right after the other. The guy twirls the dispenser in his fingers like a gunslinger and sticks it back in his catsup holster. The family cheers. When he stands up, turns around, Danny signals for him.

The vendor spots Danny and starts toward him. But then he freezes. The two of them lock eyes, stare at each other for a few long seconds.

At first the vendor's just a familiar face under a familiar Padres cap. A memory Danny can't quite place. But then he realizes it's the big Mexican scout.

But what's he doing slinging hot dogs? Shouldn't he be up in the press box? At the end of the dugout writing things down about opposing pitchers?

The scout lowers his head and slowly backs out of Danny's aisle. A couple hungry college kids whistle for his attention, but he doesn't acknowledge them. He walks out of the section and heads down into the concourse.

Danny turns to Uno, makes sure that he's still staring at the action on the field. "Be right back," he says quickly, and makes his way out of the row.

2

Danny moves toward the concourse, spots the scout walking with his case of hot dogs about twenty yards ahead and calls out: "Hey!"

The scout keeps walking, doesn't turn around.

Danny jogs to catch up, touches the guy on his arm. "Hey. You're the scout we always see, right?"

He slows a bit, turns to Danny.

Danny points to the hot dogs. "Why you selling hot dogs?"

"It's my job," the scout says in a slight Mexican accent.

Danny shoves his hands in his pockets. "I thought you were a scout."

The guy shakes his head.

"But you go to games. I remember you were always in the bleachers at my school, watching Kyle Sorenson."

"I was there to watch you."

"Me? I wasn't even playing."

The guy nods, looks around. He motions for Danny to follow him.

They weave through the long lines at the concession stands and duck through an unmarked door. The scout sets down his hot dog harness next to a few others, leans against a big steel table and folds his arms. Stacked neatly behind him are hundreds of packages of hot dog buns.

He shakes his head, stares down at the black-and-white checkered tiles, sighs. "He asked me if I could watch over you. While he's away."

Danny looks back at the scout, a frown coming over his face.

The scout pulls off his Padres cap, smoothes his thick black hair peppered with gray and pulls the cap back on. "Your dad asked me if I could. I said yes, of course."

Danny's stomach drops. His entire body goes numb, limp. Like he's paralyzed. His dad? He feels light, like he could just float away at any second. He sits down in a metal chair by the door and stares at the stacks of hot dog buns.

"He saved my life one time, your dad," the scout says.

Danny can feel his heart banging against his chest, climbing into his throat. He wonders if the scout can hear his heart, too. He looks up at him, leaning against the table there. Not a scout but a hot dog vendor. Somebody who knows his dad. Maybe knows where he is right now. Today. He wants to ask, but he can't get the words out. He doesn't want to know the answer.

The scout shakes his head, raps his knuckles on the table. He takes a deep breath and looks down at his huge hands.

Danny doesn't move. He stares up at the guy with a blank expression now. There's a long silence and then Danny says: "How'd he save you?"

The scout picks up a pack of buns. He looks down at Danny, wipes a hand across his face. "He always brags on you, you know. Goes on and on about what a great kid you are. A great player, too, he tells everybody."

Danny stares back, hardly able to listen and hanging on every word.

"But everyone says this about their kids. You get pulled away like that you only remember what you wanna remember. He's right, though, your dad. I been watching, you really *are* a good kid. A great ballplayer."

Danny looks away. His thoughts are scattered all over the place. Or maybe he *has* no thoughts. An empty head. Nothing. He stares at the packs of buns piled on the table. There must be hundreds of them. How many people get to see something like this? he wonders. All these buns behind the scenes. He stands up, walks over to the end of the table and picks up a pack, squeezes. Sets it down. He remains very still for a couple seconds, feeling the blood moving through his veins. Hearing the sound he makes as he swallows. Like there's a tiny microphone in there. "How'd he save you?" he says, focusing on the buns.

The scout runs his hands down his face again. "You will move back to Leucadia soon. He told me your mom is coming back."

Danny nods.

"Tell you what, you ask *her* these questions."

Danny turns to face the scout. "I don't wanna ask her."

The scout looks into Danny's glassy eyes, nodding. "Okay," he says. "Okay. This is the truth, Danny. One day I got jumped by a bunch of black guys. In front of everybody. They tried to kill me. Your dad was the only one who stepped in. He beat two of them real bad and the others backed away. They never did this to me again. And me and your dad turned into friends."

Danny sits back down in his chair.

"This happened in prison," the scout says. "I will never forget this."

Danny focuses on the buns. His chest is hardly moving with his breaths. He pictures his dad's face the last time he saw him. Wouldn't make eye contact. Hung his head as they sat in silence. Said he was going away. Ensenada, Mexico.

Someone rattles the doorknob from outside, but it's locked. They knock.

Neither Danny nor the Mexican scout moves. After a few more seconds the person walks away.

Danny looks up at the guy, says: "He never went to Mexico."

The scout looks at Danny. He sighs, shakes his head. "He's still in prison."

Danny stares back at the scout for a while, trying to think. But no thoughts come.

3

Danny scoots past the people in row D and sits back down next to Uno. He doesn't say anything. Simply watches the game like everybody else. Except he's not really watching the game. His head is flooded with words he doesn't know how to process. And he's exhausted for some reason. Completely drained. Like he could curl up on his cot and sleep for days.

Two Padres are on base—first and second. The Dodger pitcher spins around and throws the ball to the shortstop, who has snuck behind the lead runner at second base. The base runner slides in just under the tag and the ump calls him safe. The crowd reacts when the replay on the scoreboard shows how close it was.

Uno turns to Danny, gives him a quick nod, goes back to the game. "What took you so long, D? You droppin' a deuce?"

Danny shakes his head.

"And I thought you was supposed to get us some dogs, man. How you gonna come back here all empty-handed?"

"I forgot."

"You *forgot*?" Uno turns to him with a frown. "Hey, man, you all right?"

Danny nods. "Yeah." He puts on a smile.

Uno nods, slowly turns back to the game. The next Padre hitter cracks one high into the air, toward left center field. The crowd rises as the ball carries all the way to the wall, but at the last second the center fielder reaches up from the warning track and snags it for the third out. The air is let out of the stadium. Organ music comes on over the PA.

Uno reaches down for his soda, takes another long sip. As he puts the soda back down he gives Danny an intentional elbow to the ribs. "Oh, damn, D. My bad." He spreads out, knocking Danny's arm into his own lap. "You is kinda all up in my space, though."

Uno palms Danny's head, shakes it around a little and lets go. "Lighten up, D," he says.

Danny puts on a bigger smile.

"You know, I been watchin' the game real close," Uno

says. "And trust me on this, you better than some of these pitchers right now, man."

"I don't know about that," Danny says.

"Trust me."

But for the first time in the past three years he doesn't care who's better than who at pitching. It doesn't matter anymore.

4

The second Danny gets home he ducks into the bathroom, locks the door behind him. He paces back and forth in front of the mirror, trying to think. He rips his shirt over his head and stares at his frowning face in the mirror, his thin neck, skinny brown chest. His face is so scrunched up in confusion it looks like he's about to cry, but he's not. Doesn't feel the urge to cry at all. In fact, he doesn't feel anything. He's hollow, like the sound inside a seashell. He holds up his arms, scans all the scars on the pale inside part. Then he digs his nails into his left one, watches his face in the mirror. But he can't feel anything. He digs deeper, draws blood. Nothing.

It's not that his dad's in jail. It's that nobody told him. Like he's a little kid. He digs into his arm even deeper.

There's a knock on the door. "Danny?" It's Sofia.

"I'm in here," Danny says, and he digs deeper.

"Open up, cuz."

Danny still can't feel the pain. He's numb. Not even a real person. Needs to get deeper. He opens the medicine cabinet, shuffles through pill bottles, ointments, half-used tubes of toothpaste. Grabs a pair of tweezers.

"Danny, open the door."

He holds his left arm against the sink and runs the sharp part of the tweezers across the inside. Goes back and forth in a straight line. Back and forth again. A thin trickle of blood starts creeping out.

"Danny!"

He goes back and forth with the tweezers, again and again, staring at himself in the mirror, until the pain finally shoots up into his brain. He grits his teeth but then a strange sense of calm comes over his face. It hurts. He feels it.

"Danny, open the door. I'm not playin'!"

"One minute," he says. His eyes bug out when he looks down at his arm, sees the thick line of blood now flowing. He drops the tweezers in the sink and turns on the water full blast. Washes the blood off. Scrubs the wound with soap and then puts it under the stream of water again. But the line of blood comes back even thicker. It's all over the sink now, too.

"Open the door, Danny!"

"One second."

"Open it now!"

He reaches out for the toilet paper roll, pulls a wad and holds it to his arm. Rinses out the sink. His arm hurts. He feels it. The blood is quickly soaking through the toilet paper so he wads up some more, a second layer. Sofia's pounding the door now. She shouts: "Open the fucking door, Danny!"

Danny opens the door and tries to scoot past Sofia, into her room, but she shoves him against the wall. Takes his arm and pulls the toilet paper away from his wound. She makes an awful face and looks up at him. "Jesus, Danny. What'd you do?" Tears start forming in her eyes, one falls down her cheek. She doesn't wipe it away. She pulls him into her room and lays him on his cot, closes the door.

"Jesus, Danny," she says again.

"I'm sorry," Danny says.

Sofia shakes her head. Another tear darts down her cheek. She pulls a towel from her closet, holds it against his arm. Stares into his eyes. She shakes her head again. "But you didn't do nothin' wrong."

Danny closes his eyes. Opens them.

"Danny!"

"What?"

"You don't got nothin' to do with him bein' in trouble."

Danny tries to sit up, but Sofia pushes him back down.

"You didn't do nothin' wrong."

"I know."

Sofia presses a hand to his forehead. "You didn't do nothin' wrong, cuz."

Danny can feel the pain in his arm. He closes his eyes. Opens them.

"You didn't do nothin' wrong."

"I know."

"Listen to me!" Sofia shouts. "You didn't do nothin' wrong."

"I must have," Danny says.

"No, you didn't."

Danny takes a deep breath and closes his eyes. Opens them.

"You didn't do nothin' wrong."

This time Danny closes his eyes and keeps them that way. Sofia tells him he didn't do anything wrong over and over. In his ear. Occasionally touching a hand to his forehead. And then she goes quiet, too. She just sits there with him, holding the towel against his arm. And after a while she falls asleep, her head heavy against his towel-covered arm. Her breaths long and deep. And soon Danny falls asleep, too, lying on his back on the cot. And when they wake up the next morning, neither says a word about what happened.

The Last Hustle
of the Summer

1

Danny and Uno sit side by side on the Coaster. Outside their window the North County coastline flashes by: Torrey Pines, La Jolla, Del Mar, Solana Beach, Cardiff by the Sea. Danny eyes the campsites through the long chain-link fence, the little beachside restaurants and surf shops. The quaint motels and record shops and sleepy beachside parks. How long has it been since he's seen this side of San Diego? The peace and quiet. The white people living in comfort. He has on his Vans, a pair of baggy jeans and a long-sleeved button-down shirt to hide the bandage on his arm.

Uno elbows him. "I'm bringin' shit full circle on you, D." He pulls his new Padres cap tight over his forehead. The bill flat as a pancake and set slightly crooked. Tag still dangling from the top.

Just then the Coaster pulls up to a palm-tree-lined stop and the doors slide open smooth. Uno looks out the window, at the name of the stop, then down at a piece of paper where he's scribbled down his notes. He leaps out of his seat, clutching his duffel bag, and grabs Danny by the shirt and they both slip out of the train car just as the doors slide closed.

It isn't until Danny's standing on the familiar platform, the Coaster scooting away behind his back, that he recognizes where he is. Leucadia. He's never taken the train here.

As he and Uno start across the parking lot toward the street, he thinks about how different things will be next school year. He feels so much older now. More experienced.

And suddenly it dawns on him what Uno's up to. He stops dead in his tracks, says: "Kyle Sorenson?"

Uno laughs and stumbles ahead. After standing there a few seconds Danny follows.

They turn left onto Santa Fe, and Danny feels it wash over him—he's back home. They pass familiar fast-food joints and gas stations filled with white people, the giant nursery that runs flush against the freeway underpass where groups of faceless Mexican men hover in the shadows, hoping for work. There's such a division in Leucadia. The wealthy white people and poor Mexicans. He's never really understood how separate the two races are until now.

2

Danny and Uno walk up the long driveway of Leucadia Prep, find the entire baseball team still on the field. Coach Sullivan's there. He's messing with the bill of his cap and barking instructions at one of his pitchers. A kid named Barker's hitting off a tee in front of a squatting assistant coach. Roger and Joe are taking turns fielding grounders and firing to first. Marcus is in shallow right field stretching out his back with the help of a female trainer.

But most importantly, Kyle's there. He's wearing an Atlanta Braves practice jersey and demonstrating his trademark batting stance to a couple younger players.

Danny and Uno walk right up to the fence along the third-base line, Danny's old spot, and watch.

After a few minutes, Coach Sullivan blows his whistle, signifying the end of practice. All the players hustle toward the mound and huddle around their coach. Sullivan looks over a clipboard and then addresses his team in a low, deep voice.

Uno points through the fence at Kyle. "That him?"

Danny nods.

They watch Kyle walk up to the huddle squeezing a Gatorade bottle, the green stream of liquid arcing into his open mouth.

"How'd you know he'd be here?" Danny says.

Uno smiles. "You know I got my sources, D."

Danny nods. He's surprised to find that he doesn't feel even a little bit nervous. He feels calm. Maybe it's taken real life getting so *real* for him to realize baseball's just a game.

"He's workin' out with these guys till the team and his agent agree on a deal. You know he tryin' to get like twenty-five mil, right?"

They remain against the chain-link fence studying Kyle. He looks pretty much the same. Maybe a little thicker from lifting weights.

"Sick school," Uno says. "Everything's brand-new, man. Check out that field."

Danny tries to look at his high school field from Uno's perspective. And what he sees is almost embarrassing. It's too beautiful.

Uno pushes away from the fence. "Follow my lead, D." He unlatches the gate and struts out onto the field holding his duffel bag.

As Danny passes through the gate after Uno, the circle of players stack their hands, shout "Team!" and break their huddle. Most of them head directly for the pile of bags near the third-base dugout. Coach Sullivan hangs near the mound for a bit talking to a couple younger players. When he spots Danny and Uno walking onto the field he loses his train of thought and trails off.

Uno tosses his bag down in shallow left and holds his catcher's mitt out for the ball. Danny tosses the baseball to him and backpedals several yards. He and Uno throw the ball back and forth in silence, aware that the entire Leucadia Prep team has turned to watch them.

Coach Sullivan starts toward left field. He stops a few feet away from Danny and Uno and watches, arms crossed, a curious smirk on his face.

After a few minutes he says: "You're back, huh, kid? I asked some of the guys about you, but they said you were transferring schools."

A few guys catch up to their coach.

Danny tosses the ball back to Uno, shrugs.

"D ain't transferrin' nowhere," Uno pipes up, snatching the ball out of the air and tossing it back. "He comin' right back here for his junior year."

Sullivan nods, glances at Marcus. "Well, that's good news. We said we were gonna try it again, right?"

"Anyway," Uno says, tossing the ball back to Danny, "we fittin' to challenge your boy."

A kid named Joe turns to the team catcher, Marcus. "What's *that* supposed to mean?"

Marcus looks to Uno. "What do you mean, 'challenge'?"

"I'm puttin' money on D strikin' out your boy."

Coach Sullivan raises his hands and backs up slowly. "Whoa there, big fella," he says. "Now, I didn't hear that last part you just said. Matter of fact, I'm gonna go sit up in the bleachers right about now, look over some of my practice notes." He turns to Marcus and shrugs, walks off the field.

Marcus waits until Sullivan's out of earshot, says to Uno: "How much you talking about?"

"Thirty bones," Uno says.

"Yeah?" Joe says. "Who you wanna challenge?"

"Mr. Big League."

"Kyle?"

Uno nods, catches a toss from Danny. "All he gotta do is put it in play 'fore D strikes him out. That's it. A fair ball."

The guys all look at each other, snickering. Joe motions toward Uno. "This guy for real?"

Uno pulls a wad of money from his front pocket, peels off a twenty and a ten and holds his money up. "I got a Jackson and a Hamilton says how real I is. Less you wanna make it *two* Jacksons. 'Cause we could do that, too."

"You guys don't wanna mess with Ky," Marcus says to Danny. "You know that."

"He wouldn't be into it, anyway," Joe says. "He's about to be in the bigs."

Barker steps to Uno. "You even know where you are, dude? Kids at this school find twenties under couch cushions. Why would he do it?"

"Shut up, Barker," Marcus says.

"What? I'm just telling him. How's he supposed to pitch in that shirt, anyway?"

Marcus turns to Danny again. "You don't really wanna challenge Kyle, do you?"

Danny glances at Uno and then goes back to Marcus. "Yeah," he says. "I do."

Barker's eyes go wide. "He speaks!"

Joe megaphones a hand around his mouth, yells: "Hey, Ky! Dude, you're gonna wanna hear this!"

Uno looks at Danny. A little grin comes over his face and he punches the inside of his catcher's mitt.

Barker looks to Marcus, says: "Dude, I thought he was a deaf-mute."

"Didn't say a word all through tryouts," Roger says.

Marcus turns to Danny. "Since when did you start talking?"

Uno spits, says: "Check it, yo, does your boy wanna throw down or what?"

Joe meets Kyle halfway, catches him up as they continue toward Danny and Uno.

Kyle stops a few feet from Danny and folds his arms Coach Sullivan style.

"Remember this guy?" Joe asks him.

Kyle looks Danny up and down a couple times and shakes his head.

"Come on, Ky," Marcus says. "He's the kid who used to watch us practice all last year. Remember?"

"I don't think so," Kyle says. "Maybe."

"One of the only wetbacks they let in the school," Barker says, turning to Joe and Marcus. "How could you forget?"

Uno stops his arm in the middle of his throwing motion and points at Barker. "Careful, money. I can't have nobody disrespectin' my boy's nationality like that." Uno turns to Kyle. "Yo, let's squash the whole reunion scene, man. I don't care how much signing bonus you 'bout to get, I got forty bones says my boy D could strike your ass out."

A smile breaks over Kyle's face, and he stares Danny in the eyes. Without looking away, he says: "All right. Give the money to Marcus to hold."

Danny stares back. He feels no sense of fear whatsoever. There's a newfound calm inside his head. He can sense it. Something has changed.

Barker pumps his fist and points at Uno, says: "Get ready to lose your life savings, dude."

3

Danny locks in on Uno's first sign: fastball. He nods, grips the baseball. Fingers the seams. He glances at all the guys leaning against the dugout, watching. Goofing on each other. Pointing at a pack of passing girls. He glances at Coach Sullivan sitting at the very top of the bleachers, arms spread on the bleacher behind him, hat resting halfway up his thinning hair. His two assistants chatting a bleacher below. One of them pointing at something in the newspaper.

Danny goes into his windup, fires a two-seam fastball that screams out of his fingertips and pops Uno's waiting mitt, just off the plate.

Kyle watches Danny's first pitch all the way into Uno's leather, hardly moves his bat off his shoulder.

Uno tosses back, drops a second sign: curve.

Danny pulls in a deep breath and nods. He searches his stomach for butterflies but there's nothing. How can he be this calm? He's pitching to Kyle Sorenson. He goes into his windup, delivers a looping curve in the dirt.

Kyle doesn't bite on that one, either.

Uno traps the errant pitch and stands up out of his crouch, takes a couple steps toward the mound. He brings his mitt up to his cheek and says: "You cool, D. Remember 'bout the train!" He tosses the ball back and returns to his spot behind the plate.

One of the guys on the fence calls out: "Thought you wanted to challenge him, dude! Throw a damn strike!"

Somebody else yells: "Kid's scared to death! Look at him, he's shaking like an epileptic!"

Everybody laughs.

Danny reads Uno's next sign and nods. He fires another fastball, this one heading for the black of the inside corner.

Kyle takes his first rip of the afternoon. He swings with malicious intent, but a little too early—drives a laser into foul territory on the third-base side. The batted ball sends Kyle's teammates scattering out of the way, ducking for cover, as it smashes off the face of the home dugout and skips into left field.

"Strike one!" Uno calls out from behind his borrowed mask.

Danny watches the ball roll all the way to the fence, ricochet off the chain-link, and die a spinning death just inside the warning track. A foul ball, counts as a strike. But it's also the best contact anybody's made against him all summer.

Danny turns, fishes for Kyle's eyes, but Kyle cuts away, studies the barrel of his bat. Tucks it under his arm and pulls at both batting gloves.

Uno reaches into his bag for another baseball and tosses it out to the mound. Lays down another sign: slider.

Danny nods. He's got a strike on Kyle Sorenson. A third of the way there. But having watched him all season, having *studied* him, he knows Kyle's actually better once he's down a strike or two. Danny glances over at the section of fence he used to stand behind. Watching. Writing mental letters to his dad. If only he knew all that bragging and boasting was getting sent to a prison. His dad wouldn't have come home no matter *what* he wrote in those letters. Because he couldn't.

Danny goes into his windup and lets go of a nasty slider, a pitch that bottoms out at the very last second.

Kyle takes another ferocious swing and . . . misses. The follow-through of his fruitless rip corkscrews him into the ground and he barely catches himself with his right hand before falling on his butt.

"Strike two!" Uno calls out.

Kyle backs out of the batter's box, checks his bat again. He looks out at the mound, at Danny, smiles a little, then goes back to his bat.

Uno hops out of his crouch, points at Danny and pumps his fist. "One more, D! One more!" He reaches into his mitt for the ball, tosses back.

Danny snatches the toss out of the air and circles the mound. Toes the dirt. Digs in with his Vans. Grips the baseball. One more. Fingers the seams.

"One more!" Uno calls out again as he moves back behind the plate.

One more.

All the guys on the fence fall silent for Danny as Kyle steps back into the batter's box. As Coach Sullivan gets up and moves halfway down the bleachers, his assistants following closely behind. As the sun slips behind a thin patch of clouds, thin shadows creeping across the infield like ghosts, passing over home plate and then disappearing over a cluster of portable classrooms.

Danny tunes everything else out. Even his dad. It's not about him anymore. It's about something bigger. His talent. The power of a train rumbling over a bridge. He concentrates on Uno's sign. Nods. Breathes in deep. He goes into his windup, delivers his best fastball of the summer right down the pipe. Right through the jugular. A knife piercing a Thanksgiving day turkey at his grandma's house. And as his perfectly delivered baseball screams toward Uno's waiting mitt, Danny sees it all as a slow-motion blur of red and white. Big blob of a hitter at home plate. Shadow of a catcher and nobody in the stands. As the pitch rips through the warm air Danny is alive. Awake. Capable. He feels. He's let go a pitch that's a sure third strike against anybody else. But this isn't anybody else. It's Kyle Sorenson. Best hitter he's ever seen in person. Batted .567 during his senior season. Thirty-two home runs. Seventy-eight RBI. National high school player of the year according to almost every newspaper and magazine that cares. Third overall pick in the MLB draft.

And even though Kyle's clearly behind the pitch, so far behind his swing isn't so much a swing as a little chop, he still manages to get a tiny piece of it. He fouls it off and stays alive.

Uno chases the foul ball to the backstop, scoops it and lobs it back to Danny. He holds up an index again, shouts: "One more, D!"

Danny digs into the dirt, considers where he's at: Leucadia Prep's perfect mound, facing Leucadia Prep's best hitter, in front of Leucadia Prep's head coach. The guy who cut him. And he needs one more strike. Just threw his best pitch and Kyle still touched it. He looks at Kyle, sees the smile on his face. And Danny smiles, too. If only on the inside. Because this is so much fun. Pitching to Kyle. Pitching to Uno. Pitching when almost everything else in life is so hard to figure out. But not this. This is just a game. Two guys with smiles trying to get the better of each other. This is simple. This makes sense. This is what he loves.

Danny pulls out of his bag everything he has. He winds up, delivers a fastball that burrows through the strike zone like a groundhog, a curve that starts at Kyle's face and ends near his ankles, a slider that zips in on fingers, a change that fizzles like flat soda, a knuckle that dances across stage like a pantomime, a cutter that cuts in on Kyle's knees and another fastball and then a curve and then a slider and another fastball and a slick change and finally a split-finger that drops out of the strike zone at the last second like a picked-off duck.

But even though every one of these pitches is better than the last, is more polished than Coach Sullivan could've ever imagined, is as close to perfection as Uno's ever witnessed; even though every one of these pitches upsets Kyle's balance, wobbles Kyle's knees, tricks Kyle's mind and challenges his faith; even though with each passing pitch the guys against the dugout cheer louder while at the same time wear expressions that betray a growing doubt, a dwindling belief; in spite of Danny's very best stuff, Kyle somehow manages to stay alive, somehow manages to hang in there, to protect the plate, and he does so by getting a little piece of every pitch. The terrifying home run hitter produces a series of weak foul tips. But he stays alive.

After the thirteenth straight foul ball Uno jogs out to the mound to hand-deliver the next baseball. Kyle steps out of the box, glances at Sullivan in the stands. They both nod.

Uno spins the seams of the baseball around in his fingers, flips up his mask. "Yo, you know way more about baseball than my dumb ass. But I want you to listen for a sec."

Danny nods.

"You foolin' 'im on every one of them pitches. He barely hangin' with you."

Danny nods.

Uno holds out the baseball for Danny, drops it in his mitt. "You realize what that says about you already, D? He the best, right? If you think about it, man, you *already* won. This last strike just be gravy."

Danny pulls the ball from his mitt. Tucks his glove under his arm and rubs the ball in the palms of his hands.

"Now go on and gimme some of that gravy, D."

Danny nods.

"You know 'bout black folk and they gravy, right?"

Danny nods.

"Gimme a side of that shit, D. I'm gonna sop it all up with a biscuit. Run my tongue all up and down the plate."

Danny smiles.

Uno winks, flips down his mask, hustles back toward the plate and goes into his crouch. Kyle steps in, taps the end of his bat on the plate a couple times and looks up.

4

Danny knows this is what it all comes down to. His summer in National City. The workouts with Uno. The fair. The house parties. The hustles. Uno's money for Oxnard. There's forty bucks on the line. Eighty bucks stuffed inside Uno's brand-new Padres cap, pushed against the backstop behind home plate.

Danny peers into the sky. Like he would when he used to stand behind the fence, watching Leucadia practice. He searches the pale blue sky for a hawk, but there aren't any hawks. The sky's perfectly empty. Just the blue and a bright orange sun. Even the thin patch of clouds has passed. He's on his own now. Not just for today, for this next pitch, but forever.

Danny looks in at Uno's sign. Nods. Goes into his windup. Lets go of the hardest fastball he's capable of throwing. A pitch that explodes from his fingers and barrels toward Uno's waiting mitt.

But Kyle jumps on it. He keeps his head down, his eyes

locked in, his powerful swing compact. He drives the bat through the middle of the strike zone and makes solid contact, sprays a little liner to the opposite field, right where a second baseman would be standing. The ball touches down on the infield dirt, skips into right field and dies a few feet in front of the warning track.

Danny's stomach drops. He's lost.

He lowers his head and turns toward home plate, where everybody quickly gathers around Kyle. They shout his name and give him high fives and slap him on the back.

Suddenly Uno steps out from the middle of them and shouts: "Double or nothin'."

Everybody goes quiet, stares at Uno.

"You serious?" Joe says.

"Come on, man," Marcus says.

Uno reaches into his pocket for his money wad, pulls it out. He counts out eighty more dollars and drops the bills right on home plate.

Danny watches Coach Sullivan stand up in the bleachers, start toward the playing field, but Kyle puts his hand up and he stops.

"You really wanna put more money down?" Kyle says.

"Wha'chu think I just did?" Uno says back.

Kyle looks at Marcus, then back at Uno. "Okay, let's do it."

Marcus scoops up Uno's money and dumps it in his hat by the backstop. The rest of the Leucadia guys head back to stand along the dugout hooting and hollering. Kyle pulls his batting gloves tight, looks up at Coach Sullivan again.

Uno points at Danny. He holds his finger there for a few long seconds and then walks back behind the plate, goes into his crouch.

Kyle steps into the batter's box, touches the plate with the end of his bat and takes a couple little practice swings.

Danny looks in at Uno's sign, nods. He goes into his windup and delivers a looping curve. Kyle waits on it, though. Takes a vicious swing that crushes the ball, produces a tremendous sound. The crack of bat against ball, the thunder of aluminum penetrating all the way to the baseball's rubber core. A gunshot blast. And in a flash Danny's curve is redirected high into the blue North County sky.

Danny spins around to watch its towering flight. To watch it soar above the outfield grass, over the center-field fence. To watch it touch down near the back of the empty faculty parking lot, bounce over the locked gate and skip across the street, into somebody's yard.

A home run. But not just a home run. Not just a lost bet or a failed hustle. An answer.

All the guys along the dugout erupt. They storm Kyle at home plate and slap hands and hoot and holler and laugh at how far the ball traveled.

And Barker marches right over to Uno's Padres cap and picks it up. He scoops out the stack of cash, hands it to Kyle, then flings the empty cap into the dirt near Uno's feet and says: "Now get your black ass outta here."

Uno throws off his mask and charges Barker with clenched fists, but he's quickly cut off by four or five Leucadia guys. He points over their shoulders at Barker, shouts: "Yo, you better check yourself, punk. You 'bout to get a beatdown."

Barker's backpedaling and shouting back: "Bring it, dude! I ain't afraid of no blacky!"

Danny steps off the mound as they continue to yell at each other. He walks toward the commotion without thinking. Watches Barker spit in the direction of Uno and shout a couple more slurs. He starts jogging toward the scene, toward Barker.

Everybody's shouting over each other, to the point that nobody can hear anybody else. And Marcus is reaching down for Uno's cap. He's brushing it off with his fingers and holding it out for Uno, but Uno's too busy shouting at Barker to notice.

And right after Barker spits again, Danny reaches him. He punches Barker in the face. Spins the kid around.

Barker touches a couple fingers to his lips and looks at the blood. He takes a step toward Danny and throws a wild right, but Danny ducks it, hits the kid again. Harder this time, in the eye.

Barker goes down. He tries to stand up but quickly falls back down. A couple Leucadia guys rush toward Danny, grab him by the arms. Coach Sullivan flies down from the bleachers, his coaches in tow. He yells for everybody to calm down.

Danny turns around when he feels somebody shoving the Leucadia guys off him. He expects to find Uno, but it's Kyle. "Go on," he says. "Coach'll call you."

Danny looks at him without saying anything.

Kyle turns and releases Uno. He looks at Danny again, says: "You got great stuff, man. I'm serious. Coach'll call you." He waves them off, and Danny and Uno grab their things and hustle from the field as some of the Leucadia guys shout after them.

Danny and Uno keep jogging, though. Out the gate and back down the long parking ramp toward the Coaster. And as they're jogging Danny thinks about what's just happened. The pitches he threw. The swing of Kyle's bat. The money in Barker's hand. The punches he landed. When he stepped off the mound a second ago something died inside of him, because he lost, but now he feels something brand-new taking its place.

Stripping Tile
and Slinging Tar

1

Uno looks up from his plate, laughing, says with his mouth half full: "Then he straight-up socked white boy in the mouth. Pow!"

"No way," Sofia says, turning to Danny. "Really?"

Danny smiles, nods.

"You shoulda seen 'im," Uno says. "Racist cat tried to get up all quick but he was loopy. He spun around like a cartoon character, fell right back on his ass."

Everybody laughs, including Liberty—even though Uno's pretty sure she hasn't understood anything he's said.

"D gots my back," Uno says. "That's what's up."

It's a few hours after their failed hustle, and Uno and Danny are sitting at Uncle Tommy's kitchen table with Sofia and Liberty, finishing up a pan of chicken enchiladas with refried beans and rice. They're sipping coffee mugs of white wine from the box Cecilia opened before she and Tommy went out for dinner and a movie.

Sofia explained how it would all play out to Uno just this morning. Her dad promised he and Cecilia would be out of the house so they could have the place to themselves. No parents. "What could be better for Danny's last night," she asked Uno during the early-morning phone conversation, "than a nice dinner with his three favorite people?"

Uno laughed at her on the phone, but sitting here at the dinner table tonight, eating and drinking with everybody, he has to admit: Sofe was right. It *is* perfect. They've got some mellow hip-hop playing on the living room stereo. All the lights are off except the dim single lightbulb in the hall, a couple candles burning in the middle of the table. Uno can't imagine a better way for Danny to go out.

Sofia turns to Danny, wiping her hands on her napkin. "So, now you're a fighter, cuz? Mr. Tough Guy like Uncle Ray?" She turns to Liberty, starts explaining the whole thing over again in Spanish, but Danny interrupts her.

"I'm not like Uncle Ray," he says.

Sofia laughs a little, says: "Nah, cuz, I just meant that—"

"I'm like *me*," Danny interrupts again. "I'm just myself. That's it."

Sofia nods. She reaches across the table and touches his hand. "Okay," she says. "You're just you, cuz." She turns back to Liberty, translates their last exchange in Spanish.

Uno watches his boy. He wonders what's going through his head. If he's really talking about not being like his old man.

They talk a little more about Danny and Uno's summer hustles. All the schools they bused it to, all the players they faced, the stuff that happened. And then the topic turns to the future. Liberty says through Sofia that she's scared about next year. They're putting her in regular classes for the first time. What if she doesn't understand a word the teachers say? How's she gonna pass? Uno tells everybody about the phone call he just had with his old man, right before coming over. "'You ain't got all the money, boy?'" Uno says, mimicking his dad's way of talking. "'That's all right, boy. I got a roof needs new tile. Bring some boots, boy. Gonna have you up there strippin' tile and slingin' tar. Sunup to sundown. Twenty-four seven. You ready for some hard work, boy?'"

Everybody laughs.

"Well, this ain't really goodbye for me and Danny," Sofia says.

Everybody looks at her confused, even Liberty.

"I talked to Aunt Wendy, Danny's mom, and she lettin' me stay with them for a semester. They got this transfer program she read about."

"That's cool," Danny says.

"They ain't gonna let me into that fancy private school *you* go to, but it's all right. Me and Julia can hang out at her public school. Aunt Wendy says we gonna talk about junior colleges."

Everybody nods. Uno holds up his mug, says: "To your future, Sofe. For real." Everybody taps their mugs together and drinks.

They hang out for another hour or so, telling stories and laughing, eating, drinking. At one point Sofia leads Liberty onto the living room rug, where they dance to a string of Jay-Z songs. Uno finds an old-school Polaroid camera in a cupboard by the plates and starts taking everybody's picture. He has Danny and Liberty move super close together for the final shot. After he snaps the photo, he waves it around and shows everybody.

Eventually, though, Uno says he and Danny have to take off. They've got one more spot to make tonight.

"Wha'chu gotta do at eleven at night?" Sofia says.

"Don't worry 'bout it, girl," Uno says. "It's a man thang."

"You mean a boy thing," Sofia says, rolling her eyes.

Uno hugs Liberty goodbye. He hugs and kisses Sofia. Danny stands up, hugs Sofia. He walks over to Liberty with a shy smile. He nods at her, says: "Maybe I can visit you."

Sofia starts to translate, but Liberty cuts her off. "Yes. I like this."

"Oh, I can promise you that's gonna happen," Sofia says. "I'll bring him down myself."

"No doubt," Uno says, waving again to Liberty and Sofia.

Danny waves, too. He turns and follows Uno to the front door.

Uno lets Danny out first, steps out himself and goes to pull the door shut behind him. But just before the door latches, he hears Liberty shout: *"Espera!"*

He opens the door back up and Liberty hurries past him. She grabs Danny's face in her hands and kisses him on the lips real quick. When they separate she stands there giggling. Then Danny takes her face in his hands and kisses *her*.

Uno looks at Sofia, both their mouths hanging open in shock. Then he and Danny walk down the stairs together, across the apartment complex parking lot and onto the street that leads to the train tracks.

A New Light
on the
Recycling Plant

1

Danny and Uno are back down at the train tracks, tossing rocks to tell the future. They've already gone through four or five rounds. Danny hit five on seeing Liberty again. Uno hit three on playing organized baseball next year. Danny hit five on checking out Oxnard someday. Uno only hit two on Manny moving out of the halfway house. Danny hit five on Sofia going to college. Uno hit four on him getting along with his old man.

As they've played, the night's moved along quickly. Every once in a while Danny looks over his shoulder at the recycling plant. He remembers the night he and Liberty sat together right across the street from it. He thinks about their kiss earlier tonight. His first ever, though he would never tell Uno that.

Uno picks up his last rock and looks back at Danny. "Know what this one's on?" he says.

"What?"

"This is on me and you takin' a little trip tomorrow morning, before your moms comes down to get you."

Danny looks up at Uno, confused. "To where?"

Uno nods for a couple seconds, says: "Metropolitan Correctional Center in San Diego. See your old man."

Danny looks back at him, doesn't say anything.

Uno turns around, tosses the first rock: hits the right side. He fires the second one: misses.

"What do you mean?" Danny says.

Uno fires the third: dead center. Fires the fourth: misses. Uno turns around. "Did a little research, man. Tomorrow morning is visiting hours. Ten to twelve."

Danny hops off the track, walks closer to Uno.

"Two for four," Uno says. "Still gotta hit this last one, D. You ready?" Uno turns back around, toes the line, aims. He fires the fifth: hits dead center.

Uno turns to Danny again, shrugs. "Only if you want to, though," he says. "Your dad got transferred there six months ago."

Danny stares at Uno in silence, his skin tingling. Could he actually do that? See his dad? Would his dad want to see *him*?

Uno sits on the opposite rail, picks up a stick and tosses it over his shoulder. They're both silent for a couple minutes. Danny finally sits down, says: "You really found out where he is?"

Uno nods.

"And we could go there?"

"If you want to."

Danny sits there awhile, trying to collect his thoughts.

This is everything he's wanted over the past few years. But does he want it anymore? Over the last couple days he's decided that maybe he's okay without his dad. Maybe he can make it on his own. Even when bad things happen. But on the other hand, he's still curious. He picks up a rock by one of his Vans and looks at Uno. "I wanna go."

"Then we're goin'," Uno says. "I know the buses we gotta take and everything. Got it all written down. We'll easily be back in time for your moms to pick you up."

Danny nods.

"One last bus ride."

Danny nods.

They're quiet for a while, then Uno says: "Guess we should get back then, man. It's mad late already. We gotta get up early."

Uno drops another stick, stands up and starts down the tracks. But Danny doesn't follow.

Uno turns around. "You comin'?"

Danny shakes his head. "Let's stay," he says. "Maybe we could watch the sunrise."

A smile comes over Uno's face. He nods. "Yeah," he says. "A sunrise." He walks back toward Danny and sits back down. Picks up a stick and twirls it in his fingers.

And for the next hour or so this is where they stay. Sitting across from each other. Sometimes talking. Sometimes not. Danny tries to imagine how his dad might react to seeing him again. Will he be happy? Will he look different? Will he talk? Will he say anything about the letters? Or what happened with his mom? He touches his fingers to the part of his sleeve that covers the cut he made on his arm. He can't imagine what was going through his head when he did it. Feels miles and miles away from that now.

Across from him, Uno looks to be deep in thought, too.

Probably thinking about his own dad, Danny figures. About Oxnard and making a fresh start. Trying to envision how his life will change once he's left National City, the only home he's ever known.

It's the last night of the summer. And here they are sitting together, waiting for tomorrow. But at the same time, not wanting to waste any of tonight on sleep.

A little later Danny's pulled out of his head when Uno tosses a rock against his arm. He points toward the recycling plant, where the first few rays of sunlight are creeping over the industrial mass. Danny stares at the dull haze of morning. And Uno's dad was right. It really *is* something. In a National City kind of way. The plant is ugly, a giant eyesore in the middle of the city, but it's beautiful, too. It's a part of the landscape, and he feels lucky to be awake to see it like this.

The two of them sit in silence and stare at the pale colors slowly fingering their way into the dark sky, around the recycling plant. Even when they hear the rumble of a distant train, neither of them moves. They stay with the sky. The moment. Soon they'll have to get up, get out of the way. They'll have to leave the tracks altogether and hop on the specific bus Uno has written down. The one that'll take Danny to the prison for visiting hours, where he and his dad will sit across from each other for the first time in over three years. And his dad will say something to him. He'll actually hear his voice. And after that the summer will be over. And his and Uno's lives will continue on in different directions. To different schools in different cities. But for now Danny's happy right where he is. Sitting on the train tracks. With his best friend. Watching a sunrise.

ACKNOWLEDGMENTS

I'd like to thank the following people for helping make this novel possible: my agent, Steven Malk, for his patience, guidance and heated sports rants; Krista Marino, who helped me mold a collection of unorganized, passionate ideas into a real book; everybody at Random House, for their hard work and support; Spencer Figueroa, my best friend and creative sounding board; Matt Van Buren, who has read and commented on every page in this book (*three* times); Brin Hill and David Yoo, for being so honest in their work and friendship; Rob Jones, who's been in my literary corner from the start; Albert de la Peña, for talking books with me for hours (and inspiring thousands with his recent on-screen performance); Roni de la Peña, for inspiring me to be somebody; Tina Gonzales and Erica Lopez, who helped me paint in the color of street Spanish; Gretchen Wolfe, Tanya DiFrancesco, Elliott Smith, Sufjan Stevens, Saul Bellow, Denis Johnson; and Caroline Sun, the prettiest, smartest, most talented Brooklyn girl one could ever hope to meet—and I met her.